MEASLE
AND THE
MALLOCKEE

Ian Ogilvy

Illustrated by Chris Mould

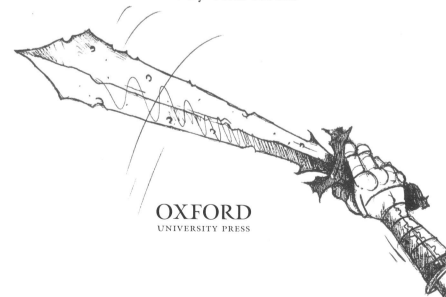

OXFORD
UNIVERSITY PRESS

OXFORD
UNIVERSITY PRESS

Great Clarendon Street, Oxford OX2 6DP

Oxford University Press is a department of the University of Oxford.
It furthers the University's objective of excellence in research, scholarship,
and education by publishing worldwide in

Oxford   New York

Auckland   Cape Town   Dar es Salaam   Hong Kong   Karachi
Kuala Lumpur   Madrid   Melbourne   Mexico City   Nairobi
New Delhi   Shanghai   Taipei   Toronto

With offices in

Argentina   Austria   Brazil   Chile   Czech Republic   France   Greece
Guatemala   Hungary   Italy   Japan   Poland   Portugal   Singapore
South Korea   Switzerland   Thailand   Turkey   Ukraine   Vietnam

Oxford is a registered trade mark of Oxford University Press
in the UK and in certain other countries

British Library Cataloguing in Publication Data

Data available

ISBN-13: 978-0-19-271978-2
ISBN-10: 0-19-271978-5

1 3 5 7 9 10 8 6 4 2

Typeset by Palimpsest Book Production Limited,
Polmont, Stirlingshire

Manufactured in China by Imago

As ever—Barnaby and Matilda

CONTENTS

MATILDA

Splat!

Something wet and warm—and very, *very* slimy—smacked against Measle's right cheek. It stuck there for a moment and then began to slide slowly down his face.

'Matilda Stubbs—you stop that this *instant*,' said Nanny Flannel, as firmly as she could without sounding cross.

Matilda Stubbs took no notice. She reached into the bowl in front of her and scooped up another handful.

'Tilly . . .' said Lee Stubbs, in a warning voice. Measle noticed, much to his disgust, that his mother—sitting on the far side of the kitchen table and thus well out of range of slimy wet stuff that whizzed about the place—was grinning openly at Matilda.

Matilda Stubbs grinned back at Lee, showing off her collection of teeth. There were six of them, all fairly new and all in the front of her mouth, and Matilda liked showing them to people whenever possible. Then she turned her attention back to Measle. She raised her hand above her shoulder and prepared to throw again. And Tinker, Measle's little black-and-white terrier, started to edge closer and closer to Matilda's high chair. As far as Tinker was concerned, you simply couldn't have *enough* wet, warm, and slimy stuff whizzing about the place—and the more that came whizzing his way (and then into his open mouth) the better.

'Sam—our daughter is misbehaving,' said Lee. 'Please do something about it.'

'Hmm? What?' said Sam Stubbs. He was hidden behind his morning newspaper and the only way to tell that he was there at all was when, occasionally, his hand would sneak round from behind the paper to pick up the coffee cup on the table in front of him.

'Our daughter, Sam,' repeated Lee. 'She's being evil again.'

'Evil, eh? Oh, good for her,' muttered Sam from behind the paper.

Lee sighed.

By now, Matilda's arm was slowly moving backwards, to a spot somewhere behind her shoulder. Measle knew from experience that, when the arm stopped, the missile that was clutched in her hand was only a second away from being launched in his direction.

Tinker, sensing that, at any minute now, some wet, slimy, and very tasty stuff was about to be let loose right here in the kitchen, began to wag his stumpy little tail so fast that it became a blur.

Measle sighed and put the piece of toast he'd been eating down on his plate.

'Tilly—cool it,' he said, glaring at Matilda with his pretend-fierce face.

Matilda Stubbs stopped the slow, backward movement of her arm and stared solemnly at Measle. Then she said, 'Blobba?'

'Yes,' said Measle, relaxing his face a little. '*Blobba*. Now, either put it down or eat it, Tilly. Just don't throw it at me, OK?'

'Goomba zoody gurk,' said Matilda, firmly—but she lowered her arm, opened her tiny fist, and stared intently at the congealing lump of porridge in her hand. Then, smiling blissfully, Matilda Stubbs began to rub the porridge into her hair.

Tinker's ears drooped in disappointment—and Nanny Flannel shrieked and ran for a washcloth.

With the danger past—at least for the moment—Measle felt safe enough to wipe his face with his napkin. Then he picked up his toast again and went back to getting on with his breakfast.

Matilda Stubbs had come to Merlin Manor nine months ago. She had arrived, snuggled in the arms of her mother, in a taxi that had driven them both from the local hospital. Then, for the next nine months, Matilda Stubbs had done what all babies do. She'd slept, she'd eaten, she'd cried and—in Measle's opinion—done awful, *dreadful* things in her nappies. Sam had once said that his darling little daughter was little more than a loud noise at *one* end, and an icky mess at the *other*—and Measle thought that was exactly right. Meanwhile, Matilda Stubbs had grown steadily into a chubby little baby girl, with piercing green eyes, spiky brown hair, six small, pearly white teeth, and a throwing arm of devastating accuracy.

Matilda adored her big brother. Whenever Measle was in the room, Matilda had eyes only for him. Measle was the one she showed her teeth to most often. Measle was the one she addressed most of her remarks to, and lately—having discovered how to throw stuff—Measle was the one she chose to throw it at. (Matilda's reasoning was that, since she rather liked rubbing her food in her hair, then her wonderful big brother would probably like some on *his* head too.)

Right now, however, Matilda was busy with her own affairs. Measle noticed that Matilda was trying to stuff as much porridge as she could into her ears before Nanny Flannel came back with the face cloth. Measle turned to his parents to tell them what Matilda was up to but, as usual, they were no good in an emergency like this. Lee was too busy laughing and, as for Sam—well, he was hidden behind his newspaper and completely oblivious to everything that was going on around him.

The newspaper suddenly started shaking, as if it was going through a small earthquake.

'I don't believe it! Justin Bucket? *Justin Bucket?*'

'What about Justin Bucket?' gasped Lee, raising her face out of her hands and trying hard to stifle her laughter.

Sam lowered his newspaper. There was a look of angry bewilderment on his face.

'The most appalling thing has happened,' he announced. 'You'll never believe this—but Justin Bucket is the new Prime Magus of the Wizards' Guild.'

'*What?* You're not serious?' said Lee—and Measle noticed that not only was his mother no longer laughing, she wasn't even smiling either.

Sam nodded. 'Quite serious. I knew the idiot was one of the candidates—but I was certain that there was no way he could ever get *elected*. I was sure that Toby would win in a landslide!'

'Who's Toby?' asked Measle, taking a big bite of toast.

'Toby Jugg,' said Sam, 'is the fellow who should, by rights, be the new Prime Magus of the Wizards' Guild. He's the wizard everybody *assumed* would be elected—which is why I'm finding it hard to believe how Justin, The-Biggest-Fathead-In-The-Wizarding-Fraternity, Bucket has managed to beat him. Poor old Toby—he must be sick as a parrot!'

'We know Toby Jugg slightly,' explained Lee. 'He seems very nice. He's rich, too. He's got lots of houses, all over the place.'

'Is that why he should've been the Prime Magus?' said Measle, chewing thoughtfully.

Sam laughed. 'No, son, of course not. Money doesn't enter into it. No, Toby should be Prime Magus because he's the best man for the job, that's all.'

'Did you vote for him, Mum?'

Lee shook her head. 'I would've done, if I was qualified to vote. But I'm not. You've got to be a wizard to vote.'

'Or a warlock,' said Sam slowly. The newspaper was back in front of his face now and he was staring intently at the election story. 'Listen to this,' he muttered. 'Here's a list of the new members of Justin's Advisory Board.'

'Advisory Board?' said Lee. 'Since when has the

Prime Magus of the Wizards' Guild had an Advisory Board?'

'Never—until now, it seems. Listen—"Sir Peregrine Spine, Tully Telford, Dorian Fescue, Ermintrude Bacon, and Quentin Underwood".'

'But, Sam—' said Lee, her eyes very wide. 'Aren't they all—'

'All warlocks, yes.' Sam lowered the paper again. He stared round at his family, a worried frown creasing his forehead. 'This isn't good, you know.'

'Whassamatter?' mumbled Measle, through yet another mouthful of toast. (Very few things could distract Measle from his breakfast toast. His years of living with Basil Tramplebone—and being half-starved to death by the horrible wrathmonk—had made him determined never to go hungry again. But there was something in his father's manner that made Measle sit up and want to listen.)

'The matter is, son,' said Sam, '(a) try not to talk with your mouth full and (b) a warlock can't be elected Prime Magus of the Wizards' Guild. It's against the rules. Warlocks like power too much and they often reach very high levels of power in ordinary life. Sir Peregrine Spine is hugely rich, Tully Telford is a top lawyer, Dorian Fescue owns a whole chain of supermarkets, Ermintrude Bacon has a string of sausage factories—and Quentin Underwood is a junior minister in the government. Well, that's fine for them—but it's not fine when it comes to leading our Guild. We've always had just plain, ordinary wizards before, who don't care about power much.'

Measle swallowed his toast. 'So this Bucket bloke—he isn't a warlock, then?' he said.

'Justin? No, he's not clever enough for that. He's just an ordinary wizard. A pretty pathetic one, if you ask me. But—and it's a *big* "but"—now he's got all these very powerful, very ambitious warlocks all apparently "*advising*" him. And what sort of advice do you suppose he'll be getting, eh?'

Measle—who had no idea—shook his head.

'Then I'll tell you, Measle,' said Sam, gloomily. 'The *wrong* sort of advice, that's what. The sort of advice that'll make the warlocks even stronger than they are now. The sort of advice that—if Justin Bucket listens to it (and, knowing him, he will)—could easily change the Wizards' Guild out of all recognition. I don't like it. I don't like it at all.'

Nanny Flannel had come back into the room and was now busy cleaning the porridge out of Matilda's ear. She said, 'Well, never mind what you like or what you don't like, Sam—it's time Measle and I were off.' She turned to Measle and jerked her head towards the kitchen door. 'Put your helmet on, dear,' she said. 'I'll be with you in a minute.'

Measle whistled to Tinker, who scurried out from under Matilda's high chair. Then they both went out into the big hallway of Merlin Manor, where a row of brass hooks lined the wall near the heavy front door. Measle took a motorbike helmet down from a hook and jammed it on his head. The helmet was bright red, with orange flames painted on it. Measle swung his school bag over his shoulder and, with Tinker trotting beside him, he went out of the front door and down the wide steps that led to the drive.

The motorbike that was standing there waiting for him was big and black and shiny, and so was the sidecar attached to it. It had once belonged to the giant wrathmonk, Buford Cudgel—but now it belonged pretty much to Nanny Flannel, since she was the only one in the Stubbs family who rode it regularly. When Buford Cudgel had owned the bike, it had been a filthy, broken-down, smoky old thing. But now it was clean and shiny and in tip-top condition and Nanny Flannel used it to take Measle to school.

Measle and Tinker hopped into the sidecar. It was cramped in there and Tinker had to sit on Measle's knees—which was fine, as far as Tinker was concerned. Tinker didn't mind where he sat, or how uncomfortable it was, just as long as he got to ride in the sidecar when the old lady and the smelly kid went to school. He liked the feeling of the wind in his face and was quite proud of the way his ears flapped when they went fast.

A few moments later, Nanny Flannel bustled out of the front door. She was all bundled up in a long leather coat, and a pair of leather gauntlets encased her hands. Her own helmet was already on her head. Nanny Flannel's helmet was silver and had a sticker of a skull and crossbones stuck on the front of it.

Nanny Flannel, who was surprisingly agile for somebody of her great age, hopped into the saddle and pushed the starter button. The engine rumbled into life and, with a roar, the big motorcycle combination sped off down the long drive.

Usually, Measle and Nanny Flannel didn't talk much on the way to school. There was too much noise, what with the thunder from the engine and the whistling of the wind—but, this time, Measle had a couple of questions that couldn't wait.

'NANNY!' he roared, shouting over the thumping sound of the engine. 'HOW COME I'M NOT A WIZARD?'

It was a question that had been bothering Measle for some time but the opportunity to ask it had never really presented itself. The whole subject of wizarding was usually avoided in the Stubbs household and, most of the time, Sam and Lee behaved as if they were perfectly ordinary people—so Measle had been hesitant to bring it up. And the longer he left the matter *un*asked, the harder it was to ask it. But now, with this latest news and his dad's obvious anxiety about the future of the Wizard's Guild, Measle decided it was now or never.

'WHAT WAS THAT, DEAR?' screamed Nanny Flannel, without taking her eyes off the road ahead.

'ME! WIZARD! WHY NOT?'

Nanny Flannel risked a quick glance down into the sidecar.

'I DON'T KNOW, DEAR!' she yelled. 'WHY *SHOULD* YOU BE?'

'BECAUSE I'M A WIZARD'S *SON*, NANNY!'

Nanny Flannel steered the motorbike to the side of the road, brought it to a quick stop, and switched off the engine.

'Now then—why aren't you a wizard?' she asked, pulling her helmet off her head and shaking out her grey curls. 'Why are you asking me? Why not ask your father?'

Measle shrugged, uncomfortably. 'Well—you know—he might be disappointed—that I'm *not* a wizard.'

Nanny Flannel laughed. 'He's not disappointed, dear. He's relieved. So's your mum.'

'Relieved? Why?'

'Because being a wizard is not all that wonderful, dear. As to why you're not a wizard—well, as far as I understand it, being a wizard's son or daughter does mean that there's quite a good chance of being a wizard yourself—but it's not *guaranteed*. On the other hand, being the son or the daughter of a perfectly ordinary mother and father doesn't mean that you're *not* going to be a wizard. There are plenty of members of the Guild whose parents have no magical qualities at all. In fact, I'm told that there are thousands of wizards out in the world who have no idea whatsoever that they *are* wizards!'

'Does that mean—that I *might* be a wizard, then?'

Nanny Flannel shook her head. 'No, dear. You're not. Any more than I am. No, you're an ordinary boy.'

'Oh,' said Measle, in a disappointed voice.

Nanny Flannel rapped gently on the top of Measle's helmet with her gauntleted fist.

'Oh, don't sound all sad, Measle dear,' she said. 'There's nothing wrong with being an ordinary boy. You should be very glad you're *not* a wizard. It isn't an easy life, you know. Wizards face dangers that ordinary people know nothing about.'

'What—dangers like the ones *I've* faced?' said Measle, staring straight ahead.

There was a pause while Nanny Flannel thought about this. Then she said, quietly, 'Yes, dear. Just like the ones you've faced.' Then she pressed the starter button and the big engine rumbled back to life—and they drove the rest of the way to school in thoughtful silence.

Later in the day, when school was finally over, Measle waved cheerfully to his friends and swung out through the school gates, his bag bouncing against his shoulder blades. Nanny Flannel was there, a few yards down the road, sitting astride the big motorbike. The bike's engine was throbbing steadily and, as Measle sauntered towards it, Nanny Flannel waved and then beckoned to him firmly. Measle quickened his pace. As he drew nearer, he saw that Tinker wasn't in his customary place in the sidecar and that, behind her helmet visor, Nanny Flannel's usually cheerful face was dark with worry.

'What's the matter, Nanny?' said Measle, taking his own helmet out of the open sidecar and jamming it on his head. 'Where's Tink?'

'He's busy,' muttered Nanny Flannel.

'Busy?'

'With *visitors*!' said Nanny, spitting the word out of the corner of her mouth. 'Hop in, dear.'

'What sort of visitors?' said Measle, squeezing himself into the sidecar.

'Unpleasant ones,' muttered Nanny Flannel. 'That's why Tinker's busy with them. He's keeping an eye on them. Oh—and you know these visitors, Measle.'

'I do?'

Nanny Flannel nodded sourly. 'Mr Needle and Mr Bland. Remember them?'

Measle remembered them. They were the two representatives from the Wizards' Guild who had come to Merlin Manor when Lee had been kidnapped by the gang of wrathmonks. The two men had been cold and unhelpful. Then, later, after Sam had trapped the last four wrathmonks in a magical net, Mr Needle and Mr Bland had been the ones to take them away in a white van—although, even then, with the Stubbs family triumphant and victorious, neither of the Wizards' Guild representatives had been particularly nice about it.

While Measle had been doing his remembering, Nanny Flannel had pulled away from the school and now they were thundering their way out of the small town.

'WHAT DO THEY WANT?' shouted Measle.

Nanny Flannel didn't reply. She just looked ahead, her mouth set in a grim line—and drove a little faster than usual.

When they got home, Measle and Nanny Flannel left the motorbike at the foot of the stone steps in front of Merlin Manor and met Lee coming out of the door. Lee held Matilda in her arms and there was a worried look in her eyes.

'What's going on, Mum?' said Measle.

'I don't know, darling. Your dad's in his study with Mr Needle and Mr Bland. And they've locked the door.'

'But—what do they want?'

'Your guess is as good as mine. They just turned up on the doorstep an hour ago and, when Dad opened the door, they barged in waving a bunch of papers and demanding that they talk to him in private—'

Lee broke off—because here, marching out of the front door, came Mr Needle and Mr Bland.

Mr Needle was tall and thin and dark. Mr Bland was short and round and blond. Both men wore dark suits, sunglasses, and bowler hats—and each man carried a black leather briefcase and a furled umbrella. As they passed by Lee and Measle and Nanny Flannel, Mr Needle and Mr Bland tipped their bowler hats, and then continued down the front steps of Merlin Manor, their twinkling black shoes making a sharp, tap-tapping noise on the ancient stones.

When the white van disappeared out of the distant gates at the far end of the long driveway, Measle and Nanny Flannel and Lee—with Matilda in her arms—went back into Merlin Manor and hurried to Sam's study. They found him there, sitting behind his desk, his face pale and his lips compressed. Tinker was at his feet. In Sam's hands there was a sheaf of papers. Sam looked up when they came in and Measle saw real anger in his father's eyes.

'What was that all about?' said Lee.

'An *Inquiry*,' said Sam, his voice trembling with

fury. 'That's what it was all about. There is to be an Inquiry—and we are summoned—by those two dim little office boys—to answer its questions.'

'*Whose* Inquiry, Sam?'

'The Wizards' Guild. We are summoned to appear before the Wizards' Guild! Well, by its latest committee, actually. This committee calls itself—' and Sam peered at the top page of the sheaf of papers—'yes, here we are—this committee calls itself "*The Isle of Smiles Investigation Committee*" and is made up of some very interesting people indeed. *Very* interesting. Guess who?'

Lee thought for a moment and then her face cleared. 'Oh dear. Quentin Underwood?'

Sam nodded. 'He's one of 'em.'

'Dorian Fescue?'

'Yup.'

'Ermintrude Bacon?'

'Trudy will be there.'

'Tully Telford?'

'He's the leading interrogator.'

'Sir Peregrine Spine?'

'Every languid, lanky bone.'

'And—and Justin Bucket?'

'He's the presiding chairman.'

'But what do they *want*, Sam?' said Lee, shifting Matilda on to her other arm. 'What's this Inquiry all about?'

Sam shook his head. 'Well, other than what happened on the Isle of Smiles, I have no idea, my love,' he said. 'And, since what happened on the Isle of Smiles turned out to be a triumph for the Wizards' Guild—not to mention for the Stubbs family, too—I can't imagine *what* they're all steamed up about. But steamed up they seem to be. All I know is, we have to be at the committee rooms, in the Wizards' Guild building, on Sunday night at ten o'clock sharp, to answer any—and all—questions they choose to ask us.'

'Us?' said Lee, faintly. 'Who's us?'

'The whole family.'

'What—*all* of us.'

'Yup. Every single one of us. Even Tinker. Don't ask me why.'

'What about Tilly? And Measle? Ten o'clock at night is far too late for them to be doing *anything*, let alone going to some ridiculous Wizards' Guild affair.'

'Oh, the committee doesn't care about that,' Sam grinned wryly. 'And all I can hope,' he said, with as much cheerfulness as he could manage, 'is that Tilly will find something nice and wet and sticky to throw at the whole lot of 'em—and Tinker will bite 'em all on the bum.'

THE INQUIRY

The big, dark-green Stubbs car, with its dragon skull mascot gleaming white on the front of the long bonnet, rumbled its way down the city road. It was late on a Sunday night and most of the city traffic had disappeared from the dark streets.

Sam Stubbs spun the wheel and the car turned a corner.

'There it is,' said Sam, quietly. 'The Wizards' Guild.'

Measle was sitting, with Tinker perched on his knees, in the back seat behind his mother—and between Nanny Flannel and a sleeping Matilda. He stared up at the tall building with a look of intense disappointment on his face. Measle had never been here before and he didn't know quite what to expect—but the building they were approaching seemed to be just another dull pile of red bricks, exactly like all the other buildings that surrounded it.

'Oh,' said Measle, flatly. 'I thought—'

'What did you think, son?' said Sam, over his shoulder. 'That the Wizards' Guild would look different from all the rest of the offices?'

'Well—yes.'

'What—all sparkly, with magical rainbows and shooting stars all over the place?'

'No, Dad, *course* not,' sighed Measle, in the sort of voice you use when a grown-up says something stupid. 'But—well, I thought it might stand out a bit, that's all.'

'It's not supposed to stand out, son. In fact, we want it to look exactly the same as all the rest of the buildings around it, if possible. That way, it doesn't draw attention to itself, you see. And, if you think that's boring, wait till you see what it's called.'

Sam parked the car and everybody got out. Nanny Flannel put Matilda, still fast asleep, into her pushchair and then they all walked the short distance to the big revolving glass doors at the front of the building. As they pushed their way through them, Sam pointed to a brass plate screwed to the wall. 'THE SMITH, JONES, BROWN INSTITUTE FOR THE STUDY OF CORRUGATED CARDBOARD' it read, in large, engraved letters.

'The dullest name they could come up with,' explained Sam.

'But—they don't *really*, do they?' said Measle.

'Don't what, son?'

'Study corrugated cardboard?'

'Well . . . er . . . *sort* of.' Sam laughed quietly, because now they were in the grand lobby of the building and there was a big, uniformed man, with a shaggy, walrus moustache that straggled all the way across the bottom half of his red face, sitting behind a large desk. The man was staring at them enquiringly.

Sam bent his head and whispered in Measle's ear. 'If you come here during the week, and wander around all the offices we've got here, you'll find hordes of young people all peering intently at different bits of cardboard, looking like they're really busy studying the stuff. Of course, they're only *pretending* to study—just in case anybody gets too curious about us, you see. They're really apprentice wizards, doing their six months of official corrugated-cardboard-study duty. I did it myself, years ago. I've never been so bored in all my life.'

The uniformed man had stood up and was now leaning across the desk, peering at the Stubbs family with suspicion. Then, a moment later, his face cleared.

'Mr Stubbs, is it?' he said, a grin appearing under his bushy moustache.

'Hello, Fred,' said Sam, leaning over the desk and shaking the man's hand. 'It's been a long time. How are you?'

'Can't complain, sir. 'Ere for the business in hand, are we?'

'If you mean this stupid Inquiry, Fred—yes, we are.'

Fred's red face became a little less red and a small, worried frown appeared on his broad forehead.

'Not so loud, Mr Stubbs,' he said, looking nervously around the lobby. 'Things 'ave changed a bit round 'ere, see?'

Sam nodded gloomily. 'So it would seem, Fred.'

Fred tapped the side of his nose three times and nodded knowingly. Then he lowered his head towards Sam and muttered, '*And*, Mr Stubbs, sir—walls 'ave ears, if you know what I mean?' Fred straightened up and tapped his nose again. Then he glanced over Sam's shoulder and caught sight of the rest of the Stubbs family. The frown disappeared.

'Hello, Mrs Stubbs,' he said, cheerfully. 'You're lookin' extremely well, if I may say so. And is this young Measle, what we've 'eard so much about?'

'That's him, Fred,' said Lee, smiling at Fred. 'And this is the newest addition to the family—her name's Matilda. And you know Miss Flannel, don't you?'

'Miss Flannel! A pleasure as usual!'

Nanny Flannel nodded curtly and sniffed loudly—a sure sign

that, while Fred the Lobby Guard might consider that what was happening was a 'pleasure', Nanny Flannel judged the whole business to be a thorough nuisance and certainly well past everybody's bedtime.

Fred turned his attention to somebody who seemed a little more pleased to meet him. Tinker was wagging his tail in a friendly sort of way and Fred bent down and patted him on the head.

'And I'm guessing this is the famous Tinker?'

'You guessed right, Fred,' said Sam. 'Now— where are we supposed to be going?'

Fred straightened up. 'It's down in number 13, Mr Stubbs, sir,' he said, in his official lobby guard voice.

Sam led his family across the lobby to a row of lifts. One of the lifts' doors were open and they all clustered inside. Among all the usual buttons on the panel by the door, there was one that was a little larger than all the others. It was bright red and had the words *'FOR USE IN CARDBOARD EMERGENCY ONLY'* engraved on its surface.

Sam pressed it.

The lift dropped. The drop went on for quite some time and Measle began to wonder just how deep they were going. It was clear that they were going a lot deeper down into the earth than any normal lift would take them.

At last there was a hissing sound and Measle felt the lift slow down. A few moments later, they came to a gentle stop and the doors slid open.

There was an immensely long corridor, lit by overhead fluorescent strips, which bathed the whole area with a harsh, white light. The corridor narrowed away in the distance, its walls broken by a succession of heavy oak doors on either side.

The corridor was empty, apart from a large crowd of people about twenty metres away, who all turned their heads and stared as the Stubbs family emerged from the lift.

'That's where we're going,' muttered Sam, jerking his chin in the direction of the crowd. 'Looks like we're expected, too.'

The Stubbs family walked down the long corridor. When they got near the crowd, a figure detached itself and strode towards them, both hands extended in welcome. Measle saw that the man was about the same age and height as his dad—but there was something about him that made Measle a little uncomfortable. The man's face was tanned, as if he'd just come back from a sunny holiday—or perhaps had spent a lot of time under a sunlamp. He had a headful of gleaming, wavy, jet-black hair. He had a broad forehead, a straight, narrow nose, a smiling mouth, and a firm and jutting chin. His eyes were a dazzling sky blue and they were very bright and shiny too—and, to Measle, they looked a little odd. The man appeared to be smiling in the friendliest way possible and the skin at the corner of his eyes was wrinkled in the way that showed that the smile was genuine—

but there was something curiously blank about the man's eyes, as if there was little or nothing going on in the brain behind them.

'My dears!' called the man, coming up to them and taking both Lee's hands in his own. 'My dears—how *lovely* to see you! Sam, old chap—you look *frightfully* well! And Lee—*lovelier* than ever! No need to ask how you both are—the very *pictures* of health!'

The man turned his empty, dazzling eyes to Nanny Flannel.

'And *dear* Miss Flannel—it's been *too* long!'

'No, it hasn't,' muttered Nanny Flannel, under her breath, so that only Measle, who was standing closest to her, heard the words.

Sam Stubbs stuck out his hand. 'Well, Justin,' he said, 'let me say congratulations on winning the election. Well done.'

So this, thought Measle, *is Justin Bucket—the new Prime Magus of the Wizards' Guild—and, I don't know why, but I don't think I like him very much.*

Justin Bucket threw back his handsome head and his long, wavy black hair whipped around his face.

'Oh, goodness!' he exclaimed, just loud enough so that the small crowd of people behind him would be able to catch every word. 'Thank you *so* much. And—can you imagine my surprise? I was sure dear old Jugg would get it—but then I managed to *squeak* through at the last minute! I don't *deserve* it, really and truly I *don't*!'

There was a long, rather awkward pause, during which Justin Bucket slowly realized that not a single member of the Stubbs family was about to tell him that he *did* deserve it—but Sam and Lee were still smiling at him in a friendly way, so Justin decided to ignore the silence and carry on being charming.

'And this, I take it, is young Measle Stubbs?'

Measle felt his small hands being wrapped in Justin Bucket's large ones. Justin Bucket's hands were cold and limp and slightly damp.

'Well, well, young man—you've been having some *jolly* extraordinary adventures, haven't you? Eh? *Eh?*'

Measle wasn't sure whether Justin wanted an answer, or whether the man was just making hearty, conversational noises, so he simply smiled and nodded and then ducked his head in an embarrassed sort of way.

'And what's *this* I see? A *baby*, I do declare!'

'This is Matilda, Justin,' said Lee.

Justin bent down and put his face close to Matilda's. 'Charming,' he said, grinning like a crocodile with a low IQ. 'Absolutely *charming*!'

Justin brought his right hand forward and tickled Matilda under her chin—and Matilda ducked her head in a quick, smooth movement, opened her mouth and, using every one of her six new teeth, bit down hard on Justin's forefinger.

'Owwww!' shrieked Justin, jerking his hand away.

'Oh, Tilly—that was very, very naughty!' said Lee, in a choky, gaspy kind of voice—and, a moment later, Measle saw his mother turn away, her shoulders shaking with laughter.

'Matilda Stubbs—you apologize to the nice Prime Magus this instant!' said Sam—and Measle heard, quite distinctly, the same suppressed laughter in his dad's voice.

'Duwwa wuwwa,' said Matilda, cheerfully.

'Nicely spoken, Tilly,' said Sam, grinning affectionately at his daughter. 'And I'm sure the nice Prime Magus forgives you now.'

Nanny Flannel had other concerns. 'I do hope your hands are quite *clean*, Mr Bucket?' she said, loudly—and several members of the nearby crowd snorted with poorly-concealed laughter.

Justin Bucket tucked his throbbing hand into his armpit and backed away, a sickly smile plastered on his face.

'Ah, the *dear* Stubbs family,' he said, through gritted teeth. 'As amusing as ever!'

Matilda shouted, 'Gubba dubba doodoo!' and then waved her small fists in Justin's direction. Justin tried a careless chuckle but it emerged from his mouth as a sort of choking gurgle. 'Well—if you'll excuse me—' he mumbled, then he turned on his heel and marched off towards the nearest door. As he neared it, a short, round, blond man detached himself from the crowd, darted forward and yanked the door open, holding it as Justin swept past him and into the room beyond. Then the man approached the Stubbs family, his face twisted into what he hoped looked like a welcoming smile—and Measle saw, with a start, that it was Mr Bland.

'Ah, Mr Stubbs—and Mrs Stubbs,' said Mr Bland. 'Splendid, splendid—right on time, right on time— I do believe the committee is almost ready for you now, so if you'll kindly take your seats?'

Mr Bland suddenly noticed Tinker, who was lurking by Measle's feet.

'Is that animal not on a lead?' he said, peering a little nervously at Tinker, who responded by curling one lip back from the right side of his mouth and giving Mr Bland a quick look at some of his best teeth.

'He's very well trained, Mr Bland,' said Sam. 'He'll only bite you if he thinks you're being nasty to us.'

'Oh,' said Mr Bland. He took a slow, careful step backwards and then, keeping an uncertain eye on Tinker, he motioned them all through the door, into a huge room with a low platform at one end. Rows of chairs took up most of the rest of the large space. On the front of the platform was a long, desk-like structure, with pads of paper and pencils and glasses of water on it. Behind this structure was a line of six chairs, all but one of them occupied at the moment. Measle noticed a pale, pudgy, middle-aged woman, with too much make-up on her round face, sitting on the far right—and a very tall, very thin, distinguished-looking man, with a mane of silvery hair, sitting on the far left. Between them sat three other people. A young man with a long, yellowish face and smooth, glossy black hair. Next to him, there was a short, tubby little man with a bald head and a pair of thick glasses balanced on the end of his snub nose, and, beside him, a man who looked so dull and ordinary and utterly unremarkable that Measle found his eyes sliding off him—and on to Justin Bucket, who, at that exact moment, was easing himself into the chair in the middle of the line. Measle saw that Justin's chair was just a little taller and a little wider—and a touch more ornate—than anybody else's. Measle also saw, with a start of recognition, that dark, thin Mr Needle was standing behind Justin's chair and was, at this moment, helping Justin to sit down in it.

Measle also noticed that all six people now sitting behind the long desk were wearing black gowns, of the sort that schoolmasters used to wear, and that all of them had small, round, black velvet caps on their heads, with little velvet flaps that covered their ears.

'Now then,' said Mr Bland, herding the Stubbs family further into the room, 'if Mr and Mrs Stubbs would kindly take those two chairs in front of the platform?' Mr Bland pointed towards a pair of plain wooden chairs that stood, all by themselves, in the area immediately in front of the raised platform. Then Mr Bland turned to Measle and Nanny Flannel. 'And if young Master Stubbs and Miss Flannel—and the baby and the . . . ah . . . the animal—if you would all kindly take those stairs at the far end of the room and find seats for yourselves up in the gallery and hold yourselves in readiness for any questions that the committee might see fit to address to you.'

Mr Bland waved his hand towards the opposite end of the long room and Measle turned and saw that there was a sort of balcony there, high up off the floor, with a narrow staircase leading up to it on one side.

Measle turned to look at his dad and Sam smiled and nodded and said, 'You'll get a good view from up there, son. Go on, get a seat at the front.'

Measle allowed a worried look to cross his face—and Lee saw it.

She bent down and kissed Measle on the cheek.

'We'll be fine, darling,' she whispered. 'Go on—and don't let Tilly or Tinker do anything awful, all right?'

They both glanced down at Matilda in her pushchair. Matilda had gone back to sleep.

The room was beginning to fill up now, as the crowd began edging their way inside. Some took seats in the area behind the two lonely chairs and others went to the far end and climbed the stairs to the gallery. Sam grinned encouragingly at Measle and then he and Lee turned and sat down together in the two wooden chairs. Nanny Flannel tapped Measle on the shoulder.

'Come on, dear,' she said, quietly. 'Let's do as we're told, shall we?'

When they reached the bottom of the narrow staircase, there was an immediate problem with Matilda's pushchair. The problem was solved by a man who arrived at the foot of the stairs a moment later. The man had a cheerful smile, a bumpy broken nose, a short beard, and a great mane of curly brown hair, with little flecks of grey running through it, that fell to his shoulders. He had the broadest shoulders Measle had ever seen. Measle thought he looked like a mixture between a middle-aged rock star and a professional boxer.

'Well, hello there, Miss Flannel,' the man cried, in a jovial voice. 'Fancy seeing you! I swear you look younger and lovelier every day!'—and Measle saw (to his astonishment) that Nanny Flannel's face was turning pink with pleasure.

'Ooh—Mr Jugg!' stammered Nanny Flannel, smiling broadly and clasping her hands under her chin. 'You are so *naughty!*'

Mr Jugg. The name registered in Measle's mind. *Toby Jugg. The candidate who should have been elected Prime Magus of the Wizards' Guild. Mum said he was nice—*

'Now, Miss Flannel,' chuckled Toby Jugg, 'you know you're my favourite lady in the whole wide world, don't you?'

'Oooh, Mr *Jugg!*' Nanny Flannel's face had turned a bright red and her whole little round body was squirming with pleasure.

Measle stared—this was a Nanny Flannel he'd never seen before. Nanny Flannel was always cool and calm and collected. She was the sensible centre of the Stubbs family. She was never, *ever*, flustered by anything—

Until today, it seemed.

Nanny Flannel did a little more squirming and twittering and blushing—then she glanced down at Measle and saw him looking at her, with his mouth open. Nanny Flannel gave her head a little shake, as if trying to shock her brain into working normally again. Then she took a deep breath and became herself once more.

'Oh, Mr Jugg—this is Measle and his sister Matilda. Measle—say hello to Mr Jugg.'

Measle stuck out his hand and the man took it in his own. Unlike Justin Bucket's, Mr Jugg's hand was warm and dry and hard with muscle.

'Hello, Measle,' said Mr Jugg. 'Heard a lot about you. All good stuff, too. A real pleasure to meet you.'

'Same here, Mr Jugg,' said Measle, feeling that he meant it.

'Oh, call me Toby,' said Mr Jugg. 'Now then, let's see about this young person and her pushchair, shall we?'

Toby Jugg bent down and picked up the pushchair—with Matilda in it—as if the thing was a feather. Then he trotted up the narrow stairs, with Measle and Tinker and Nanny Flannel close behind. Nanny Flannel said, 'Oh, do be careful, Mr Jugg!' But she needn't have worried. Toby Jugg seemed to be as strong as a carthorse and Matilda remained fast asleep.

When they reached the gallery, Toby found them seats right at the front. He pulled a couple of chairs out of the way and made room for Matilda's pushchair. Then Nanny Flannel, Measle, and Tinker sat down next to her, and Toby took a seat at Measle's side.

Measle couldn't see the faces of the audience, since they were below him and all facing in the opposite direction. The only faces he could see were those of Justin Bucket and the five members of the committee.

Measle felt a gentle nudge in his ribs.

'A pretty dim-looking lot,' whispered Toby into Measle's ear. 'Wouldn't you agree?'

'Who are they?'

Toby snorted. 'That's the Advisory Committee. Ridiculous bunch! See the piggy-looking woman on the end? That's Ermintrude Bacon—a good name for her, don't you think? The glossy chap next to her, with the face like a bowl of custard, is Dorian Fescue. The little bald fellow with the bottle specs, shuffling all the papers, is Tully Telford—he's the lawyer and he'll be asking the questions. Then there's Justin Bucket himself, a fathead if ever I saw one. The boring-looking bloke next to him is Quentin Underwood and the long piece of string on the end is Sir Peregrine Spine.'

Measle found himself smiling at Toby's short but accurate descriptions. Ermintrude Bacon did look a bit like a pig, Dorian Fescue's face was exactly the colour of custard, and Sir Peregrine Spine, while looking very grand and important, had the sort of long, skinny body that looked as if you could (if you really wanted to) tie a knot in it.

'Dad says they're all warlocks,' said Measle, bending his head close to Toby's, so that they wouldn't be overheard.

Toby nodded. 'Every man-jack of 'em,' he whispered. 'Except for Justin Bucket, of course, who simply doesn't have either the brains or the power to be one.'

'Dad says you should have been Prime Magus, not Justin Bucket,' said Measle.

'Your dad's very kind,' said Toby, cheerfully. 'But I lost fair and square. Mind you, if I *had* won there wouldn't be any Advisory Committee. I can't stand those ruddy warlocks.'

'How can you tell a warlock from a wizard?' said Measle.

Toby turned his head and stared at Measle in surprise. 'You mean—you don't know?' he said, his voice registering surprise.

Measle shook his head.

'But—did Sam or your lovely mum never tell you?'

'No,' said Measle. 'Well, I've never met any warlocks, you see—not yet, anyway. And we don't really talk about it at home—wizarding stuff, I mean. I think it's because I'm not one.'

'Well, lucky old you, that's all I can say,' said Toby, gently clapping Measle on the back.

Nanny Flannel leaned round Measle and hissed, 'That's what I told him, Mr Jugg.'

'Quite right too, Miss Flannel,' said Toby. Then, turning back to Measle, he said, 'All the same, I think you ought to be able to tell the difference between a wizard and a warlock, don't you? I mean—you never know when it might come in handy.'

Measle nodded and Toby went on in a low voice. 'Right. Now—look over the balcony and down at the tops of everybody's heads down there.'

Measle leaned forward and stared down at the sea of heads below him.

'Now,' he heard Toby's voice, whispering in his ear, 'have a look at the tops of their ears.'

Measle peered down—looking for ears. There were plenty for him to pick—so many, in fact, that he wondered what exactly he was supposed to be noticing. Several audience members—in particular the women among them—had hats or hair that covered their ears, so Measle ignored them and concentrated on only the visible ones.

'Notice anything different about any of 'em?' said Toby, under his breath.

No, not particularly, thought Measle. *Ears are ears, and that's all that can be said about them—no! Wait a minute! Over there, by the wall—that young man's got a pair of ears that are definitely different from everybody else's! The tips are dark grey—almost black! As if somebody's taken a paintbrush, dipped it in a bottle of ink, and then dabbed the very tips of the man's ears with the bristles. How weird!* And now that Measle had seen one, he began to notice that several of the younger audience members, both men and women, had black (or *almost* black) tips to their ears—

'See anything different?' whispered Toby.

Measle raised his hand, his finger extended—and he was about to point directly at the man by the wall when he felt Toby's hand on his.

'No pointing, Measle,' said Toby. 'Not among wizards and warlocks, at least. We might think you were about to do a spell, you see—and that makes us nervous. Now then—are you looking at that chap sitting near the wall?'

'Yes,' said Measle. 'The tops of his ears are sort of black.'

'Well spotted. The Gloomstains. All warlocks develop them. The bigger and blacker the Gloomstains, the more powerful the warlock. A few of the younger warlocks quite like showing off their Gloomstains, but older, more powerful warlocks prefer to keep 'em hidden. That's why the Advisory Committee are all wearing those silly little caps, see?'

'But Justin Bucket's only a wizard,' whispered Measle. 'Why is he wearing a cap too?'

'So that he'll look the same as the rest of 'em, of course,' said Toby. 'Old Justin always rather fancied himself as a warlock, you see—but he simply hasn't got the brains for it. Let me give you a bit of advice, Measle. Never, ever trust a person whose hairstyle covers their ears.'

Measle thought about that for half a second—then his head whipped round and he stared at Toby, his eyes filled with a sudden suspicion. *Toby's hair fell to his shoulders and it completely covered his ears!*

Toby's face split into a wide grin. He brought both his big hands up and lifted the two curtains of hair away from his face—and Measle saw that Toby's ears were as pink as his own, without a trace of grey or black about them.

'All right?' said Toby.

'Sorry,' muttered Measle.

'Don't be sorry,' said Toby, firmly. 'You were quite right, Measle. That's the point I was trying to make, see? Nobody, not even me, can be trusted in this wizarding world of ours.'

Measle wanted to find out more but there was a sudden banging sound of wood on wood. Measle turned and looked down at the raised platform, where Justin Bucket, standing tall in front of his ornate chair, was whacking a small wooden mallet on the counter in front of him. The hubbub that had filled the room died away and all heads turned towards the platform.

'This Inquiry will come to order,' called Justin, in a pompous voice. He glared around the room, daring anybody to make a sound. Then he sat down and turned to the tubby little man on his right. 'Mr Telford—if you please.'

Tully Telford got to his feet and peered down at a sheet of paper in his hand.

'In the matter before us this evening,' he began, his voice high-pitched and a little squeaky, 'namely, the events that occurred at the Isle of Smiles—the committee is composed of myself, Tully Telford, and Miss Ermintrude Bacon, Mr Dorian Fescue, Mr Quentin Underwood, and Sir Peregrine Spine, with Prime Magus Justin Bucket in the Chair. Here to furnish the committee with *their* version of the facts are Mr and Mrs Stubbs. I, as Chief Interrogator, will commence the questioning.'

'Commence the *nonsense*,' muttered Toby in Measle's ear.

Tully Telford leaned forward, staring fiercely down at Sam and Lee.

'Mr Stubbs,' he said, in his squeaky voice. 'You sent a report to the Guild, describing events that you *claim* occurred both near your home of Merlin Manor and on the Isle of Smiles. In your report, you *claim* that you were rendered helpless by a group of wrathmonks and that your wife was kidnapped by them. Is that correct?'

'Yes,' said Sam, calmly.

'And that, subsequently, your wife was removed to the Isle of Smiles which, at that time, was undergoing winter maintenance and was therefore deserted, other than for the presence of a few key

THE ISLE OF SMILES

personnel, all of whom had been petrified by the
aforementioned wrathmonks, by means of a
Gorgon's mummified snake head?'

'Yes.'

'And, subsequently, you stated that your wife
was held prisoner by a magical being calling itself
the Last of the Dragodons . . .'

Measle found his attention drifting. All that was
happening down there was a re-telling of the story
of the Dragodon—and he *knew* all that. He
sneaked a sideways glance at Toby Jugg and
whispered, 'Can I ask you something?'

'Shoot,' whispered Toby.

'Why don't *wrathmonks* have black tips to their

ears? Because, before they go mad, they're warlocks, right?'

Toby smiled. 'You know about wrathmonks' rain clouds, don't you? Well—where do you suppose they come from?'

'What—you mean they come from their *ears*?'

'Well, the colour does. When the madness overtakes 'em, the Gloomstains fade away and then reform in the air, in the shape of a black wrathmonk cloud overhead. And it's lucky for us that they do, because no amount of hair—or even the biggest hat in the world—can conceal a ruddy great rain cloud, can it?'

The voices below were becoming louder. Measle turned away from Toby and looked over the edge of the balcony. He saw, to his surprise, that Sam was now on his feet, shouting and shaking a forefinger in the direction of the six robed figures on the platform. Lee was pulling gently on Sam's wrist, trying to get him to sit down again.

'Untrue!' roared Sam, his finger stabbing the air in the direction of Tully Telford. 'My son has no magical powers whatsoever! Any suggestion that he has is a lie!'

'Then how do you explain it, Mr Stubbs?' shouted Tully Telford, his little round face red with anger. 'How do you explain the ease with which he overcame, not just the wrathmonk Basil Tramplebone, but *seven other* wrathmonks, all equally powerful and all bent on his destruction?

And not only did your son overcome them—he also, according to your report, managed to defeat and then destroy an actual living, breathing Dragodon and his actual living, breathing dragon as well! How did he manage all that, Mr Stubbs—*without magical powers of his own?*'

'He managed it, Tully,' said Sam, through gritted teeth, 'by being brave and resourceful and imaginative and quick-thinking—and perhaps by being just a little lucky, as well! Why can't you idiots accept that?'

'Insolence will get you nowhere!' snarled Tully, brandishing his papers in a shaking hand.

Lee was still pulling at Sam's sleeve and now Measle could hear her urgent whispering. 'Sit down, Sam—please sit down!'

Sam allowed himself to be pulled down into his chair, but Measle could see that his dad was shaking his head in obvious disgust.

'May I interject for a moment, Mr Prime Magus?' said Ermintrude Bacon, in a sweet and sickly voice. It was, thought Measle, the sort of voice you might use when talking baby talk to a toddler.

'The chair recognizes Miss Ermintrude Bacon,' said Justin, graciously.

'Thank you, Mr Prime Magus. I can't help noticing that Mr Stubbs is becoming just the *weensiest* bit *tense*—and we know what can happen when a wizard becomes tense, don't we?'

There was lot of nodding heads and rumbles of

agreement. Then Ermintrude went on, 'Adding to my unease, is the fact that *Mrs* Stubbs—the celebrated Manafount—is seated right next to her husband. May I remind everybody that a Manafount can produce a never-ending supply of mana to his—or, in this case, *her*—married partner! This means that Mr Stubbs could perform an unlimited number of harmful enchantments whenever, and upon *whomever*, he chooses!'

'Oh, don't be ridiculous, Trudy,' said Sam. 'I'm not going to do anything of the sort.'

'In which case,' said Ermintrude, ignoring Sam and now smiling sweetly at Justin Bucket, 'in which case, I would feel a *tiddly-widdly* bit safer if they were separated.'

There was a short, hurried consultation between the six members of the committee and then Justin rose to his feet and banged his little hammer again.

'Mr Bland—Mr Needle—would you be so kind and place the dividing screen between Mr and Mrs Stubbs?'

Measle watched as Mr Bland and Mr Needle—both of whom had been standing discreetly at either end of the platform—produced a folding wooden screen from a cupboard at the back of the room. They carried it to where Sam and Lee were sitting and then they slid the screen between the two chairs, so that Sam and Lee could neither touch, nor see, each other any more.

'Oh, thank you so much, Mr Prime Magus,' trilled Ermintrude. 'I do feel a teeny weeny bit more secure now.'

'May I continue now, Mr Prime Magus?' said Tully, rustling his papers impatiently.

'Please do, Mr Chief Interrogator.'

'Thank you. Now—leaving aside for the moment the distinct probability that Measle Stubbs does *indeed* possess magical abilities—and also leaving aside the whole question of the small dog in the case—a dog which appears to me to be an almost *unbelievably* remarkable animal—I now turn to you, Mrs Stubbs. Would you deny, Mrs Stubbs, that a number of illegal acts were performed by both your son Measle and by yourself?'

'Illegal acts? What are you talking about, Mr Telford?' said Lee in a quiet, calm voice.

Tully shuffled through his papers, picked one from the pile, and began to read.

'Illegal Act Number 1: unauthorized use of a Guild vehicle by a minor. Illegal Act Number 2: breaking into an area—by both a minor and a Manafount—which had been declared off-limits by this Guild. Illegal Act Number 3: considerable damage done, by both minor and Manafount and *dog*, to human-owned equipment on the property known as the Isle of Smiles.'

Tully Telford took a deep breath and adjusted his spectacles. Then he went on, 'Illegal Act Number 4: the unwarranted—and unapproved—eradication of a Dragodon, a species of wizard thought to be long extinct and therefore of considerable interest to this Guild. Illegal Act Number 5: the unwarranted and unapproved eradication of an actual dragon, a species of creature also thought to be long extinct and therefore also of considerable interest to this Guild—'

'Wait a minute,' came Sam's voice. 'Wait just a minute! What do you mean, "*unwarranted*"? And what do you mean, "*unapproved*"? My wife and my son were about to be *eaten*! May I point out that—with only seconds before their deaths—there wasn't exactly any *time* to get Guild approval!'

'No, Mr Stubbs, you may not point it out!' squeaked Tully, fiercely. 'This Court—I mean, this *Inquiry*—is only concerned with the breaking of a number of laws of the Wizards' Guild, of all of which infractions you and your family are shown to be clearly guilty—'

Tully Telford's voice began to trail away, because he was slowly becoming aware of the sudden gasps of astonishment—and the stifled sounds of choked-back laughter—that were now starting to come from every member of the audience in that great room. At exactly the same moment that he noticed the change in behaviour from the audience, he started to feel a strange sensation in the area of his ears. There was a sort of gentle flapping, a kind of soft fluttering, as if a little bird was trying out its new wings—a soft, velvety little bird, flapping its baby wings, trying to take off for the very first time from its nest—a nest that just happened to be *on top of the Chief Interrogator's head*!

DISORDER
IN THE COURT

Tully Telford raised both hands and touched the pair of soft velvet folds that hung from the little black cap on his head. They were moving! Moving up and down! Fluttering and flapping against his ears!

The laughter from the audience became louder and less stifled. Tully glanced to either side of him—and saw that all the other members of the committee also had their hands raised, their fingers touching the velvet flaps on their caps, and every little flap was moving up and down, up and down—

'Whoever is responsible for this childish behaviour,' said Tully, loudly, his eyes glaring round the room, 'whoever is responsible for this, would he or she kindly desist? This is a serious matter, and this Court—I mean, this *Inquiry*—will be not be trifled with!'

Nothing changed. If anything, the ear coverings on every little cap began to flap faster and with greater strength and, try as they might, the committee members found themselves unable to keep them under control. Faster and faster they flapped—and now the committee members could actually feel a breeze on their cheeks as the beating of the little cloth wings became more and more powerful.

It was Ermintrude Bacon's cap that was the first to leave her head and fly round the great room. Ermintrude had dropped both her hands for a moment, letting go of her cap, and the little thing seemed to jump at this opportunity for escape, because it did literally that—it jumped off her head and soared up towards the high ceiling. It looked, thought Measle, staring up at it with astonished eyes, just like a small, black bat.

'My cap!' wailed Ermintrude.

'This tomfoolery must stop immediately!' thundered Tully. 'Mr Prime Magus—if you would kindly bring this Court—I mean, this *Inquiry*—to order!'

Justin Bucket rose to his feet and picked up his little wooden mallet—and, in doing so, he let go of one side of his own cap. The flaps over his ears blurred in a sudden powerful effort and his cap wrenched itself from his head and darted up to join its fellow that was hovering near the ceiling.

The laughter from the audience was getting out of hand. Adding to the din was Justin Bucket. He was now whacking the desk in front of him as hard as he could with his little mallet and shouting, 'Order! *Order! ORDER!*' at the top of his voice, but nobody seemed to be paying him any attention. Sir Peregrine Spine—with a look of despair—gave up the battle to keep his cap on his head and let go of the wildly beating flaps and, instantly, his cap zoomed up to join its two companions.

The remaining caps began to beat their wings even more powerfully now and it became harder and harder for the rest of the committee to hang on to them. Tully Telford let his go when he began to feel himself being lifted off his feet—and, with his ears revealed, Measle saw that Tully Telford's Gloomstains were, indeed, a little bigger and blacker than anybody else's in that great room.

Dorian Fescue and Quentin Underwood quickly surrendered too, letting their caps fly from their heads and join the little group of fluttering objects high above them.

Most of the audience were howling with unsuppressed laughter now, tears running down their cheeks, neighbour clutching neighbour, fingers pointing, feet stamping—and, up on the platform, Justin was pounding his little hammer and screaming, 'Order! ORDER! *ORDER!*'

Tully Telford was on his feet, screeching, 'This is intolerable! THIS IS *INTOLERABLE!*' Ermintrude Bacon, looking bewildered, was trying to pat her disarrayed curls back into place. Dorian Fescue was staring up at the ceiling with his mouth wide open. Quentin Underwood was smiling vacantly, like a person who's been told a joke he doesn't understand but pretends he does—and Sir Peregrine Spine was shaking his head angrily and drumming his fingernails on the desk in front of him.

Tully Telford pointed a shaking finger down at Sam Stubbs. 'It's you!' he shrieked. 'You're doing this, aren't you?'

'Not me!' shouted Sam, his voice raised over the hubbub of laughter that roared from behind him. 'Nothing to do with me!'

'If it isn't you,' screamed Tully, 'then who is it?'

'You tell me!' yelled Sam. 'You're the warlock, Tully! I'm just a lowly wizard—what do *I* know?'

Tully Telford's stout body seemed to swell and his face grew very red. He raised his eyes to the fluttering caps high above and yelled, 'I have had quite enough of this nonsense! *Incognate Encanto Negatobile!*'

The flaps on the small round hats suddenly stopped fluttering and, a second later, all six caps began to fall back towards the floor. They landed, with soft, lifeless little plops, in the area exactly between Sam's and Lee's chairs and the front of the platform.

Tully Telford sat down. 'Mr Bland—Mr Needle,' he said, quietly, 'would you kindly retrieve our head coverings and return them to their respective owners?'

Mr Needle and Mr Bland stepped forward and advanced towards where the six caps lay still. When they reached the spot, Mr Bland and Mr Needle bent over and reached for the caps—and, as they did so, the flaps started moving again. But this time, instead of fluttering like wings, the flaps acted like little pairs of legs, lifting the caps off the floor and balancing them there. Mr Bland made a grab for the nearest one and it suddenly moved, the two flaps waddling it away from his outstretched hands. Mr Needle reached for the next and it too scurried away, out of his reach.

There was no laughter now in the great room. Instead, a wondering hush fell over everybody. Every person there was realizing the same disturbing fact. Turning the caps into little flying objects had been *one* spell; giving them legs was—without a doubt—a *second* enchantment. And that meant that there was more than one practical joker in the room because wizards and warlocks (and even wrathmonks) can perform only one major spell in twenty-four hours, and the flying hats—and now the *walking* hats—were both quite major enchantments, even if both examples were, in the eyes of an infuriated Tully Telford, thoroughly childish.

'Mr Needle—Mr Bland, we are *waiting*!'

Mr Bland stayed where he was and Mr Needle began to walk slowly round to the other side of the collection of caps. When he arrived at the opposite side from Mr Bland, he nodded at his companion and both men began to advance on the waiting hats. When they got as close as they dared, they paused.

'On three, Needle?' said Mr Bland in a quiet, calm voice.

'On three, Bland.'

'On three it is. One—two—*three*!'

Mr Needle and Mr Bland jumped forward, both men diving towards the caps with arms outstretched—

And the caps scattered in all directions, looking (Measle thought) like a nest of tarantulas that had been suddenly disturbed. Mr Needle and Mr Bland

landed together, with a thump, on the bare and empty floor.

'Mr Needle—Mr Bland, if you would both kindly stop wasting this Court's time!' shouted Tully Telford.

Justin Bucket tapped Tully on the arm. 'I say, Tully,' he said, 'it seems to me that there must be more than *one* rascal doing this.'

'Of *course* there is more than one, you *idiot*!' squeaked Tully, pulling his arm away from Justin's hand. Then, realizing that, perhaps, this wasn't the way the audience expected a member of an Advisory Committee to address the Prime Magus of the Wizards' Guild, he changed the tone of his voice to one of oily politeness. 'And, Mr Prime Magus, rest assured, we shall of course get to the bottom of this nonsense and, when we do, the two troublemakers will be severely punished—'

Tully broke off, because what was happening out on the floor of the great room was now bordering on pandemonium. Mr Needle and Mr Bland were running this way and that, each man frantically trying to snatch at least one of the scurrying caps. The caps themselves were doing an efficient job of keeping from being snatched and several of them had taken to slithering under the seats of the audience members, some of whom found the scuttling black things so disturbing that they had climbed to safety up on to the seats of their chairs.

There was a sudden rustling, scuttling movement as the six little caps emerged from their various hiding places and ran together into the middle of the floor. Once again, Mr Needle and Mr Bland advanced towards them, arms outstretched—

And all six little caps turned a bright, brilliant—almost luminous—*pink*.

Ermintrude Bacon screamed.

'So!' shrieked Tully Telford. '*Three* of you, are there? Three childish hooligans! I demand that you all put a stop to this tomfoolery this *instant*!'

Tully's words had no effect whatsoever. The little flaps on the caps began to flutter like wings again, lifting them off the floor and raising them steadily up towards the ceiling—but, this time, instead of flying wherever they wanted, the six pink caps formed in a line, marshalled like a row of soldiers. The line rose slowly and, as it climbed through the still air, it moved towards the front row of the gallery. When the line reached the level of Measle's nose, it stopped—and the six little caps hovered there in front of him.

Tinker, sitting close to Measle, cocked his head to one side and let out a short, sharp bark.

'*Proof!*' screamed Tully Telford, on his feet again, one trembling finger pointed up at Measle. '*Proof* that the boy has powers! See how he controls them? Undoubtedly with the help of his unnatural dog! And the Flannel woman is probably one of his accomplices!'

Sam and Lee had twisted round in their chairs and were staring up at Measle with their mouths open. Measle shook his head furiously at them. He wanted to shout, to yell—*It isn't me! I'm not doing anything!*—but the words wouldn't come. He looked wildly around him and saw that everybody up there in the gallery, including Nanny Flannel and Toby Jugg, were staring at him with wonder and fear in their eyes—

And then, quite suddenly, Measle knew.

At first glance, it looked as if the line of little pink caps was hovering directly in front of Measle. But they weren't.

They were hovering directly in front of Matilda's pushchair.

And Matilda was awake.

THE MALLOCKEE

Matilda's bright green eyes were fixed on the line of caps and she was smiling happily at them, showing all six of her little pearly teeth. Her chubby arms were waving and her feet were kicking—

The caps began to dance up and down and, as they did so, a bouncy little tune began to play, the individual notes apparently coming from each cap as it bobbed in the air. Measle recognized the tune at once. It was Matilda's favourite. It was from a CD that Sam and Lee had bought for her. The CD was called *Tunes For Toddlers* and the song was called 'The Whistling Pony'.

And, because Measle was now staring, wide-eyed and open-mouthed, at his sister, all the eyes that had been on Measle began to shift—slowly—from him to Matilda. As they did so, a deep silence fell over the great room—

'Tilly!' hissed Measle—and Matilda turned her head and stared at him with her bright green eyes.

'Tilly! Cool it!'

'Googa?'

'Yes! *Googa!* Stop it, Tilly! Stop it now!'

Matilda grinned. Then she turned back to the line of caps and waved her hands. The caps stopped bobbing up and down and 'The Whistling Pony' died away. The pinkness faded to black and, a moment later, all six caps floated slowly down towards the floor. At the last minute, they veered towards the platform and then settled themselves in a row, each cap resting on the counter in front of its respective owner.

The silence was profound. Nobody in that great room moved so much as a muscle. The stillness was broken finally by Justin Bucket.

'I say, everybody,' he said, his voice echoing in the hush, 'what . . . um . . . what on earth is going on?'

Tully Telford turned his head and glared hard at Justin. 'What is going on, Mr Prime Magus? *What is going on?* Surely it's painfully obvious! The Stubbs family have trained a Magus Infantum, which is against every rule, ancient and modern, in the book!'

'A what?' said Justin, blankly.

'A *Magus Infantum*! An infant wizard! A most dangerous creature! And, not only have the Stubbses produced this . . . this . . . *appalling* thing, but they also seem determined to make a mockery of these proceedings! No doubt Mr Stubbs began it, then Mrs Stubbs took over—'

'I'm not a wizard, Mr Telford!' said Lee, firmly.

Tully Telford waved a dismissive hand. 'The idiotic prank was continued by the Flannel woman—'

'You silly little man!' shouted Nanny Flannel, furiously. 'How dare you call me "the Flannel woman"? And, anyway, I haven't got a gram of magic in me!'

Tully ignored the interruption. 'And the vulgar performance was then taken over by young Measle Stubbs and his canine accomplice, and then finally by his Magus Infantum sister! This sort of behaviour will not be tolerated by this Court! I demand that this Court be respected! I demand that the Stubbs family be punished! I further demand that—'

A steady banging sound—of wood on wood—started from somewhere at the very back of the room. As Tully Telford's voice died away, Measle leaned forward and craned over the edge of the balcony—and there, emerging from the shadows, came the figure of a little old man. He was small and thin and bent, his gnarled right hand clasping a knobbly walking stick which he was banging rhythmically on the wooden floor. From his vantage point a few metres above him, Measle could see that the old man's white hair was cropped short and that his ears were free of Gloomstains. He shuffled forward slowly and Measle saw that all the eyes in the room were following the little man's progress.

It took a while, but at last the old man reached the front of the platform. Tully Telford stood up and leaned over the front of the counter—and the little old man muttered a couple of sentences up at him, too quietly for anybody but Tully to hear. Measle saw Tully's eyebrows shoot to the top of his forehead—then he saw him nod in a respectful way. Tully straightened up, stared out at the audience, and announced, 'The committee recognizes His Worship, Supreme Justice Lord Octavo, who wishes to address a few remarks to this Court. I mean, this Inquiry.'

Lord Octavo turned and faced the audience— and now Measle could, at last, see the old man's face. It was deeply wrinkled. The nose was a sharp and bony beak and the beady black eyes beneath the heavy white eyebrows shone with intelligence. Measle watched as the old man surveyed the people in front of him. Then Lord Octavo lifted his gaze to the gallery—and, a moment later, those clever old eyes fastened on Measle's face.

'Ah—there you are.' The voice was quiet and

calm and friendly. 'May I ask, young man, if I am addressing Master Measle Stubbs?'

Measle nodded nervously, aware that every eye in that great room was now fixed on him.

'A pleasure to make your acquaintance, Master Stubbs. My name is Lord Octavo. I'm the Supreme Justice of the Wizards' Guild. It sounds a very grand job, doesn't it? And I suppose it *is* quite grand. I help to decide what's right and wrong, you see. Not here—this is just an Inquiry into some rather strange recent events—but when somebody has done something really wicked, I'm one of the people who decides what to do about it. That's why they're letting me interrupt, you see. Now then, would you mind answering a couple of questions?'

Measle nodded uncertainly. He had no idea whether this little old man meant him harm or not—but, so far, Measle rather liked what he saw.

'Thank you, Master Stubbs. Now—the small child next to you, in the pushchair? She is your sister?'

'Yes, sir.'

'And what is her name, Master Stubbs?'

'M-Matilda, sir.'

'And can you tell me, Master Stubbs—it's a little hard for me to see from down here—is young Matilda asleep at the moment?'

Measle glanced down at Matilda. Her eyes were closed, her head was lolling to one side, and she was breathing steadily, her little chest moving gently up and down.

'Yes, sir.'

'I am glad to hear it, Master Stubbs. She must be quite tired after all her exertions. For an adult wizard, casting spells can be a gruelling business. For a child, it must be truly exhausting.'

'A Magus Infantum!' said Tully, loudly.

'Now that, Mr Telford, is where you're wrong,' said Lord Octavo, quietly. 'Miss Matilda Stubbs is not a Magus Infantum. What Miss Matilda Stubbs is—well, she's something a great deal more *extraordinary* than a Magus Infantum. And a great deal more dangerous, too. I wonder if any of you can guess what she is?'

The six members of the Inquiry committee bent their heads towards each other and held a hurried, whispered discussion. There was a lot of nodding of heads and an equal amount of shaking of heads as well. Then Tully Telford straightened up and said, 'Ah . . . well . . . we admit that we have no idea what you're talking about, Lord Octavo. Would you be so kind and tell us?'

Lord Octavo smiled a wintry smile.

'Fellow wizards and warlocks, please, listen very carefully to what I have to say. What I have to tell you is profoundly disturbing—but I must ask that you all remain very calm and, above all, very *quiet*. There must be no shouting, no panic, no rush to the exits. Do I have your agreement to these conditions?'

There was a nervous murmuring from the audience and a general nodding of heads.

'Thank you. Now then—unlike all these clever warlocks on the platform here behind me, I am nothing more than a simple wizard. Well, perhaps not altogether *simple*—because there is one thing I can do that they cannot. I can detect the origins of concealed spells. I can *sense* where they come from. Today, this small talent of mine has revealed something truly extraordinary. Today, my fellow wizards and warlocks, we are in the presence of something wonderful, something unique, and something that has not been seen in a very, very long time.'

Lord Octavo paused again. There was an impatient rustling in the audience and Justin Bucket leaned forward and said, '*Frightfully* sorry, Lord Octavo, to be so dim—but what exactly hasn't been seen in a very, very long time? And where is it?'

Lord Octavo slowly raised one hand and pointed his gnarled old finger up at the gallery.

'It is there, Mr Bucket. Up there in the gallery. At present, it is asleep in its pushchair and therefore—for the moment, at least—relatively harmless. I can only hope it stays that way.'

'What—you mean the Stubbs baby?' said Justin, absent-mindedly rubbing the finger that Matilda had bitten earlier.

'The same,' said Lord Octavo.

'The Magus Infantum?' said Tully.

Lord Octavo smiled a small, weary smile and turned to Tully Telford. 'Mr Telford, I have already informed you that little Miss Stubbs is *not* a Magus Infantum.'

'Then what *is* she?' said Tully, irritably tapping the desk in front of him with a pencil.

'Miss Matilda Stubbs is, I believe, a very terrible creature. She is—and I am quite sure of this—she is a *Mallockee.*'

A mumbling, rumbling muttering sound went round the great room as the audience tried out the word.

'*What did he say? . . . Mallockee? . . . What's a Mallockee? . . . Never heard of a Mallockee . . . Any idea what the old chap's talking about? . . . Mallockee? . . . Mallockee? . . . Mallockee? . . .*'

Lord Octavo held up two wrinkled hands and the muttering died away. Then Lord Octavo looked up towards the gallery, caught Measle's eye—and smiled at him.

'See what being very old and reading lots of books does for you, Master Stubbs?' he called. 'I know things that nobody else here knows!'

Lord Octavo dropped his gaze from the gallery and swept his eyes round the great room.

'Is this, in fact, the case?' he demanded. 'Am I the only one here who knows of the Mallockee?'

An uncomfortable silence fell over the great room. Nobody wanted to be the first to admit their ignorance, so everybody held their tongue, hoping that somebody else would be the first to speak. When nobody did, Lord Octavo shook his head sorrowfully.

'Scholarship—and the love of learning—are disappearing so fast. Such a pity. In my young day, education was something we all yearned after—'

'Excuse me, Lord Octavo,' said Sam, twisting round in his seat to stare angrily at the old man, 'excuse me, but my wife and I are understandably anxious to learn what exactly you are accusing our daughter of being?'

Lord Octavo made a small bow in Sam and Lee's direction. 'My apologies, Mr Stubbs,' he said, gently. 'You're quite right. I have a tendency to ramble. So—to the point. As we all know, wizards and warlocks—and even those contemptible wrath-monks—can perform only one major spell in a twenty-four hour period. But the Mallockee has no such limitations. The Mallockee can perform spells without stopping, until he—or she—becomes too exhausted to continue. Also—and this is most interesting—a Mallockee doesn't need incantations for its spells. All a Mallockee has to do is *think* the spell—and it's done! This is what I detected a few moments ago. All those spells—those *silent* spells—involving those little hats of yours—the flying and the walking and the colour-changing and the music-making—they all emanated from one source. *One source only*.

They emanated from that little girl up there in the pushchair, currently sleeping the sleep of the exhausted. And it occurs to me that we are extremely lucky.'

'Lucky, Lord Octavo?' whispered Ermintrude Bacon.

'Yes, indeed, Miss Bacon. Extremely lucky. So far, the child seems to possess a charming and playful personality. Can you imagine what might have happened if she was a poisonous brat?'

Tully Telford was on his feet again. 'Lord Octavo!' he cried. 'Are you seriously asking us to believe in a magical entity with no boundaries to its powers?'

'Yes, I am, Mr Telford,' said Lord Octavo, quietly.

'Impossible! For a start, where does it obtain an endless supply of mana?'

'From *itself*, Mr Telford. You don't seem to understand—a Mallockee is both a wizard, *and a manafount*!'

Tully gulped. 'But—such a being would have powers beyond reason!'

Lord Octavo nodded. 'Indeed he—or she—*would*, Mr Telford. And may I remind you to try to speak as quietly as possible, since a Mallockee *asleep* is considerably less dangerous than one which is awake.'

Tully took a deep breath and shook his head angrily, but when he spoke, it was in little more than a whisper. 'Lord Octavo, this Mallockee creature—why have none of us *heard* of such a thing?'

'Because, Mr Telford, first, nobody reads books any more, and second, there hasn't *been* such a thing for several thousand years. Indeed, such a thing has been impossible for several thousand years. In fact, it was thought that such a thing could never occur again. And yet—it has. This is no random event, you understand. A Mallockee does not simply come by chance—it is *created*.'

'You mean—this was done on *purpose*?'

Lord Octavo turned and looked at Sam and Lee. He stared at them for several seconds, with a quizzical expression on his lined old face. Then he seemed to make up his mind about them and abruptly shook his head.

'In this case, I believe not, Mr Telford. In the distant past, it's true to say that the very few Mallockees that appeared were made on purpose. But I believe that, in *this* case, the sequence was a series of catastrophic accidents, nothing more. However, these accidents have led to the appearance among us of a genuine Mallockee.'

'But—but—how did this happen, Lord Octavo?' stammered Tully.

Lord Octavo turned slowly and pointed at Lee.

'There's your answer. Mrs Stubbs. She is the mother of the Mallockee—and therefore its creator.'

'But *how* did she create this Mallockee?'

Lord Octavo shrugged his narrow shoulders. 'In

the same way that all Mallockees are created—and, when I say "all", I am referring to the only three known cases in all of wizard history. A Mallockee is created when a Manafount is to become a mother. The Manafount simply bathes herself in the blood of a dragon. She absorbs a vast amount of mana from the dragon's blood, which overloads her *own* mana production. This enormous volume of mana in her system has to go somewhere. It goes to the unborn baby. When the baby later arrives in the world, it is a Mallockee.'

There was the sound of nervous muttering all around the room. Lord Octavo took a few shuffling steps towards Lee, who was staring at him, wide-eyed with astonishment.

'My dear Mrs Stubbs,' he said, in a kind voice, 'none of this is your fault. You and your son were in great peril from a gigantic dragon. When the sea water came rushing into that great cave, it killed the dragon—and you were forced to swim for your lives. You can hardly be blamed for the fact that much of what you were swimming in was dragon's *blood*. And in doing so—and without meaning any harm—you have produced a Mallockee, an extraordinary magical being, not seen on earth for several thousand years, simply because of a—how shall I put it?—a general scarcity of Manafounts and an even greater, and worldwide, *shortage of dragons*!'

There was a very long silence, while everybody

in the great room thought about what Lord Octavo had said. The silence was broken by Sam. He stood up abruptly, the legs of his wooden chair scraping on the bare floor.

'Well,' he said, in a business-like voice, 'now that all this has been cleared up, we'll be off, I think. It's *very* late—well past my children's bedtime in fact—and, since we've got a long drive ahead of us, I reckon we ought to make a start. Thanks so much for having us. Come on, my love—'

Sam was beginning to step out from behind the screen that separated him from Lee, and Lee herself was starting to rise out of her chair—

'Wait!'

The sharp, almost shouted word had come from the distinguished-looking, silver-haired man at the far end of the line of chairs on the platform. He leaned forward on the counter, his long, thin hands clasped under his chin.

'Please, Mr Stubbs—Mrs Stubbs—please sit down,' said Sir Peregrine Spine, his voice smooth and soft and polished. 'Much as I understand your urge to leave, I'm afraid that this Inquiry is far from over, particularly in light of these recent revelations.'

Sam and Lee glanced at each other over the top of the dividing screen. Sam gave a small shrug, winked at his wife, and then slowly settled back in his chair. Lee did the same. Sir Peregrine Spine said, 'Thank you so much, Mr Stubbs—Mrs Stubbs.' Then he turned and looked down at the small, bent figure in front of him.

'Lord Octavo—'

'Sir Peregrine?'

'Are you quite positive about all this?'

'There really is no other explanation.'

Sir Peregrine raised his noble head and looked out at the packed room.

'If I could ask you all to bear with us for a few moments? I request that this Court will allow the committee a moment of consultation?'

Nobody seemed interested in raising any objection to this, so, for the next few minutes, all six members of the committee leaned towards each other and whispered intently.

Up in the gallery, Measle did a bit of whispering of his own.

'What's happening, Nanny?'

Nanny Flannel shook her head and shrugged her shoulders. 'I don't know, dear. But don't worry. Your mum and dad will sort it out.'

But will they be allowed to? thought Measle. *I don't like the look of those whispering faces down there.* He glanced down at his sister. Matilda was fast asleep and, from the look of her, Measle guessed that she wouldn't wake up for several hours.

Measle looked at Toby. 'Did you know about Mallockees?' he said. 'I mean, before?'

'Never heard of 'em. Mind you, if Lord Octavo says they existed, then I for one believe him. He's read more books than me, and your dad, and your mum, and half a dozen other wizards put together—'

There was some movement down below. The committee members were settling back into their chairs.

Measle watched as Justin Bucket beckoned to Mr Needle and Mr Bland. Both men hurried to Justin's side, bent their heads, and listened intently to what Justin was saying. Then they nodded sharply, straightened up, and marched briskly out of the room. Justin Bucket waited until both men had disappeared. Then he turned and looked out over the room.

'Thank you all *so* much,' he said, nodding his handsome head in a friendly way. 'If you would all be *terribly* kind and remain in your seats for a few more minutes, we'd all be *terrifically* grateful. The secretaries won't be gone for long—they are simply consulting a reference book on our behalf to help us *verify*, as it were, all these remarkable theories. So interesting, isn't it?'

The audience members began a soft murmuring among themselves and each one of them, at one point or another, glanced up at the gallery, trying to catch a glimpse of the sleeping baby. The seconds, then the minutes, ticked by—

The door to the corridor burst open with a crash. Six very big figures, dressed in black uniforms, strode into the room. They wore jet-black helmets and jet-black boots and their eyes were obscured behind darkened visors.

Behind them came Mr Needle and Mr Bland. Mr Needle pointed at Lee and Mr Bland pointed at Sam. Two of the burly figures marched silently up to the two wooden chairs. One man grabbed Lee by an arm and dragged her out of her chair. Sam jumped to his feet and swept the dividing screen to one side. He reached for Lee—but it was too late. The second figure had wrapped a pair of massive arms around Sam and was pinning his arms to his sides. A third man approached the struggling figures. He had something in his hands—no, *two* somethings, Measle saw with horror. They were a pair of neck-sized rings, like dog collars, made of some sort of dull grey metal, with a hinge set in the outer circle. When this third man reached Sam, he lifted one of the rings, pulled it open, and snapped it round Sam's neck. Then he turned and did the same to Lee. Sam and Lee were pushed roughly back into their chairs. Nobody bothered to pick up the dividing screen that now lay flat on the floor and Measle watched as Sam reached out his hand towards Lee—who reached out *her* hand and grasped Sam's—

'*Stasimus exertico fortegilimus!*' yelled Sam—

And nothing happened.

The only effect of Sam's shouted spell that Measle could see was a dim flash of blue light that travelled from Sam's finger tip; but, instead of zipping away from him, the light travelled in the opposite direction, up Sam's arm and then disappeared—as if it was somehow being swallowed up, up into the metal ring around his neck.

By this time there was a certain degree of panic in the great room. At least half the audience seemed desperate to get out of there and were now streaming out of the rows of chairs and heading fast for the door—and Lord Octavo himself shuffled forward towards Sam and Lee, his lined old face creased with concern but, when he got within a couple of metres, one of the uniformed men stepped forward and pushed him backwards with such sudden force that the old man staggered and almost fell.

Measle was out of his chair, standing with both hands on the rail in front of him and staring with horror at what was going on down below. Out of the corner of his eye he saw two more of the black-uniformed men start towards the foot of the stairs. One of the men held three metal hoops in his gloved hands—

Measle turned back—and saw that Toby Jugg was bending over Matilda's pushchair and undoing the buckles that held the little girl in place. Then, a moment later, Toby was lifting the still-sleeping Matilda out of her seat. With his free hand, he clicked the catch that held the pushchair open. The chair folded and Toby scooped it up—

'What are you *doing*?' blurted Measle.

Toby threw a hurried look in Measle's direction. 'We've got to get her out of here, Measle! And—and you, too, come to think of it!'

'But what about Dad?' blurted Measle. 'And Mum?'

'I can't help them, Measle! But I can help you and your sister! Now come on!'

Toby turned to Nanny Flannel and spoke urgently into the old lady's face. 'Miss Flannel, I can get them away but we've got to move fast and I can't manage you as well. Trust me, I'll keep 'em safe—just a couple of days—I'll sort it out, but right now there's no time for anything but getting them away, all right?'

Nanny Flannel was instinctively shaking her head but then she seemed to change her mind. She looked up at Measle, then at Matilda nestled in Toby's strong arms, and then she started making shooing gestures with both hands.

'Go on, Measle dear!' yelled Nanny Flannel. 'Go with Mr Jugg!'

'But—'

'Go on! It'll be all right! Look after Tilly! Oh—wait!'

Nanny Flannel reached into her old black handbag. She pulled out a small plastic bag and tossed it to Measle. Measle caught it and felt the hard little oval shapes inside—

Jelly beans!

'Just in case you get hungry, dear!' shouted Nanny Flannel.

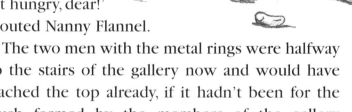

The two men with the metal rings were halfway up the stairs of the gallery now and would have reached the top already, if it hadn't been for the crush formed by the members of the gallery audience who were trying to get *down* the same narrow stairs and out of the door.

'Come on, Measle old son,' muttered Toby, tucking Matilda and her pushchair under one muscular arm and grabbing Measle by the other. 'No time to lose!'

Measle felt himself being hustled against the flow of people, all of whom were pressing forward to get to the top of the stairs. Toby was dragging him through the mob, heading as fast as possible towards the wall that was furthest away from the stairs. It looked, to Measle, like a perfectly blank wall and he wondered why they were trying so hard to get there—but then, a moment later, he saw that there was a door there, a hard-to-see, flat-faced door that was painted the exact same colour as the wall that surrounded it.

Measle and Toby pushed clear of the last of the people who were streaming in the other direction and Toby reached out, grabbed the door handle and yanked it open. Measle glanced backwards and saw that the two uniformed men were standing over Nanny Flannel. They seemed to be barking questions at her and then one of them looked up and saw Measle and Toby—

Then Measle felt a strong hand pull him through the opening.

Toby slammed the door shut. He was just reaching for the heavy iron bolt at the top when, suddenly, there came a frantic scratching from the other side. Before Toby had time to slam the bolt home—and without bothering to ask if this was a good idea—Measle yanked open the door, and a small, black and white, fuzzy bullet shot through the opening.

'Not the dog, Measle!' said Toby, in a voice filled with exasperation. 'We can't take the dog as well!'

Measle felt a sudden welling of anger. *All these people, telling my family what we can do and what we can't do—I've had enough!*

'I'm not going without him,' said Measle.

Toby growled like an angry old lion and then, a moment later, grinned and shook his head in surrender. He pushed the bolt into its socket with a thud.

'All right,' he said. 'That should hold them for a bit. Just make sure the little guy doesn't slow us down, OK?'

'Slow us down?' said Measle. 'Have you seen him run? It's more likely he'll speed us up!'

Toby laughed. Then he looked upwards and said, 'Come on, now, Measle, old son—we've got a bit of a climb ahead of us. And we'd better get started. That bolt won't hold them for long.'

Measle saw that he and Toby were at the bottom

of a deep well. There was a cast-iron spiral staircase set in the middle of the well and, when Measle tilted his head backwards and looked up, he saw that the staircase was immensely tall. Far, far above him, the column of winding iron steps narrowed to a point and then disappeared altogether in the far-off darkness.

'We've got to get to the top of that,' said Toby, cheerfully. 'Think you can manage it?'

'But where are we going?' said Measle.

Toby seemed to read his thoughts because he said, quickly, 'Look, Measle, your mum and dad will be all right. But it seems to me that they might come down a bit hard on you and the baby.'

'B-but why? What did we do?'

'Between the two of you, an awful lot, old son. They already think you're a secret wizard. They now believe your sister is that thing old Octavo said—'

'A Mallockee.'

'Right. There are a bunch of tests they can do—none of them very pleasant, I'm afraid. I think we ought to keep you both clear of all that. And, once I've got you to safety, then I can work on getting your mum and dad out of there as well. OK?'

Measle nodded slowly. He felt terribly confused. Everything had happened so fast, he hadn't had time to stop and think—

There was a sudden pounding on the door and

muffled shouts from the room beyond. Toby grabbed Measle's arm.

'Come on, Measle. Run now—talk later!'

Toby led the way to the first step on the towering spiral staircase—and they began to climb.

Escape!

By the time Measle had climbed the first two hundred iron steps, his legs were trembling, his lungs bursting, and his heart was pounding so hard in his chest that it felt as if it might, at any moment, jump clean out of his body.

He had to rest. Measle paused, panting. He closed his eyes, bent his head, and pressed his burning forehead to the cold iron of the handrail—

Far below, there was a heavy crash—and the sound of splintering wood.

Tinker growled.

Measle heard Toby's footsteps coming back down the stairs towards him and, a second later, he felt Toby's strong hand on his arm.

'Come on, Measle,' said Toby, quietly, 'we can't

stop now. They're through the door. We've got to keep going. I'll give you a hand. Come on.'

Far below them, there was the distant sound of heavy boots on iron steps. Measle felt Toby's hand grab his own and start to drag him upwards—and, with Toby taking at least some of Measle's weight, the endless placing of one foot above the other became a little less difficult and he found himself climbing faster and more easily than before. Tinker scurried upwards, close by Measle's dragging feet. He didn't seem to be tired at all.

The sound of their pursuers far below them certainly helped to speed all three of them up and up and up, higher and higher and higher—and Measle began to wonder just how high this staircase was because, along with the trembling legs and the burning lungs and the pounding heart, now he was getting really rather dizzy from the continuous circular movement of climbing the endless spiral—

And the sound of pursuit continued far below them, not getting any louder but not getting any quieter, either, just a steady pounding of boots on metal—

Clang—thump—clang—thump—clang—thump—

Measle felt as if he'd been climbing for ever, for all his life, in fact, and, quite probably, that's all he'd be doing for the *rest* of his life, too—

Just climbing. Round and round and round.

Up.

And up.

And up.

And up—

And then, quite suddenly, they were at the top.

They had reached a small iron platform. There was a concrete ceiling two metres above their heads and, in front of them, a heavy iron door, with the sort of horizontal bar at waist height that you push to open.

Toby slammed his free hand against the bar. The door sprang open and he pulled Measle out into a dark, narrow alley, bounded on both sides by high brick walls. Tinker slipped through the narrow opening and Toby pushed the door shut. Then he glanced left and right, and, panting hard, he said, 'Looks like the coast is clear, Measle. But it won't be for long. Come on.'

Measle's legs felt as if they were made of hot marshmallows but he managed to stumble along, close behind Toby's stocky figure. There was dim light at the far end of the alley and, when they neared it, Toby slowed down and motioned to Measle to do the same. They both shrank against the rough brick of the high wall and Toby inched forward and then peered round the corner. Then he reached back and took Measle's hand again.

'OK, Measle. My car's just down the street. Think you can make it?'

Measle started to say that he probably could, but then there was no more time because, from behind them, came the sound of the iron door being smashed open and a gruff voice that yelled, 'Oi! You! Stop right there!'

Toby yanked so hard on Measle's hand that Measle thought his arm was going to be wrenched out of its socket. Together, they burst out of the alley and into the dimly-lit street. The street was empty of people and Toby ran, dragging Measle behind him, towards a low, black car that was parked about twenty metres away. Tinker galloped at their sides. They reached the car in a few seconds. Toby pulled open the door and bundled Measle inside. Tinker jumped in and dropped down into the shadows by Measle's feet. Toby threw the pushchair into the back seat and thrust the sleeping Matilda into Measle's arms. Then, in one fluid movement, he slid into the driver's seat and slammed his door shut.

'Oi! You! Stop!'

Measle glanced back through the car's rear window. The owner of the gruff voice was just emerging from the alley; a huge man, encased in black, his hands holding a metal hoop—

Toby jabbed his thumb against a big red button in the middle of the dashboard and the car's engine rumbled to life.

The car jumped forward, its tyres squealing. They roared off down the dark street and Measle, looking backwards, saw the black-uniformed figure get smaller and smaller and smaller—

Toby drove fast—*just like Dad*, thought Measle—through the dark city streets. Soon they were in the suburbs and, twenty minutes later, they were racing through the open countryside.

'Where are we going?' said Measle, staring out into the darkness.

'Somewhere safe,' said Toby. 'Somewhere far away, too.' There was a short silence and then Toby said, quietly, 'I'm sorry about what happened back there, Measle—I mean, I couldn't have done anything about Sam and Lee, but I'm sorry about not being able to get Miss Flannel out of there too.'

'I don't think we could've done anything,' said Measle glumly, picturing Nanny Flannel trying to drag herself up that endless staircase.

'Probably not—but I'm afraid it means you're going to have to look after your sister all by yourself.'

The next hour passed in silence, with only the sound of the car's powerful engine to keep them company. They were racing up a motorway now and it was Toby who broke the quiet. He glanced across to Measle and said, 'We've got a long way to go, Measle old son. There's a motorway café up ahead. Do you fancy something to eat? I could murder a cup of coffee myself.'

'Sure. Thanks.'

The café was bright and cheerful and—this late at night—fairly empty of customers. Measle found a table and, with Matilda sleeping peacefully in her pushchair beside him, sat down at it. Toby went to the counter and bought Measle a Coke and a ham sandwich and a big mug of black coffee for himself.

Measle ate his sandwich and drank his Coke but they didn't make him feel any better. Instead, he felt tired and depressed. If he could only get those images out of his head: those disturbing images of black-uniformed men roughly grabbing his mother and father—

'Mr Jugg?'

'Toby, Measle, call me Toby.'

'Oh, right. Toby. What were those ring things the men had?'

Toby sniffed in disgust. 'Those are Wrathrings. They use 'em on beastly wrathmonks, to restrain 'em. The rings absorb spells, you see—a captured wrathmonk with a wrathring round its neck can't cast magic. I must say, I never thought I'd live to see the day they were used on innocent *wizards*!'

'They were going to put one of them on me, weren't they? And on Tilly too?'

Toby nodded seriously. 'Looked that way, didn't it?'

'Would it work on a Mallockee, though? If she's so powerful, I mean?'

'I don't see why not, old son. The principle's the same, no matter how powerful you are.'

Five minutes later, they got back into the big black car and started up the motorway again. After a few miles, Measle began to feel quite sleepy—it was very late, long past his bedtime and it had been an exhausting and emotional day—so, holding tight to Matilda and with the comforting feeling of Tinker's compact little body between his feet, Measle lay back against the car's soft leather upholstery and closed his eyes. He felt himself beginning to drift away—

There was just one more question—

'Where are we going, Mr Jugg—I mean, Toby?'

'We're going to one of my homes, Measle. It's way out in the wilds, about as far away from everything as you can get. There isn't another house for a good five miles around. It's called Caltrop Castle.'

'You've got a *castle*?'

'Yup. I hope you like it—because you'll be staying there while I sort out this mess. Now, we've got a long way to go, Measle. See if you can get some rest.'

And, with the thought that he was going to be staying in a real castle floating about in his head, and with the steady, muffled roar of the big engine in his ears, Measle quite soon fell fast asleep.

CaLTROp CaSTLe

For Measle, waking up in the morning was usually a swift affair. One minute he would be asleep, the next he'd be wide awake and ready for whatever the day had in store for him.

But not this time.

This time, waking up was like floating slowly upwards from the bottom of a lake. At first, there was nothing but a soft, velvety blackness. Then, slowly, a gentle light began to press against his closed eyes—and the soft light was getting brighter and brighter and brighter—and now he could feel the touch of some sort of material against his fingertips—a smooth, fine-textured cloth of some kind. It smelt fresh, as if it had come straight from a laundry—(*sheets, perhaps?*). His head seemed to be resting on something soft and squashy—(*a pillow!*). There was a weight on his legs, a warm weight that felt familiar—and now the weight was moving, as if it had a life of its own. The weight shifted off his legs and moved up towards his head. There was a snuffling sound in his ear—then something warm and wet flapped against the side of his face and a breath—a very *doggy* sort of breath—wafted over his nostrils.

Measle's eyes opened a crack.

Tinker was standing over him, staring down into Measle's face, his fuzzy head cocked to one side and his stumpy little tail a wagging blur.

'Hello, Tink,' muttered Measle blearily and rubbing the sleep from his eyes. Then he pulled himself up against the pillows and stared around him in wonder.

He was in a big, airy room, full of light that streamed in through a tall window set in the far wall. The glass in the window was made up of small, diamond-shaped panes that were held in place with lead strips, just like the kind of window you'd expect to see in a very grand old house. There were heavy, dark green velvet curtains on either side of the window and the window frame wasn't made of wood—it was arched at the top and made of a warm, sand-coloured stone.

Whether the rest of the walls were also made of stone, Measle couldn't be sure, because they were completely covered, from floor to ceiling, by dark wood panelling. On the right-hand wall, and set into the panelling, there was a huge fireplace. A couple of comfortable-looking chairs and a big squashy sofa stood square on to the fireplace, on either side of which were bookshelves that reached to the high ceiling. Measle saw that several of the bookshelves on one side of the fireplace had been removed, to make room for a large television set. The bed itself, where Measle lay propped up against the pillows, was a wonder. It was huge, with four carved wooden posts, one at each corner. When Measle raised his eyes and looked straight up, he saw that the four posts held up a sort of canopy, made of the same dark green velvet that framed the window. This canopy formed a false ceiling above his head and, hanging from the supporting frame, was a pair of green velvet drapes that reached to the floor on either side of the bed. These drapes were held back by heavy brass hooks but Measle saw that, if you unhooked the curtains, you could draw them all the way round the bed, enclosing yourself completely in a little private room of your own.

Where on earth am I? thought Measle—and then, slowly, the memories began to filter back into his brain that was still sluggish with sleep.

Caltrop. Caltrop Castle! He was safe in Caltrop Castle! He and Tinker—and Tilly! Where's Tilly?

Measle looked frantically round the huge room. He saw Matilda's pushchair first—and there, next to it, was a high-railed wooden cot. Matilda was standing up inside it, peering at him with a serious look on her face. Matilda was still in the clothes she'd been wearing yesterday—

Oh, no, thought Measle, *she's going to be all stinky and I'm going to have to change her nappy—*

With a sinking heart, Measle slipped out from between his sheets, went to the cot, lifted Matilda out, and then carried her back and laid her on his bed.

A moment later, Measle saw that there was no need to change Matilda's nappy at all.

Matilda's nappy was as fresh and clean and dry as if she'd just put it on.

'Ah,' said Measle, slowly. 'How did you manage that, Tilly?'

How Matilda had managed it was quite simple, in a magical sort of way. She had woken up, in this strange cot, in this strange room—with that familiar damp and uncomfortable feeling that meant she needed changing. When nobody came anywhere near her, she'd pulled herself upright and, holding tight to the cot rail, had looked around the room. She'd seen her big brother sleeping soundly in the enormous bed. She'd seen Tinker, curled up at Measle's feet. She'd said, 'Brocka-brocka-brocka!' quite loudly, several times, but Measle didn't wake up and Tinker had simply lifted his head, glanced at her, and had then gone back to sleep. Matilda had tried the crying trick next—a bit of 'Waaah! Waaah! Waah!' usually worked and got everybody's attention—but not this time, it seemed. Measle hadn't moved a muscle and now the damp, uncomfortable feeling was getting worse and where was Mum when she needed her?

And then, with nobody taking any notice of her at all, Matilda had simply decided to stop the nasty, damp feeling all by herself. She decided to *make it go away*.

And it did.

She'd felt a little sleepy after making it go away, so she lay back in the cot and had a little nap—and then, an hour later, she'd woken up again and had pulled herself up and had stood there in her cot, waiting patiently for somebody to come and take some notice of her.

Measle lifted Matilda off the bed and put her on the floor. He glanced quickly round the room, to make sure there was nothing there that could hurt her. Then, satisfied that there wasn't, he went to the window. The first thing Measle noticed about the window was that it didn't open. There were no catches, no hinges—it was just a tall expanse of lead strips and diamond-shaped pieces of glass. Measle thought about this for a moment and then decided that perhaps windows in old castles weren't supposed to open. He peered out through one of the diamond-shaped panes. There was a flowerbed under the window, then a broad gravel drive and, beyond that, a sweeping lawn that ended, a hundred metres away, in a dark, glassy lake. Beyond the lake, and forming the horizon, was a line of distant pine trees. There seemed to be no sign of life out there, so Measle turned his attention back to the room. On the wall opposite the fireplace was a door. Measle padded across and opened it—beyond was a bathroom, bigger by far than any at home, tiled in a dark green marble. Measle crossed to the wash basin—there was a brand-new battery-operated electric toothbrush, just like the one he had at home, propped up in a glass and, next to it, a tube of toothpaste— and the toothpaste was the same brand he used at home, too.

Measle brushed his teeth and washed his face and hands and then left the bathroom. He dressed himself in yesterday's clothes and jammed his feet into his old sneakers. He checked to see that Matilda was all right—she seemed quite happy, busily trying to see if Tinker's tail was properly attached to Tinker's body, and Tinker was letting her do it, because having his tail pulled by Matilda, and without doing any growling while it was happening, usually meant that he was given a tasty treat later.

As Measle was shrugging on his leather jacket, there was a knock on the door. Toby was there, a friendly smile under his broken nose.

'Hi, Measle old son,' he said. 'Did you all sleep OK?'

'Yes, thanks,' said Measle, holding the door half closed because Tinker was right behind him and wanting to get out.

'Um . . . I think Tinker needs to go outside. Can we go out into your garden?'

Toby rubbed his beard and said, 'Ah—well, the thing is, Measle, I don't want you wandering around outside. Caltrop Castle is a funny place. Those woods—well, let's just say there are things out there you wouldn't want to meet. You're a long way from Merlin Manor, you understand. But there's a solution, old son. We've got an *inside* garden here at Caltrop, and that's perfectly safe. Come on, I'll show you. Bring your sister, too.'

Measle lifted Matilda into her pushchair and, pushing her in front of him, followed Toby out into the corridor. Tinker trotted at their heels. They walked down a long passage, all panelled in the same dark wood that was in Measle's bedroom. There were various doors leading off the passage, all closed and, round one corner, Measle spotted an enormous suit of jet-black armour, complete with a sword held upright in its gauntleted hands. The armour stood on a black marble plinth and it was so huge that Measle guessed that it must have been made for a real giant of a man.

The passage twisted and turned—left, then right, then left again—then Toby stopped abruptly outside a door that looked just like all the others, except that it had the word 'JARDIN' painted on it in small gold letters.

'That's French for "garden",' said Toby. 'This place was built a long time ago by a very famous French wizard, the Duke of Touffou. That's him up there.'

Toby pointed to an enormous oil painting that hung on the opposite wall. It was a portrait of a tall, dark man, with long, straight black hair that framed a pale, narrow face. The man's eyes were dark and piercing and, wherever you stood, his eyes seemed to follow you. He was dressed in a long crimson robe and was standing by a twisted tree, one hand resting on a crooked branch. Beyond him, in the background, a herd of cows grazed in a distant field.

'The Duke of Touffou was a very early Prime Magus—when the Wizards' Guild was just beginning,' said Toby. 'The story is that he discovered that this area was full of natural magic—and so he built Caltrop Castle on this very spot. And there's something else in the painting, too—I wonder if you can find it?'

Measle looked more closely at the picture. He saw the duke, the twisted tree, the fields stretching away into the distance, the herd of cows in the background—

'Look for a cave, Measle.'

Measle's eyes flickered all over the great expanse of painted canvas—*cave? What cave? Oh!*

There, up near the left-hand corner—a distant cliff—and, in the side of the cliff, a dark, irregularly-shaped opening.

The entrance to the cave was dark, but something even darker seemed to be lurking in its depths. Measle could just make out a vague shape that was a shade blacker than the shadows that surrounded it—and then he saw the twin points of light, set close together, points that seemed to slant upwards at their outer edges—

They looked like the eyes of a cat.

'What is it?' said Measle, gazing up at the picture.

'That was the duke's murderer,' said Toby. 'A very nasty and dangerous denizen of the local woods. People called him Gobbin Good.'

'Called him *what*?' said Measle, trying not to smile. *'Gobbin Good' sounded rather like 'Robin Hood'* —

'I'm afraid he wasn't very funny,' said Toby, who had caught the trace of a grin on Measle's face. 'His name might have been a bit like the outlaw of Sherwood Forest's—but he wasn't like Robin Hood at all. He was quite the opposite, in fact. For a start, he was always spitting, which was why he was called "Gobbin", you see. I don't think Robin Hood did all that much spitting, do you? And, while Robin Hood was an exiled nobleman who stole from the rich and gave to the poor, Gobbin Good was a murderous grimling who stole from the poor and kept it all for himself. Not only that, he always killed his victims after he'd robbed them. With a powerful crossbow, usually from a long way off. That's how he got the duke. Shot him in the back, which was the only way he could have got the better of such a powerful wizard, of course.'

'What did he look like?' said Measle, squinting up at the painting and trying to see more detail in the dark shape in the cave.

'Horrible, so they say,' said Toby. 'All bent and twisted, with a face that would give you nightmares. Not something you'd want to meet down a dark alley, that's for sure. Now, come on, old son—let's see about this garden, shall we?'

Toby twisted the handle and threw the door wide open.

The little garden was perfect. It was about twenty metres by twenty metres, with shrubs and flowerbeds and little pebbled paths—all surrounding a small, perfectly-manicured lawn with a stone fountain in its centre. Water tinkled in the fountain. High overhead was a frosted glass ceiling, through which a soft sunlight filtered down. Matilda expressed her approval of the place by making crowing noises.

'It's not very big, I'm afraid,' said Toby. 'But then neither is your dog. Perhaps he won't mind too much, eh?'

Tinker didn't seem to mind at all. After the usual sniffing around to find exactly the right spot, the little dog did his business and then trotted back to Measle.

'You can come here whenever you like,' said Toby. 'Just remember the word "Jardin" and you'll have no trouble finding it.'

As they walked back to Measle's room, Toby said, 'Now—I'm afraid I'm going to leave you for a while, Measle old son. I've got to get back to town and see what I can do about this mess. I can't do it from here, you see. No phone, no fax, no email at Caltrop. They don't work here. It's all the magic around us—it acts like some sort of interference. So, I'll be gone for a couple of days. Just make yourself at home. Read a book. Watch TV. Wander about as much as you like—but don't try to go outside. OK?'

'OK. Thanks, Toby.'

They reached the door to Measle's room and Toby clapped Measle gently on the back and said, 'Right—well, I'd better make a start, eh? Enjoy yourself—and I'll see you in a couple of days.'

Toby waved his hand cheerily, marched quickly off down the long passage, turned a corner and was gone.

Measle sat on the edge of the four-poster bed, rocking Matilda gently back and forth in her pushchair. He stared out of the tall window, trying hard not to think about the terrible situation that he and his family were in. The whole business of his parents' capture was so scary—and he hadn't been able to do anything to help them—and he had no idea where they were and, come to that, he had no idea where *he* was, either—and now he had the awful responsibility of looking after Matilda, too.

Miserable and frightened as he was, Measle couldn't help feeling a little hungry. And then he realized that, if *he* felt hungry, then so would Matilda. What could he feed her? All he had were his jelly beans—he could feel the comforting pressure of the lumpy plastic bag in his trouser pocket pressing against his thigh. He didn't take the bag out of his pocket, though. Measle didn't want Matilda to see it, because then she'd want some—and Measle knew that you didn't feed a nine-month-old baby jelly beans. They could choke her to death.

And Tinker was hungry too. He was sitting on the floor at Measle's feet, looking up at him expectantly. *Oi! Smelly kid! Wot about a little dog, then? Wot about a poor, hungry little dog, what has had nuffink to eat for ever and ever and ever? Wot is starvin' to death down here!*

Both Tinker's and Measle's thoughts were interrupted by a strange scratching, scrabbling, tapping sort of sound, that seemed to come from the other side of the bedroom door. It was the sort of sound that made you wonder *what* exactly was on the other side of the door and—whatever it was—what did it want?

'Come in,' called Measle—and Tinker stopped pretending he was a starving dog and concentrated on being a fierce watchdog instead. He flattened

his ears against his head and began a low growling in the back of his throat.

For a moment, the scratching, scrabbling, tapping sound stopped. Then it started up again—*scratchscratch, scrabblescrabble, taptap*—

'Come *in*!' shouted Measle. Tinker curled one side of his lip, exposing two of his best teeth.

Scratchscratch, scrabblescrabble, taptap—

Measle got off the bed and crossed over to the door. He put his ear against it and listened. Now, in addition to the scratching and the scrabbling and the tapping, he could hear something else. It was the sound of heavy breathing.

Measle reached for the doorknob, twisted it, and pulled the door wide open.

Standing there in the passage—and glaring at him with a pair of cold, fishy, eyes—was a very small, very skinny—and very damp—little wrathmonk.

MR IGNaTIUS NIGGLE

Measle's first instinct was to reach into his pocket and find a yellow jelly bean. Ever since Nanny Flannel had taught him how to use the magical things, Measle had known that biting down on his least favourite jelly bean (in Measle's case, they happened to be the lemon-flavoured ones) was probably the best thing to do when faced with a wrathmonk. But there wasn't time to *find* a yellow one—and anyway, invisibility for thirty seconds wasn't much good right now since he had Matilda to think of too.

The little creature standing out there in the passage was no taller than Measle and appeared just as skinny—but he had the bone-white face of a real wrathmonk and a pair of staring eyes that looked as if they should belong to something lying on ice in a fishmonger's shop. And, when his thin lips parted and he grinned a humourless grin, he exposed—on either side of his mouth—his two sets of pointed yellow teeth.

The rest of the creature was wrathmonk-ish too. He wore a shabby black suit that was several sizes too small for him. His limp hair was a mousy colour and was stuck flat to his head and parted in the middle. His ears were pointed, his nose was thin and hooked, and his round, fishy eyes were rimmed with red, which made him look as if he'd been crying.

The oddest thing about him was his rain cloud. All the wrathmonks that Measle had come across so far in his short life had black rain clouds hovering over their heads. A black rain cloud was the sign of a wrathmonk—but these rain clouds never came indoors. They were always too big to fit inside a house. So, when a wrathmonk entered a building, his rain cloud stayed outside, dribbling its rain down on the building's roof and not on its wrathmonk owner's head.

This little creature was less fortunate. His rain cloud was very small, no larger than a man's fist, and it hovered over the wrathmonk's head and drizzled a constant stream of very small raindrops down on his head and shoulders. The tiny cloud didn't produce enough water to *soak* the wrathmonk beneath it, but it generated enough to make the creature's hair permanently wet and the whole top-half of its body very damp. In fact, when Measle looked a little closer, he saw that there was actual moss growing on the shoulders of the shabby black suit and that the collar was streaked with a bright green slime.

Measle saw all of this in a horrified fraction of a second and he was about to slam the door in the little wrathmonk's face, when the creature opened its thin gash of a mouth and said, 'Mumps?'

Measle stopped his hand from hurling the door shut. 'What?'

The wrathmonk sighed irritably. '*Mumps?*' he repeated. 'Is dat your name—"Mumps"?'

'No—it's Measle.'

'Funny. I fort Mr Jugg sssaid it was Mumps.'

'No. Measle.'

The wrathmonk frowned crossly. 'Well, I don't care. I'm going to call you Mumps. Dey is both nasssty diseases, ain't dey? Huh? Just like *you*, huh?'

Measle nodded politely, being careful not to anger the creature.

The wrathmonk sniffed. 'Mr Jugg sssaid I got to do wot you tells me to do.'

'What?'

'Wossamatter? You deaf or sssumfing? MR JUGG—SSSAID—I GOT TO DO—WOT YOU TELLS ME—'

The little wrathmonk was interrupted by Tinker. Having given the nasty-looking creature out in the passage a long, hard stare, Tinker made up his mind that the occasion called for some serious protest and so he let loose with a succession of furious, teeth-baring, lip-curling snarls and barks.

The wrathmonk cocked his head to one side and peered round Measle and down at Tinker.

'I don't like dat, Mumps,' he said nervously. 'You better ssstop it doing dat—or I'll breave on it, sssee if I don't.'

To Measle, there was something oddly un-frightening about this little creature. He was so small and so damp and so wretched—and his rain cloud was so ridiculously tiny—that Measle felt brave enough to step out into the passage and close the door behind him. The sounds of Tinker's fury diminished by half.

'Who are you?' said Measle, watching the creature warily.

The wrathmonk stood up straight and puffed out his narrow chest. 'I am Missster Niggle,' he said, haughtily. 'Missster Ignatius Niggle.'

'What are you doing here?'

The wrathmonk blinked several times in bewildered outrage. 'Wot am I doing 'ere? WOT AM I DOING 'ERE?' Mr Niggle's eyebrows had shot up to the top of his head and he stared at Measle with a look of huge superiority. 'I shall tell you wot I am doing 'ere! Disss is my 'ome! I live 'ere!'

'I thought it belonged to Mr Jugg?' said Measle.

For a moment, Mr Niggle looked a bit

uncomfortable. Then he shook his head irritably and several drops of rainwater flew off and spattered against Measle's face.

'Well, yesss,' said the little wrathmonk, 'it belongs to Mr Jugg all right—but dat don't ssstop it being my 'ome, does it? Dat don't ssstop me living 'ere, does it? Dat don't ssstop me working 'ere, does it?'

'You *work* here?'

For a moment, a sort of panic seemed to seize Mr Niggle. His white face twisted fantastically, all of his features looking as if they were trying very hard to put themselves somewhere else.

'Never sssaid dat,' he muttered.

'Yes you did. You said that it belongs to Mr Jugg—but that didn't stop you working here.'

Mr Niggle stared at Measle, his cold, fishy eyes blinking slowly. It was obvious that he had no idea what to say next. The seconds ticked by, the only sounds being Tinker's muffled snarls from the other side of the door.

'You *watch* it, Mumps,' whispered Mr Niggle at last. 'Jussst you *watch* it. I'll *breave* on you, sssee if I don't. I'll breave on both of you!'

Mr Niggle and Measle glared at each other for several seconds. Then Measle said, in his most reasonable voice, 'Well, if Mr Jugg says you've got to do what I tell you to do—then I'm telling you *not* to breathe on us.'

Mr Niggle's face twisted again—into another variety of fantastic contortions—while he thought about this. Then his round eyes narrowed and he said, 'Right—but, if I *did*—coo! Den you'd sssee sssumfing!'

Measle decided that silence was the best answer to this, so the pair of them stared at each other for another ten seconds without saying a word. Mr Niggle appeared to take Measle's silence as a sign that he wasn't very impressed, because he said, 'I 'ssspect you'd like to know what 'appens when I breave on you, eh?'

Measle shrugged, trying to look as if he didn't really care.

Mr Niggle frowned irritably. Then he leaned forward and put his face close to Measle's.

'Deaf. Dat's what appens. Deaf!'

'You make people go deaf?'

'No! No! Not *deaf*! *Deaf!* When I breave on dem, dey die!'

'Oh—you mean *death*?'

'Yeah—dat's what I *sssaid*! *DEAF!* Wossamatter wiv you? You deaf or sssumfing?'

Measle felt a little laugh trying to bubble its way to the surface, so he put on his most serious and respectful face and said, in an awed voice, 'You mean—when you breathe on people, they die?'

Mr Niggle shook his head, sending several drops of rainwater into Measle's face.

'No, no, no—not *peoples*! You get into 'orrible trouble if you kill peoples! I don't kill *peoples*!'

Mr Niggle bent close to Measle and, when he spoke, Measle could smell the faint but familiar smell of old mattresses, dead fish, and the insides of ancient sneakers on the wrathmonk's breath.

'Bugs!' hissed Mr Niggle. 'I can kill bugs wiv my breaving!'

'Bugs?'

Mr Niggle nodded proudly. 'Billions! Dat's how many I've killed! Billions and sssquillions of bugs! All dead, coz of me!'

Mr Niggle sighed a long, satisfied sigh. Then he seemed to have another thought, because he glanced down the passage and then said, abruptly, 'You comin' den?'

'Er . . . where to?'

Mr Niggle snorted crossly. 'De kitchen, o' course! Mr Jugg sssaid I 'ad to make you breakfassst. Come on!'

Tinker was scratching hard at the door, so Measle opened it and Tinker burst out. He peered suspiciously at Mr Niggle and then opened his mouth and started to bark at him, as if he was challenging the nasty creature to a fight. Measle bent down and put his hand on Tinker's neck and the little dog stopped barking at once.

'It's OK, Tink,' said Measle, in a reassuring voice. 'We're going to have *breakfast*.'

Tinker knew a few words. He knew '*sit*' and he knew '*stay*' and he knew '*be quiet, Tink*'. There were several others too and one of them was '*breakfast*'—which was why his ears pricked up immediately and his tail started flipping from side to side. Measle went back into the bedroom and collected Matilda and her pushchair.

'Breakfast, Tilly!' he announced and Matilda clapped her hands together and showed him her six teeth. Measle pushed her out into the corridor and when Mr Niggle saw her, he screwed up his face into a look of extreme bewilderment.

'Wot is dat fing?' he muttered out of the corner of his mouth.

'This is my sister, Matilda. I call her Tilly.'

Mr Niggle stared at Matilda for several more seconds, and Matilda stared back at him. Then Matilda decided the little man looked quite funny, so she opened her mouth and grinned at him. Mr Niggle jumped backwards.

'Wot did it do dat for?' he asked, suspiciously.

'I think she likes you,' said Measle.

This idea seemed to puzzle Mr Niggle. His face muscles started wriggling about again and he began to say something—then obviously decided against it, because he turned on his heel and, with a grumpy-looking wave of his hand, he motioned at them to follow him. So, in a little procession, Measle and Matilda and Tinker set off, close on Mr Ignatius Niggle's heels.

The passage twisted and turned, zigzagging this way and that. Several times, Measle got the impression that they had turned back on themselves and were walking back the way they had come. They went along another corridor—round a corner—under a stone archway—round several more corners—through a swinging door that was covered with green baize material—on down several more dim passages before arriving, at last, at a heavy wooden door, studded all over with large, square, iron nail heads. The door stood open and Measle, Tinker, and Matilda stepped into a great room with a high, vaulted stone ceiling. There was a big, black, old-fashioned cooking range along one wall. In the middle of the room was an ancient pine table, scarred and gouged and scrubbed, its worn surface showing its many years of use. There were several old pine chairs set round the table. Copper pots and pans hung from hooks on the stone walls and there was a big white sink, with rust stains streaking its sides.

Mr Ignatius Niggle was standing by the cooker, his arms folded across his narrow chest, staring irritably at Measle and Matilda and Tinker as they entered his domain.

'Right,' said the little wrathmonk, peering sourly at them. 'Wodja want?'

'Er ... can I have some toast, please?' said Measle. 'And marmalade? And a glass of milk? And Tilly likes cereal and milk.'

Mr Niggle sniffed and said nothing.

'And Tinker likes dog biscuits,' said Measle. 'If you've got any? And some water for him, please.'

Mr Niggle sniffed again. Then he gestured for Measle to sit down at the old pine table. Measle sat down, pulling Matilda's pushchair next to him. Tinker squatted at their feet, staring expectantly at the little wrathmonk. Mr Niggle stared back—and then, abruptly, he turned on his heel and marched out through a small door on the other side of the room. By leaning sideways, Measle could see through a crack in the door. There were shelves in there, stacked with stuff, and Measle guessed that the room was a sort of pantry and storeroom combined. Measle, Matilda, and Tinker waited in silence for several minutes. There was the sound of banging pots and pans. Then Mr Niggle reappeared, carrying a wooden tray. There were two plates on the tray, together with a couple of glasses and a pair of metal bowls.

Mr Niggle advanced to the kitchen table and dumped one of the plates and a glass down in front of Measle. Then he did the same for Matilda. Then he bent and placed the two tin bowls on the floor, in front of Tinker's nose.

With a sly and nasty little smile on his mouth, he straightened up and glared down at Measle and Matilda.

'Your breakfassst,' he announced.

Measle looked down at his breakfast. On his plate was a dusty old brick, with bits of cement still stuck to it. His glass was filled to the brim with a clear liquid that looked like water. It didn't smell like water, though—even from a metre away,

Measle could detect the strong, chemical stink of the stuff. It smelt familiar—

'Er . . . what's this?' asked Measle, pointing at his glass.

'Dat is purplepine,' said Mr Niggle, smugly. 'Lovely, lovely purplepine. Drink up.'

'Purplepine?' said Measle. 'What's purplepine?'

Mr Niggle rolled his eyes impatiently. 'Purplepine! Dat is de ssstuff wot you clean paint brushes wiv!'

'Oh—you mean *turpentine*,' said Measle.

'Dat's what I said,' muttered Mr Niggle. '*Purplepine.*'

Measle knew what turpentine was, because one of the things his mother liked doing in her spare time was oil-painting. Lee wasn't very good at it, but that didn't matter. She *liked* doing it—and Measle liked to watch her, and sometimes he helped to clean her brushes—and that was why the smell of the liquid in his glass was so familiar. The trouble was, turpentine was pretty poisonous stuff—and right now Matilda was reaching out one chubby hand towards her glass—

Measle leaned forward and shoved the glass out of Matilda's reach.

Tinker whined softly. Measle looked down at the little dog. In front of Tinker's nose was his plate. There was a brick in it, too—and the bowl next to it was full of turpentine.

Mr Niggle sniggered.

'Eat up,' he said. 'Eat up your lovely breakfasts.'

Measle's mind was racing. This was such typical wrathmonk behaviour—nasty and spiteful and pointless—only, in Mr Niggle's case, it was nasty and spiteful and pointless in a not-too-terribly-dangerous way. He was remembering all the other wrathmonks he'd dealt with before—Griswold Gristle and Judge Cedric Hardscrabble, Scab Draggle, Buford Cudgel, Mr Flabbit, and the Zagreb couple—and everything they had tried to do to him had been *extremely* dangerous. Life-threatening, in fact. And then there was Basil Tramplebone, his horrible old guardian, who had tried to turn him into a cockroach—

All very nasty stuff.

And all those wrathmonks had something in common.

They weren't very bright.

'Mmm! Yummy!' said Measle, licking his finger and then dabbing it against the dusty old brick. He lifted his finger, stuck it in his mouth and sucked it loudly. He could taste the cement dust.

'Really delicious!'

Mr Niggle looked puzzled. 'Huh?' he said, doubtfully.

'The best breakfast ever! And thanks a ton for not bringing me toast and marmalade and milk! That's what they make me eat at home—and I hate it! I only asked for it because that's what I'm *supposed* to have. But I think it's really disgusting! So does Tilly! Horrible, icky stuff! Eeeuuugh! And Tinker really hates dog biscuits, too! But bricks and turpentine—wow! Thank you very much! Thanks from *all* of us!'

Mr Niggle's expression changed from bewilderment to a look of crafty cunning. He rubbed his pale hands together and his fishy eyes darted round the big room—and Measle could see that the little wrathmonk was trying to use his brain to its fullest capacity. Measle hoped that the capacity of Mr Niggle's brain was very, very small—

Suddenly, without a word, Mr Niggle collected all the plates and bowls and glasses and put them back on his tray. He picked up Tinker's metal bowls and placed them next to the others. Then, without a word, he scurried off to the storeroom. Measle listened as a number of sounds came from beyond the small door—the sounds of cupboards opening, packages being unwrapped, cartons being opened, lids being twisted off—

Five minutes later, Mr Niggle came back into the kitchen. He carried his wooden tray, which was now filled with dishes and bowls and cups and glasses—and he marched up to the kitchen table with an air of triumph and dumped everything down in front of Measle and Matilda.

'Dere!' he exclaimed, loudly. 'Eat dat if you dare!'

On the table in front of Measle was a plate piled high with perfectly-toasted toast. There was a dish of marmalade, too, another of butter, and a tall glass of milk. Matilda had a bowl of cereal and her own glass of milk—and, on the floor at their feet, Tinker was looking with interest at a metal bowl filled to the brim with dog biscuits.

'Eeeuuugh!' said Measle, making a disgusted face. 'Are you trying to make me sick?'

Mr Niggle grinned delightedly, clasped his hands under his chin, and did a strange little hopping, shuffling dance.

'Ho, yesss!' he squealed. 'And you will eat every bit of it! Or else I shall just 'ave to breave on you! Eat! Eat!'

Measle sighed and tried to look depressed. He sneaked a sideways look at Matilda—and saw with relief that his sister was doing what she usually did with food when it was first presented to her: she was sloshing it around with her hands and not actually putting anything in her mouth. Now all that was left to hope for was that Tinker would do what Tinker usually did with a bowl of dog biscuits.

To Measle's relief, Tinker did. He took a quick sniff at the bowl—and then he turned his face up, cocked his head to one side, and stared up at Measle with his *look-at-me-I'm-a-poor-little-starvin'-orphan-doggy-wot-needs-real-human-food* expression.

'Poor Tinker,' said Measle, dejectedly buttering a piece of toast. 'He hates those things just as much as I hate this stuff.'

Mr Niggle peered down at Tinker and frowned angrily.

'Well—he's being a wicked dog, isn't he,' he announced. 'Not eatin' nuffing. A very wicked dog indeed. I shall jussst 'ave to breave on him, won't I?'

And, before Measle could do anything about stopping him, Mr Niggle took a deep breath, bent over, and puffed hard in Tinker's face.

Interestin', thought Tinker. *Very interestin'. I've smelt that smell before, lots of times. Usually a bit stronger than this—Hello? Where's my tickle gone?*

Tinker's tickle was a semi-permanent itch, usually located behind his right ear. Sometimes the itch went down his neck and occasionally he had to sit down and scratch his stomach as hard as he could because the itch had travelled down there.

But mostly the itch stayed behind his right ear and that's where it had been all morning—

And now, quite suddenly, it was gone.

(And the flea—which had been living for some time very comfortably behind Tinker's right ear—dropped, dead as a doornail, out of Tinker's wiry fur and down onto the stone floor at his feet. Several thousands of other tiny parasites—all too small to see with the naked eye—also fell dead from Mr Niggle's poisonous breath and, for the first time in his doggy life, Tinker found himself entirely free from tiny hitchhikers.)

'That'll teach 'im,' muttered Mr Niggle—and, to the little wrathmonk's satisfaction, Tinker gave up waiting for a bit of toast and wandered instead back to his bowl of biscuits. He sniffed them again, sighed—and then he picked out a single biscuit and began to crunch it thoughtfully.

Measle ate steadily through his pile of toast, carefully keeping up a series of little muttering sounds, all designed to make Mr Niggle think that he was having a hard time eating the disgusting stuff. And, all the while, Measle watched the little wrathmonk out of the corner of his eye. Measle decided that Mr Niggle didn't pose much of a threat. If the wrathmonk's spell-casting abilities were as pathetic as his breathing magic, then Ignatius Niggle wasn't going to be too much of a problem. *But it might be a good idea to find out exactly what he can do—*

'Can I ask—Eeeugh! This toast is horrible!—can I ask you something?'

'Don't sssee why not,' said Mr Niggle, looking pleased with himself.

'Well—Oh, yuck! Disgusting marmalade!—I was wondering what spells you can do? Apart from the breathing one, I mean?'

Mr Niggle stopped looking pleased with himself and, instead, adopted a look of deep sadness.

'Can't do any,' he muttered. 'Not any more. Dey won't let me do it, sssee?'

Mr Niggle lifted both hands to his neck and pulled apart the wet collar of his grubby shirt. There was a ring round his scrawny throat—a ring made out of a dull, silvery metal—

A wrathring!

Which means that Mr Niggle can't hurt me with magic, even if he wants to!

Measle decided to ask some more questions.

'Um . . . when you *could* do spells, what sort were they?'

Mr Niggle looked a little embarrassed. He sniffed nervously and rubbed his nose with the back of his hand. Then he said, in a low, sad voice, 'I could only do one.'

'And what was that?'

Mr Niggle stared at the floor and mumbled something under his breath.

'Sorry?' said Measle. 'I didn't quite catch that.'

'I sssaid—I could open fings. Doors and fings.'

Measle thought about this for a second and then he said, 'But I can do that. All you've got to do is turn the handle, see—'

'I *know* dat, Mumps,' said Mr Niggle, shaking his head irritably. 'De point is—I could open dem when dey was *locked*, sssee?'

'Oh, I see. That's very clever.'

'Ho, yesss. Dat is what I am—very clever *indeed*. Wot else do you want to know?'

'I was wondering how you came to be living here?'

Everybody likes being asked to talk about themselves and Mr Niggle was no exception. 'Ho! Well, it all come about after I was happily ended, sssee—'

Happily ended? Measle didn't think that Mr Niggle's end was particularly happy-looking, so he said, 'Happily ended?—Ugh! I hate milk!—What's "happily ended" mean?'

Mr Niggle didn't look very pleased at being interrupted.

'Happily ended? Wossit mean? It means—well— it means . . . er . . . when you've done sssumfing bad, sssee and den you get arresssted, sssee?'

'Oh—you mean *apprehended*?' said Measle.

'Dat's wot I said,' muttered Mr Niggle irritably. '*Happily ended*. Kindly do not interrubble me again—'

'*Interrubble?* What's interrubble mean?'

Mr Niggle banged both his bony white hands

down hard on the kitchen table. Obviously, he did it a little bit too hard, because he said, 'Ow!' quite loudly. Then he swivelled his big, fishy eyes round and glared angrily at Measle.

'You're doin' it again!' he hissed. 'Interrubbling! 'Ow can I tell you my ssstory if you keep on interrubbling?'

Measle dropped his gaze and stared hard at the top of the kitchen table. He did that because he realized that—if Mr Niggle went on making up all these ridiculous words—then there was a danger that he wouldn't be able to stop himself from laughing. There was something so pathetic about poor little Mr Niggle that Measle found himself actually feeling a bit sorry for the creature—*and how can I feel sorry for a wrathmonk? Well—it's weird—but I do!*

'I'm sorry,' said Measle in a humble little voice. 'I won't inter—um—I won't interrubble again.'

'Sssee dat you don't,' said Mr Niggle severely. 'Now den, where was I? Ho, yesss—I was happily ended, 'cause I done sssumfing bad, sssee? What I was doin' was—I was burglariding dis old wizard's house. You know what burglariding is, do you?'

Measle shook his head, trying hard to keep a straight face.

'Coo—you don't know *nuffing*, do you? It's when you take ssstuff wot ain't yours, sssee? Dat's burglariding. Dat's what I was, sssee? A burglarider!'

Measle nodded slowly—but his mind was racing. *So—poor Mr Niggle must have started out as a pathetic little one-spell wizard—a spell which he'd used to help him steal stuff—and being a petty thief would pretty soon have turned him into a pathetic little one-spell* warlock—*and, with a brain as hopeless as Mr Niggle's, it wouldn't have taken long before the strain of being a warlock burglar proved too much for his sanity—turning him into this pathetic little excuse for a wrathmonk!*

'Ssso,' went on Mr Niggle, 'dere I was, busy burglariding, when I got caught, sssee? Dis old wizard, he come down de ssstairs in his jimmy-jammies and he puts a big ssspell on me wot completely paraglides me—wot? Wot's ssso funny?'

'Nothing,' gasped Measle, hurriedly wiping away a tear of laughter from the corner of his eye. 'I wasn't laughing, honestly I wasn't. I got some of this horrible toast stuck in my throat. Please—go on.'

'Right—well, dere I was, completely paraglided. I couldn't move nuffing, except for my mouf. Den de old wizard, he goes and makes a fellytone call—'ere, you're doing it again! You ought to learn 'ow to eat dat toast ssstuff wivout choking to deaf!'

'Sorry.'

'Right. Jussst you be careful. Well, after de fellytone call, we sssits about and waits and dis old wizard, he tells me his name is Lord Octopus—'

Measle sat up straight. 'Lord Octavo?' he blurted.

'Dat's wot I *sssaid*, Mumps,' said Mr Niggle. 'Lord *Octopus*. Anyway, he was quite nice. Made me a cup of tea, gave me a bissscuit. Den, after a bit, dis uvver wizard come in and he had dis lady wiv 'im. Dey was quite young, not like Lord Octopus. Now, dis *young* wizard asked me a whole lot of quessstions and den he sssaid he was going to— wot was 'is exact words, now?—ho, yess, he said he was going to "*ricky-bend leaningsea*". Dat's what he sssaid to me. "I'm going to ricky-bend leaningsea," he said.'

Even after several moments of intense thought, Measle couldn't work out what '*Ricky-bend leaningsea*' could possibly mean. But Mr Niggle didn't look too upset about what had happened to him, so—

'That was very . . . er . . . nice of him. Ricky-bending leaningsea, I mean.'

'Yeah, well—I wasn't burglariding '*im*, was I? I was burglariding Lord Octopus. I even remember 'is name. It was Mr Sssam Ssstubbs—'

'That's my dad!' yelled Measle, jumping up out of his chair.

'Your dad?'

'Yes! And the lady with him—that must have been my mum!'

'Your mum?'

'Yes!'

Mr Niggle, frowning with terrific concentration,

let his small brain absorb this new information. Then, at last, his face cleared.

'Ho!' he said, excitedly. 'Ssso dat means your name is Mumps *Ssstubbs*!'

'Well—*Measle* Stubbs, really,' said Measle.

Mr Niggle waved a hand carelessly in the air. 'Measles, mumps—sssame fing! But dat's not de point! De point *is*—Mr Sssam Ssstubbs is your dad! And dat changes *everyfing*!'

'It does?' said Measle, wondering what, exactly, was going to change.

'Yesss!' shouted Mr Niggle, grinning widely and showing all his pointed teeth. 'Dat means I *like* you now! 'Cause your dad was nice to me, sssee—and he *ricky-bended leaningsea*! Dat's why I'm working here, and not—' Mr Niggle ducked his head, looked suspiciously from side to side, and then whispered hoarsely into Measle's ear, '—and not ssstuck in de uvver place!'

'What other place?'

Mr Niggle didn't reply straight away. Instead he just shook his head very hard, scattering droplets of water all over Measle and the remains of the toast. Then, looking very mysterious, he winked, tapped the side of his nose with a long, bony finger and muttered, 'Asssk no quessstions, tell no fibby-dibs.'

'Oh, right,' said Measle, trying to look wise.

Quite suddenly, Mr Niggle swooped forward and gathered up Measle's and Matilda's now nearly empty plates and glasses. He clattered them down onto his tin tray and then bent and picked up Tinker's bowl from right under the little dog's nose.

'You won't be wantin' dis nasssty ssstuff no more,' he said, sounding just a little bit apologetic. 'You can 'ave your nice brick and your lovely purplepine back.'

Measle did some very fast thinking and then— hoping that Mr Niggle had meant what he'd said about liking him now—decided to come clean.

'Well, actually—I was only joking. I don't really like bricks and turpentine, you see. Neither does Tilly. Not even Tinker.'

Mr Niggle considered this for several seconds. Then he beamed and said, 'Dat was a *joke*? Dat's *funny*! Hahahahahahahaha! Hoohoohoohoo-hoohoo!' He bent over and laughed like a mad hyena. Then, wiping his streaming eyes, he straightened up and said, 'I likes you. I do. Ssso, now you can call me Iggy.'

'Iggy?'

'Iggy. Dat's short for Ignatius, sssee? Okey-dokey?'

'Okey-dokey, Iggy.'

It was a new sensation for Measle, having a wrathmonk being friendly to him. He decided to make the most of it while the friendship lasted. His experience with wrathmonks led Measle to believe that their madness made them horribly unpredictable and likely to change their minds in an instant, so he kept himself alert and ready for anything. For instance, how would Iggy react to this request—

'Um—could I see round the castle, Iggy?' he asked.

'Sssee round *my* cassstle?'

'If you don't mind.'

It was obvious that nobody had ever asked Iggy such a thing before, because once again the little wrathmonk's face screwed itself up in a whole succession of wild grimaces as he tried to work out what his answer should be. Then, at last, the wriggling of his facial muscles settled down.

'Yesss,' he said, firmly. 'Dat would be all right. But only de *inssside*. Not de *outssside*. We can't go outssside, sssee? Dat's not allowed.'

For the next half hour, Measle and Matilda—with Tinker trotting at their heels—followed Iggy Niggle all over the inside of Caltrop Castle. It was a vast place. There were endless corridors that twisted this way and that, sometimes doubling back on themselves, then turning again and resuming their original direction. They all looked pretty much the same, too, with their dark panelling and their stone floors. Measle thought it was like being in a sort of maze and, like a maze, he never had any idea where he was.

At one point, near the end of the tour, Iggy Niggle threw open a door and said, 'Dese is Missster Juggs's rooms.'

Toby's rooms weren't very interesting. There was

a small bedroom and an even smaller bathroom. In the bathroom there were all the things you'd expect to find in a bathroom—and Iggy seemed to want to show Measle every single one of them.

'Dis is Mr Juggs's bath—and dis is Mr Juggs's toilet—and dis is Mr Juggs's basin—and dis is Mr Juggs's flannel—and dis is Mr Juggs's sssoap—' and on and on went Iggy, detailing everything down to the smallest item in a droning voice, as if he were reciting a shopping list.

A couple of objects caught Measle's eye. There was a little, flat, round silver case, full of what looked like compressed face powder—and a small brush, which looked like something an artist would use. Measle recognized it immediately—his mother Lee had several on her dressing table in Merlin Manor and, on the rare occasions when she put on make-up, she used the brushes to smooth the colour on to her cheek.

I wonder who that belongs to? thought Measle. *Perhaps Toby's got a girlfriend?*

There was nothing more to see in Toby's bare rooms, so Measle and Matilda and Tinker followed Iggy back out to the corridor. Iggy paused and said, 'Now den—wot else do you wanna sssee?'

'What about where you sleep, Iggy?' The idea of sleeping in the same building with a wrathmonk— even one as simple and unthreatening as Iggy—was a little unsettling and Measle simply wanted to know just how close Iggy's quarters were to his own room.

Iggy's face brightened.

'You wanna sssee where I sssleep?' he said, delightedly. 'Come on, den!'

Iggy waved one bony hand and set off at a terrific pace, making Measle and Tinker break into a trot just to keep up with him. Matilda, who liked it when somebody pushed her along really fast, squealed with delight and kicked her legs. They went along a dark passageway, round several corners, through a succession of doors, left and right and right and left—and Measle noticed that their surroundings were growing shabbier and shabbier. Now there were patches of damp on the ceilings and ancient, dusty spider webs in the corners. The stone flooring ended after they passed through one door and became old and dirty planks of wood, cracked and splintered with age. These dark and dingy corridors seemed to Measle to go on and on, twisting and turning and getting progressively more and more run-down. And, quite suddenly, Measle realized, with a start of fear, that he had no idea how to retrace his steps to anywhere in this vast castle, let alone back to his bedroom. He caught up with Iggy and tapped him on a wet shoulder.

'Is it much further, Iggy?'

Iggy shook his head and pointed down the passage.

Measle saw that they were approaching a dead end. The passage simply stopped, about twenty metres away, in a brick wall. At the foot of the wall,

and set tight up against it, was an old plywood tea
chest, turned on its side. As they got closer, Measle
saw that there was a puddle of water all the way
round the tea chest, like a little moat—and that the
brick wall next to it was wet and mossy and green
with slime.

'Dere,' said Iggy, proudly. 'Dat's where I sssleep.'
'You sleep in a *box*?' said Measle.
'Yesss, I do,' said Iggy. ''Ere, I'll show you.'
Iggy stepped forward and then bent in half and

wriggled himself into the box. He fitted so tightly in there that his head was twisted over to one side and he had to talk out of the side of his mouth.

'Sssee?' he said proudly.

Now Measle saw why Mr Ignatius Niggle slept in an old tea chest. The rain cloud couldn't follow him into the confined space and, unable to drop its constant load on to Iggy's head, was now forced to drift over the tea chest and dribble on the top of the box instead.

'Very nice, Iggy,' said Measle.

Iggy tried to nod but he was squashed so tightly into his tea chest that the only movement he could make was blinking his fishy eyes.

'It *is* nice, innit?' he blinked. 'Nice and dry, too. I'm ever ssso lucky, ain't I?'

Iggy did several more blinks—and then his eyelids slid down and stayed there.

'Iggy?' said Measle, wondering what was happening.

Iggy's eyes stayed tight shut, but he waved one limp hand in a dismissive sort of gesture.

'Go away, Mumps,' he said, in a sleepy voice. 'I'm all tired now, ain't I? All dis runnin' around. I'm goin' to 'ave a little nap.'

'But—how do I get back to my room?' said Measle.

Iggy opened one eye.

'You lift up one of your foots, den you make it go forward and den you put it down. Den you do de sssame fing wiv de uvver foot—den de sssame fing wiv de uvver foot—den de sssame fing wiv de uvver foot—and you go on doin' dat until you get dere.'

'But I don't think I can remember the way, Iggy.'

Iggy hissed impatiently. 'You go de sssame way dat you came!' he said. 'Now, go away!'

Iggy closed his eye and started to make snoring noises. They weren't very convincing snoring noises, so he was obviously just pretending to be asleep but Measle realized that Iggy was determined to be of no use at all.

'Come on, Tink,' he said. 'Let's see if we can get back, shall we?'

Within five minutes, Measle realized that they were hopelessly lost. He'd walked back down the damp passage, passed through several doors and turned several corners he thought he recognized—and then found himself in a small hallway which he didn't recognize at all.

And this small section of Caltrop Castle seemed, for a moment, to be particularly gloomy.

Measle was thinking hard. There was no doubt at all that he was lost. In fact, he was pretty sure that he couldn't even find the way back to Iggy's box. He looked down at Tinker, who was staring up at him with his fuzzy head cocked to one side.

Then Measle had one of his ideas. It was a small one compared to some of his others *but it might just work—*

'Tink, you want to go outside? Huh? You want to go outside?'

'*Going outside*' was one of the things that Tinker understood. At home, it meant fresh air, open skies, and grass under his feet. Here, in this shadowy place, it could mean only one place—

'Outside, Tink? Wanna go outside?'

The smelly kid was smiling and nodding his head in an encouraging sort of way so Tinker stretched, yawned, and then set off briskly back the way they had come. Measle, pushing Matilda in front of him, followed, hoping for the best.

Tinker led the way back through several doors and then veered suddenly to the right, taking them down a dark and narrow passage. There was a missing floorboard here—Measle remembered steering Matilda's pushchair round it. They had come this way before! And there—that stain on the wall that looked like an upside-down elephant— he'd definitely noticed that on the way to Iggy's box! Measle began to follow Tinker with growing confidence.

For Tinker, the problem of getting lost simply didn't exist. All you had to do was keep your nose fairly near to the ground and smell the scent you'd left behind on your way here—and soon enough you'd arrive back at your starting point. So Tinker, with his nose a centimetre off the floor, led Measle and Matilda with perfect accuracy right back to the little indoor garden. From there, it was an easy walk back to their bedroom.

The next few hours passed slowly and Measle

was terribly bored. Matilda was happy playing with Tinker on the floor, so Measle turned on the television, but it showed nothing but news. The books on the shelves were equally dull. They were leather-bound and dusty and had titles like *Accountancy For Warlocks* and *Cobbett's Property Laws As Pertaining To Wizards' Estates*.

Measle went and sat by the big window in his room and stared out at the sweeping lawn and the glassy lake and the dark forest beyond—

Not a leaf stirred, not a branch waved.

It's very quiet out there, thought Measle. *Not even a tiny breeze.*

At home in Merlin Manor, even at the dead of night, there were always sounds. Faint sometimes—and often far away—the gentle sighing of the wind in the treetops, the distant barking of a dog, the soft hooting of an owl . . .

Noise.

But not here. Caltrop Castle was silent. As silent as—well, as silent as a *grave*.

But, outside the bedroom door, things were happening.

Things were changing.

Things were being—*rearranged*.

Silently.

A CHANGE FOR THE WORSE

The morning drifted into being the afternoon.

Measle came out of a daydream in which he was rescuing his parents from an entire army of fire-breathing dragons and noticed that Tinker had left Matilda's side and was now standing hopefully by the bedroom door.

'Come on then, Tink,' said Measle, 'let's go to the garden again, shall we?'

Measle put Matilda into her pushchair.

He opened the door—

—and then he stood there, very still, his feet frozen to the floor, his eyes wide and staring, and his mouth gaping open.

The passage outside his bedroom door was— well, it was utterly *different*. Completely, totally, utterly different—*no, wait, not everything's different*—the colour and texture of the walls were the same, the floor was still made of worn old flagstones—but there was one extraordinary and, to Measle, utterly mind-boggling alteration. Where, this morning, the passage outside the bedroom door stretched out to the left and the right, so that you could pick which direction to go in, now there was no left or right. Now, the corridor stretched out in *front* of the bedroom door, making Measle's room the last door in a dead end.

'What's going on, Tink?' whispered Measle, staring in bewilderment at the corridor in front of him. A moment later, Tinker started to move. The little dog, with his nose a centimetre from the stone floor, started to trot off down the corridor—and Measle, with no choice in the matter, started to follow.

They twisted and turned, this way and that, along a succession of passages, none of which Measle—to his certain knowledge—had ever been down before. And yet everything *looked* familiar—except for the fact that the corridors and the passages and the doors were all in quite different places from those that Measle remembered from earlier in the day.

It was, Measle decided, one of the most unsettling feelings he'd ever experienced. There was that massive, towering suit of black armour—before, it had been on the right side of an arched door. But now, there was no arched door and the armour was positioned on the other side of the passage—and the passage itself turned sharply right and Measle remembered distinctly turning sharply *left* earlier that morning.

None of this seemed to be bothering Tinker in the least. He kept his nose down close to the floor and simply followed the distinctive smells of his own—and Measle's—footsteps. The scent of his own paws—and scent of the soles of Measle's sneakers—were two things that hadn't changed and, as far as Tinker was concerned, the fact that everything *else* had altered around him didn't matter in the least.

Tinker turned another unfamiliar corner and then stopped dead outside a door. The door was the same familiar garden door, with the word 'JARDIN' painted on it in small gold letters—only now, instead of being on the right-hand side of the corridor, it was on the left, next to a sharp bend in the passage, which Measle knew had not been there earlier. And now the great portrait of the Duke of Touffou was positioned right next to the garden door, instead of hanging on the opposite wall.

But it wasn't just the location of the portrait that had changed.

Something had changed in the painting itself.

The Duke of Touffou wasn't in it.

Where the tall figure of the duke had once

stood, close by the twisted tree, now there was just a smudge—as if somebody had come and wiped the figure off the canvas, leaving just a smear of dark base-paint behind.

There was another, smaller smudge in the background of the painting. There, in the distant fields—where once had stood a herd of cows— there was nothing but a faint outline.

And, in the far-off cave entrance, the twin points of light that looked like a pair of slanted eyes— they were no longer there, either.

Measle stared up at the ruined painting, wondering who could possibly have done this— and why? There seemed to be no point to it at all—

He felt a nudge against his ankle. He looked down: Tinker was staring up at him, his tail wagging fast, the expression in his eyes quite plainly saying, *C'mon, smelly kid! It's the garden, innit? Open the door an' let me out!*

Measle opened the door and Tinker darted inside. Measle followed—and was vastly relieved to see that the garden itself appeared to be unaltered. He pushed Matilda over to a stone bench and sat down. His mind was in a whirl. For a moment, he thought that perhaps he'd gone mad. How could a building as solid and as ancient as Caltrop Castle suddenly change its entire geography? Why would somebody rub a figure out of an old oil painting?

No, I'm not mad, thought Measle. *I've seen lots of weird things in my life, like dragons and giant cockroaches and flying hats—and this is just another weird thing I'm seeing, which doesn't mean I'm mad, it just means I live in a really weird world and this is the kind of thing I've got to get used to seeing all the time.*

Measle got up and he and Matilda and Tinker went out into the unfamiliar corridor. Measle looked down at Tinker and said, 'I hope you can find your way back, Tink, because I don't think I can, and Tilly *certainly* can't—'

And that was when they heard the first scream.

The scream was faint and a long way off—but Measle could still hear the terror and the panic and the desperation in it. A moment later, the scream came again.

Another scream—

Tinker growled softly and turned his head in the direction of the sound.

Another scream—

The screams were beginning to have a familiar tone to them. They were the kinds of screams you might expect to come from the scraggy, scrawny throat of a terrified little Mr Ignatius Niggle—

'It's Iggy, Tink! Come on—let's find Iggy!'

It took Measle and Matilda

and Tinker twenty minutes to locate Iggy, because they were forced to search for him using only their ears.

'He could be anywhere, Tink,' said Measle, as they stood at the start of yet another unfamiliar corridor and strained their ears for the next faint, panic-filled scream.

It came all too soon—

'Come on, Tink—this way!'

They found him at last. Iggy was in a doorway, curled up on the floor, his head buried in his arms. His tiny rain cloud hovered a few centimetres over his prostrate body, dribbling its load down on to the little wrathmonk. Iggy was moaning in terror and, as Measle and Matilda and Tinker rounded the corner and saw him for the first time, Iggy raised his head from the protection of his arms, opened his mouth, and let out another piercing, terror-filled shriek.

Measle ran to Iggy's side. He knelt down and put his hand on Iggy's damp shoulder—and Iggy screamed again and pulled away, burying his head even deeper in his arms.

'Iggy! It's me!' yelled Measle.

Iggy raised his head and opened one fishy eye.

'Mu-Mu-Mumps?' he whispered, his voice shaking with fear. 'Is dat you, Mumps?'

'Yes, Iggy, it's me. It's all right, you're quite safe.'

Iggy grabbed Measle's hand, wrapping it in his

own damp and bony one. His long, claw-like fingernails dug into Measle's palm.

'Sssumfing's happened, Mumps,' he muttered. 'Sssumfing awful! I don't know where I am, I don't know where I'm going and I don't know how to come back again! I woked up and it was all 'orrible and I ssstarted to run and now I can't find my box, can't find my kitchen, can't find *nuffing*! Wot 'appened, Mumps?'

Measle tried to pull his hand gently out of Iggy's grasp but the little wrathmonk held on tight.

'I don't know, Iggy,' he said. 'But everything's in a different place. It's all—well—it's all sort of *rearranged*.'

'Re-a-wot?'

'It's sort of changed itself around, Iggy. It's a kind of magic, I think. All the passages and the doors and things are in different places, you see.'

Iggy's eyes opened very wide and two big tears welled out of them and trickled down his cheeks.

'Oooh!' he moaned, softly. 'It's never done dat before! Not never!'

'Well, it's doing it now, Iggy.'

Iggy was now sobbing openly. 'Y-you know what dis means, Mumps?' he gurgled. 'It means we is going to ssstarve, dat's what dis means! Sssee, de kitchen is de place where all de food is! And if we can't find de kitchen, where all de food is, we is going to ssstarve!'

From behind him, still sitting in her pushchair,

Matilda said, 'Cubba doogy wump.'

Measle looked over his shoulder and saw that Matilda was kicking her feet and holding out her arms—and getting ready to make a lot more noise if some-body didn't pay her some attention pretty soon and do exactly what she wanted.

Measle knew what the kicking and arm-stretching meant. Matilda wanted a cuddle. He went over to her and unbuckled the straps that held her in place.

'Come on then, Tilly—ups-a-daisy.'

He lifted Matilda out of her chair, fully expecting her arms to curl around his neck, as they usually did when he picked her up. But her arms remained stiffly outstretched, both of them rigidly pointing at something down the passage—and Matilda wasn't looking at him, either, she was staring fixedly down the corridor, in the direction of the dead end—and her feet were still kicking, too—

'What is it, Tilly?' said Measle—and Matilda said, 'Cubba doogy *wump!*' again, only more firmly this time.

Measle turned to see what she was looking at.

There was only Iggy Niggle, sitting there in a snivelling heap on the floor, his back leaning against the wall.

Matilda's kicking was getting more desperate, so Measle carried her over to Iggy and squatted down next to him. Iggy looked up, his eyes pink with tears, and he saw this strange little creature stretching her arms out towards him, her feet kicking, her mouth smiling, lips parted, revealing six pearly little teeth.

'Wossit want?' said Iggy, shrinking back against the wall.

'I think she likes you, Iggy.'

'*Likes* me?' Iggy's eyes were even rounder than usual and his mouth was gaping open. 'Wossit like me for?'

'I don't know, Iggy,' said Measle. 'But, when Tilly likes somebody, she always wants to give them a hug. That's what she wants to do now. And you'd better let her, otherwise she'll start making a horrible noise—and I don't want her to do that, because it hurts your ears really badly.'

Very slowly and cautiously, Iggy edged forward, until he was within reach of Matilda's hands. Matilda lunged forward and threw both arms round Iggy's neck—and Measle let go of her, releasing her into Iggy's nervously clutching little claws.

Matilda liked people who took no notice of her. All too often, when she was introduced to strangers, they would want to cuddle her and kiss her and coo in her face—and, most of the time,

Matilda didn't want them to do that. Iggy had never done any of those things. In fact, Iggy had made a point of not even *looking* at her, if he could possibly help it—so Matilda decided that she liked him. Matilda was also very fond of *wet* things. She liked baths and paddling pools and porridge and cereal and she liked getting her hands into them all and having a good splash around—so Iggy, with his own personal rain cloud, was something special.

The first thing she did with him—after the hug—was to scrumple her hands around in his wet hair, until every sodden strand was standing up on end.

'Wossit doing?' whispered Iggy, holding Matilda as if she was made of the most fragile glass in the world.

'Messing up your hair, Iggy,' said Measle. 'Oh, she *really* likes you.'

Matilda *did* like Iggy— she liked him a lot. He looked so funny and she admired his cloud enormously. But there were one or two little

144

things wrong with him. His breath wasn't very nice—so Matilda changed it. She waved her hands and the smell went away. Nobody noticed—certainly not Iggy—but now his breath no longer smelt of dead fish, old mattresses, and the insides of ancient sneakers. Now it didn't smell of anything at all.

The other thing about Iggy that Matilda changed was the colour of his teeth. Matilda was very proud of her own, so, with a wave, she took the yellow stains away from Iggy's teeth and made them the same colour as hers. Nobody noticed Iggy's new teeth, either.

Matilda, having performed two little spells, felt the tiredness sweep over her. She put her head on Iggy's damp shoulder and, within five seconds, fell fast asleep.

'Is—is it dead?' said Iggy, his voice quavering with terror at the thought.

'No, Iggy. She's just asleep,' said Measle. He looked at his sister thoughtfully. 'She's been doing a lot of that lately.'

'Wot should I do wiv it?' said Iggy, squinting down at Matilda's head resting on his shoulder.

'You could carry her for a bit,' said Measle. 'She loves being carried by somebody she likes.'

A slow grin spread across Iggy's face. Nobody had ever liked him before. In fact, everybody he'd ever come into contact with had tried to get away from him as fast as possible. Certainly nobody had ever hugged him. Nobody had ever messed about with his hair. Nobody had ever fallen asleep on his shoulder—

And, in that moment, Iggy felt—for the first time in his miserable little life—actual love for another living being.

'You *sure* it's not dead, Mumps?'

'I'm quite sure, Iggy. Look—you can see her breathing.'

'Does it want sssumfing to eat?'

'Well, she might when she wakes up.'

Iggy's face fell. 'But we is lost, Mumps,' he muttered sadly. 'How is we going to find de kitchen? If we can't find de kitchen, it's going to ssstarve to deaf!' And he started to snivel again.

'No, Iggy,' said Measle, gently. 'I think we're going to be fine.' He pointed at Tinker. 'Tinker can find the kitchen. He can smell it, you see.'

Iggy stopped snivelling almost as quickly as he'd started. The corners of his lips drew themselves up in a cautious little grin, exposing his newly-whitened teeth.

And now Measle noticed the teeth. For a moment, he was puzzled. Then he realized what had happened. Obviously, it was Matilda's doing— and here she was, asleep again, and this seemed to happen immediately after his sister had performed some magic, which was rather interesting—

His thoughts were interrupted by Iggy tugging at his sleeve.

'Can we go to de kitchen now, Mumps?' he

asked. 'Coz it might wake up soon and be 'ungry—
and den it might make de 'orrible noise, mightn't
it?'

Measle clicked his fingers and Tinker's ears
pricked up.

'Dinner, Tink! Want some dinner?'

Tinker never turned down an offer of food. He
wagged his tail twice, then raised his nose in the
still air and sniffed—*There! A long way off—a
definite smell of toast! Right—follow me!*—and
Tinker set off briskly down the corridor, his nose
twitching all the way.

'Come on, Iggy!' said Measle. He folded Matilda's
chair and, trailing it behind him, set off after
Tinker—and Iggy, holding carefully to Matilda as if
she was a glass of water from which not a single
drop must be spilled, scurried along at his side.

They threaded their way through the endless
maze of corridors.

Left, right—

Right, left—

On and on and on—

And then Tinker stopped so abruptly that Iggy
almost tripped over him.

'Go on den, doggie,' muttered Iggy, prodding
Tinker on the rump with the toe of one scuffed old
shoe.

Tinker's legs didn't move. In fact, the only thing
that moved on Tinker's body was the ridge of fur
that ran all the way from his neck to the base of his

tail. This line of coarse hairs rose and stood upright, so that it looked like a little Mohawk haircut. At the same time, Tinker curled back his lips and, exposing his teeth, began a low growling.

'Wot's de matter wiv it?' whispered Iggy.

'I don't know, Iggy,' said Measle. 'But I think there's something up ahead that Tinker doesn't like.'

They were almost at the end of a corridor. Ahead of them was a T-junction, giving them the choice of turning either left or right. There was nothing to be seen at the junction itself, so Measle guessed that, whatever Tinker was sensing, it must be lurking a few metres down one side or the other. Very cautiously, he crept past Iggy and Matilda, then past the rigid, quivering Tinker. He reached the junction and poked his head forward—he looked first to the left—

Nothing there—

Then to the right—

Something there.

Something tall and thin and dark. Very tall, very thin, very dark—with a pair of piercing black eyes that gleamed in the gloom—

The figure stepped forward.

And Measle's jaw dropped.

It was the man from the painting—the Duke of Touffou—brought somehow to life! That alone was startling enough, but the most unsettling thing to Measle was the fact that the duke was quite obviously made out of *paint*. Measle could see fine cracks, criss-crossing all over the duke's face and clothes. On an old painting, the cracks simply indicate the painting's age, but on the duke, those same cracks gave his face the look of a long-dead corpse.

Somehow, Measle made his legs move. Slowly, he started to back away, and the duke smiled uncertainly and moved forward equally slowly, until he was standing in the centre of the T-junction.

'What have we here?' said the duke, in a thick accent that Measle guessed was French. 'A small boy, a small dog—and a small peasant, wiz a *very* small person in his arms! And what are zey doing here? Here in my château?'

The duke frowned. Then, quite suddenly—and for no apparent reason—every muscle in his body jerked spasmodically. The duke opened his eyes very wide, as though astonished beyond belief at what he was seeing. Then, slowly, he lowered his eyes and stared down at his own chest. Measle—who had never seen anybody behave like this before—also lowered his gaze to the duke's chest.

A short, gleaming spike of metal was sticking out of the front of the wizard's crimson robe.

The duke brought one hand up and touched the tip of the spike. Then he raised his dark eyes and stared—with an expression of deep bewilderment—at Measle. Slowly, he shook his head. Then he took one staggering pace forward and, without warning, fell forward. He didn't bend in the middle as he fell—he toppled over, as straight as a tree that had just been cut down. He hit the ground with a thump and lay still.

Sticking out of the duke's back was a short wooden rod. At the end of the rod were three black feathers.

For several moments, it seemed to Measle that the world was standing still. Nothing happened, nothing moved and, apart from his own breathing, Measle didn't hear a sound. Then, in the shadows a long way down the passage, there appeared two points of light. The points slanted up at the outer edges—

The points of light were moving, coming closer and closer—and now Measle could see a bent and shambling shape that seemed to be accelerating towards him. Measle took a step backwards—

Then the shape came into the light.

Measle gasped, because here (*it could be nobody and nothing else!*) was Gobbin Good.

Gobbin Good had a head. The head had two eyes, two ears, and a mouth. Gobbin Good also had two arms and two legs and, in between, a body of sorts—but even though the number of limbs and organs was perfectly correct, any resemblance to a human being stopped right there. The grimling looked as if he had been stitched together from bits and pieces, collected from a whole lot of people of completely different sizes. His painted skin was cracked, just like the duke's had been—but it was also lumpy and coloured a sickly shade of green, like a toad. His head was small, not much bigger than a grapefruit, and it came to a point at the top. A few strands of greasy hair hung round the thing's face—a face that, for the rest of his life, Measle would remember with a shudder. The grimling had no nose—just warty green skin where his nose should have been. His mouth was lipless and the lower jaw jutted forward, like a bulldog's. The teeth in this bottom jaw were jagged and stained, and they overlapped the creature's upper lip, like a row of crooked tombstones. Gobbin Good's eyes were yellow and slanted. He had no neck—at least as far as Measle could see—and his shoulders sloped down to a pair of long and powerful arms. The hands were huge, far bigger than they should have been, and the fingers were gnarled, with long, curved fingernails that were black with dirt. The creature's feet were huge too, although his legs were short and bowed. Covering the grimling's misshapen body were layers upon layers of tattered, filthy black rags and, in his enormous hands, he carried a massive crossbow made of iron and wood.

Gobbin Good came level with the still body of the Duke of Touffou. He nudged the corpse with one booted foot and then, satisfied that the duke was dead, he spat disgustingly, sending a glob of greenish slime to splatter against the crimson robe. Then he bent down and, with his powerful hands, reset the string on the crossbow. Once the string was taut again, the grimling looked up, concentrating his yellow eyes on Measle. He grinned cruelly, exposing even more stained and crooked teeth. Then, without a word, he reached into a quiver that was slung on his back, pulled out a short arrow and placed it into the slot on the crossbow.

Measle didn't need to be told what was likely to happen next. He looked around him for some means of escape. He saw that Iggy had shrunk back against the wall and was clutching Matilda protectively. Tinker was, as usual, standing his ground, his head cocked to one side and his tail tucked down between his back legs.

And then Measle saw that the herd of cows, which had stood in the distant background of the painting, were now shuffling forward out of the shadows.

Cows are clumsy creatures—and very curious, too. They like to see what's going on and the ones at the back of the herd have a tendency to shove and push at the ones in front of them—

As Gobbin Good slowly raised his crossbow, the cows jostled forward and one of them nudged against the grimling's right arm. Instinctively, Gobbin Good tightened his grip on the crossbow. Without meaning to, he also tightened the tension of his index finger on the bow's trigger—

There was a TWANG! and the arrow whistled across the corridor, missing Measle's nose by a centimetre before thudding against the stone wall. A look of irritation crossed Gobbin Good's face. His lips twisted in a snarl and he spat again. He pushed the nearest cow away and bent down to reset the crossbow string. In doing so, Gobbin Good was momentarily lost from view among the cattle that were now milling aimlessly round him.

Measle started to back slowly away from the jostling herd. And then he saw something that made his heart beat even faster in his chest.

One of the cows seemed much bigger than the rest. It stepped forward, away from the rest of the herd. It lowered its massive head and glared at Measle through small, reddened eyes.

And Measle realized that it wasn't a cow at all.

It was a bull.

It was huge. It had a brass ring set in its nose and a pair of wide and wicked-looking horns on its head. To Measle, it looked very big, very powerful—and, quite suddenly, very angry, too. The bull stared at Measle, then it shook its head from side to side and the horn tips whistled through the air. Its tail whisked back and forth and one hoof pawed and scraped across the stone floor. Then it lowered its head even nearer to the ground and snorted loudly.

Measle knew enough about bulls to guess what was going to happen next. And the *combined* threats of the huge animal and the murderous grimling were enough to jump-start him into action. Measle dropped the folded pushchair and screamed, *'RUN!'* at the top of his voice.

And the bull was the first to obey. It bunched the muscles in its powerful back legs and leapt forward.

Fear can make a frightened person do extraordinary things. In this case, fear made Measle run faster than he'd ever run before and it seemed to do the same thing to Iggy, too, even carrying the weight of Matilda in his arms. Tinker had always been a fast dog, so he had no trouble keeping up with their racing feet as they tore back down the corridor.

Behind them, Measle could hear the sounds of angry snorting and heavy, pounding hooves—

Left, right—right, left—on and on they ran—and, slowly, the sounds of the pursuing bull began to diminish a little. The fact was, the animal was simply too huge and heavy to handle all the twists and turns that the corridors of Caltrop Castle presented it with. It was forced to slow down to a lumbering trot to get round some of the narrower corners, so a couple of lightweight humans and a small terrier had all the advantages here. But the sounds of the bull's massive body thudding against the castle walls—and the sounds of its hooves and its snorting breath—never quite died away altogether, which kept Measle and Iggy and Tinker running for all they were worth.

Five minutes later, at the end of yet another unfamiliar corridor, once again Measle had no idea where they were. From the look on Iggy's face, neither did he. But they had to be aiming for *somewhere*, and it might as well be the kitchen; Tinker's nose should still be able to lead them there.

Panting hard, Measle said, 'Tink—dinner! Dinner!'

Tinker lifted his nose and sniffed—and once again he caught the distant scent of toast and dog biscuits. Off he ran and Measle saw, to his relief, that Tinker wasn't simply doubling back the way they had come but, instead, was setting off down yet another unfamiliar passage, which must mean that they would now approach the kitchen from an entirely new direction and that Tinker had no intention of leading them back to where the bull's stamping hooves could be heard far off in the distance.

Gasping for breath, Measle and Iggy followed the little dog, twisting once again round endless corners, zigzagging this way and that until, quite suddenly, the heavy, open wooden door to the kitchen loomed in front of them. They dashed through the gap and then Measle turned back and threw his weight against the door, swinging it shut with a ground-shaking crash. There was a heavy iron bolt next to the handle and Measle slid that home into its hasp. Then, panting for breath, he pressed his ear against the door's rough wooden surface.

There, in the distance, was the faint sound of thudding hooves.

The sound grew steadily louder.

The bull hadn't given up the chase. On the contrary, it was obviously determined to see the finish of it. And so, it seemed, was the rest of the herd, because Measle suddenly detected the sound of distant mooing—which could mean only one thing: the remaining cows had left Gobbin Good and had caught up with their leader and were now joining him in the hunt.

Nearer and nearer they came—

Then the mooing stopped. There was the sudden sound of skidding, of hooves on stone— and a hard thump that rattled the hinges of the great wooden door.

Measle, his ear still pressed hard against the door, felt the sudden impact like a light blow to the side of his head—but he resisted the temptation to take his ear from the panels. He pressed it harder against the rough surface and listened to the heavy, laboured breathing of the huge animal on the other side. Then he heard the bull move away. He heard it stop again. He heard it snort—and a single scraping thump as the bull pawed the ground.

Measle stepped hurriedly away from the door.

'I—I think it's going to charge,' he said—and, a second later, he *knew* it was going to charge, because he heard, quite distinctly, the thudding, clattering hooves coming closer and closer. Measle turned and ran back into the great kitchen. He saw, in the fraction of a second that was left before impact, that Iggy and Matilda were on the far side of the massive pine table and that Tinker was with them—

Then, behind him, there was an ear-splitting CRASH! of bull against door—and Measle threw a look over his shoulder and saw, in that instant, that the door had lost the encounter. There, standing in the splintered wreckage, was the great beast. Its sides were heaving, its eyes glowed red, its breath came snorting out of its flaring nostrils—and behind it, clustered out there in the corridor, was the rest of the herd, all milling about and waiting for their leader to make its next move.

Measle dashed round to the far side of the table, grabbed Iggy's hand, and dragged him to the storeroom door. He seized the door handle and twisted it hard but the door didn't budge.

'It's locked, Iggy!' hissed Measle. 'Where's the key?'

Iggy, wide-eyed with fear, could only point a trembling finger at the far side of the great kitchen. Right beside the shattered remains of the door, an iron hook was fastened to the wall. Hanging from the hook was a rusty key. Measle felt his heart sink. An enraged bull and a herd of nervous cows stood between them and it.

Measle saw that the only protection left to them now was the big pine kitchen table—but out there, in the middle of the huge room, it was useless. Maybe if they could somehow drag it into a corner and then get themselves behind it—

The bull snorted and pawed angrily at the ground. Then it lowered its head, took three shambling steps forward and smashed its horns against the table.

The table slid with a grating sound over the stone floor. The bull, its head wedged under the table, followed, shoving hard—and then, in a fury, it bunched the massive muscles in its neck and tossed its head upwards with a jerk, sending the table flying end over end across the room. It landed with a crash, on its side, only a metre away from where Measle and Iggy were huddled—and it landed in such a way as to form a kind of barrier, behind which Measle and Iggy could shelter.

Immediately, Measle and Iggy and Tinker hunkered down behind the table, disappearing from the bull's view.

Bulls have bad tempers and poor eyes. Once it lost sight of its quarry, the bull—still in a rage—looked around for something else to kill. All it saw was the room.

So it attacked the room.

Hidden behind the table, Measle and Iggy and Tinker listened to the sorts of sounds you might expect when a herd of cows, led by a very angry bull, invades a kitchen. There were crashings and bangings and the splintering sounds of breaking wood, the clanging of copper saucepans on stone floors, the thudding of heavy bodies against walls and tables—and, all the while, a steady, fear-filled mooing from the cows, all mixed together with furious snorting noises from the bull.

It was very noisy. It was so noisy that it woke up Matilda.

Held tightly in Iggy's arms—and all hunched together with her brother and Tinker behind a kitchen table—there wasn't much for Matilda to see. But it happened that her eyes were exactly level with a long crack that ran down the length of one of the pine boards and, once she had discovered that there was something going on in the room beyond their shelter, she leaned forward out of Iggy's arms and peered through the narrow gap.

Cows.

Matilda liked cows. She especially liked the little plastic cow she'd found at the bottom of a box of cornflakes. She liked it so much, she wouldn't go to sleep unless it was beside her on the pillow. She had also seen the cows in the big painting near the garden door. Matilda hadn't been particularly impressed by the tall dark man in the foreground, but she had noticed and admired the cows in the background. And *because* they were set in the far distance in the painting, those cows had appeared to Matilda to be very small. As small as her plastic cow, in fact.

But these cows here in the kitchen weren't little. These cows were big. And Matilda really only liked little cows—

Quite suddenly, all sounds stopped. One minute it had been all confusion out there, all crashings and bashings and clangings and snortings and stampings and mooings—and the next, a dead silence. It was as if the herd had simply disappeared.

'Wot's 'appening, Mumps?' hissed Iggy into Measle's ear.

'I don't know, Iggy. I think they might've gone.'

Very carefully, very slowly, Measle rose and peeped over the side of the table.

The kitchen looked as if ten hand-grenades had exploded in it. Apart from the massive table, there wasn't a stick of furniture left in one piece. The chairs were just scattered piles of kindling wood. Most of the pots and pans lay on the floor and were little more than dented, twisted heaps of scrap metal. A couple of the iron doors from the kitchen range had been yanked off their hinges and the floor itself was dusty with plaster, great chunks of which had been gouged from the walls by the horns of the herd.

But the herd that had done all this damage was nowhere to be seen.

Measle stepped out from behind the table and Iggy followed, holding Matilda in his arms. Matilda was yawning. Tinker trotted to Measle's side—and then his small, wiry body stiffened and, staring hard at the far corner of the kitchen, he started to growl.

'What is it, Tink?' said Measle, staring in the same direction.

A tiny flicker of movement caught Measle's eye and he stepped forward. There, in the shadow of a splintered chair seat that leaned, half-propped up against the wall—

The herd of cows hadn't gone anywhere. The herd of cows was still in the kitchen.

But now they were reduced to the size they had been in the picture. They milled around on the floor, like little guinea pigs, mooing faintly in obvious distress. The tiny bull stood apart from the rest, breathing heavily. Its head swung uncertainly from side to side, its brain trying to get to grips with the changes in its surroundings. It looked utterly bewildered.

There could be only one explanation. Measle glanced at his little sister. She was resting her head on Iggy's shoulder and her eyes were drooping.

I didn't see her wake up, thought Measle. *And I didn't see her wave her hands, either.*

Measle's thoughts were interrupted by Tinker, who growled again, more fiercely this time. Measle watched as Tinker strutted forward towards the milling cattle. The bull stopped swaying its head from side to side. It stared up at the huge, hairy monster in front of it, and the rest of the herd crowded in behind their leader.

The bull's bewilderment turned back to rage again. It didn't matter that the creature in front of it was the size of a barn—the intruder was standing its ground and challenging the bull and, under these circumstances, the bull did what bulls will often do. It lowered its head and pawed at the ground and then shook its quarter-centimetre long horns. It bunched the muscles of its haunches—and then, suddenly, it leapt forward in a charge—and the herd lowered their heads and started forward after their leader, the hooves of each tiny cow scrabbling for a grip on the stone floor—

Tinker barked once, very loudly.

The bull instantly planted both its forefeet straight out in front of itself and skidded to a stop.

Behind it, the cows jumbled and bumped and slipped to a clumsy halt.

Tinker took a step forward, pushed his nose close to the panting bull, curled his lips back and displayed every one of his best and sharpest teeth—and then barked again.

There was a moment of frozen stillness. Then the bull gave a tiny, shrill squeak of terror. It heaved its body round and charged off in the opposite direction, running straight through its own herd of cows, which scattered out of its blundering way. Then they too turned tail and stampeded after their leader. They ran alongside the wall and Tinker ambled after them, his nose close to the ground, sniffing the cow scent they were trailing behind them. Then, quite suddenly, the bull veered sideways and disappeared into a small black hole in the bottom of the wall—and, a moment later, the remaining five cows did the same. Tinker pushed his nose down at the spot and sniffed loudly. Measle ran to his side and knelt down, staring in wonder at the little hole in the wooden wainscoting. It was an obvious mouse hole, its edges gnawed smooth by little mouse teeth. Measle bent further and, pushing Tinker gently to one side, he put his ear close to the hole and heard the sound of distant mooing. The sound got fainter and fainter, until it disappeared altogether.

'Coo—wot a mess!' said Iggy, whose interest in anything he couldn't see any more seemed to drift away like smoke in a high wind. He trotted over to the shattered door and lifted the key off the iron hook. 'I gotta clean all dis up before Missster Jugg sees it, or else he is goin' to be ssso *cross*!'

Iggy scuttled over to the storeroom. He put the key in the lock and twisted it. The door opened and Iggy, still clutching tight to Matilda, disappeared inside.

Measle got to his feet and was just brushing the plaster dust from his knees and thinking how lucky they all were to have escaped this particular danger when Gobbin Good stepped out of the shadows of the corridor and sidled into the kitchen.

THE PAINTED GRIMLING

Measle froze.

Gobbin Good spat on the dusty floor. Then he lifted one side of his mouth and sneered. He pointed a gnarled finger at Measle and said, 'Gotcha! Now—gimme all your money!' His voice sounded like sandpaper rubbed across gravel.

Gobbin Good stepped forward, lifting his crossbow and aiming it at Measle's head. Measle put his hands up and stammered, 'I—I'm sorry b-but I haven't g-got any money.'

'Too bad,' snarled Gobbin Good. 'Too bad—for *you*, I mean.'

Measle began a slow retreat towards the storeroom door. His feet stumbled over something that made a clanging sound as his heel caught it.

He risked a quick glance downwards. By his foot was a battered iron frying pan. It looked pretty heavy—

Measle bent down and grabbed the handle. Then he held the pan out in front of him, like a weapon.

Gobbin Good laughed contemptuously.

'Ha! What are you going to do with that?' he rasped. '*Bat* my arrows away?'

Measle didn't answer. Instead, he kept walking steadily backwards, hoping desperately that he wouldn't trip over anything else. Gobbin Good sauntered casually after him.

Measle felt his back bump into the frame of a door—then he felt a hand grab at the collar of his jacket and drag him roughly backwards into the narrow confines of the storeroom.

Measle's head whipped round and saw Iggy, his eyes wide with fear, right behind him. Iggy was holding an old dustpan and brush in one hand. Matilda was nestled in the little wrathmonk's free arm.

Measle tried to smile in a reassuring way at Iggy and Matilda—but all he could manage was a sickly grin, because it was right about now that Measle realized that perhaps the narrow storeroom wasn't the best place to make a last stand. In fact, it was the worst place to be, because there was no room in here to dodge a speeding arrow—

It was too late now. Measle and Iggy went on backing up, until Iggy's shoulder blades touched the rear wall of the storeroom. Then they both stopped, facing the open door.

Gobbin Good was stepping through the opening. He looked around at his surroundings and then spat contemptuously on the floor.

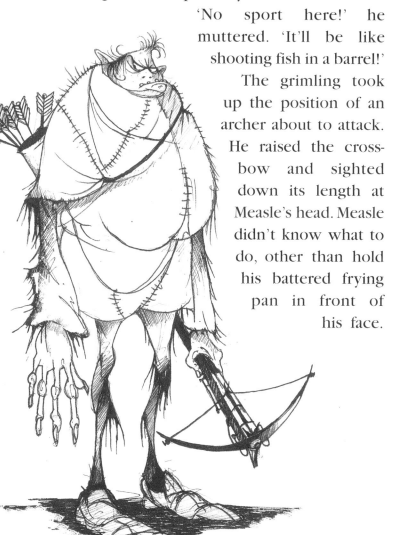

'No sport here!' he muttered. 'It'll be like shooting fish in a barrel!'

The grimling took up the position of an archer about to attack. He raised the cross-bow and sighted down its length at Measle's head. Measle didn't know what to do, other than hold his battered frying pan in front of his face.

The only trouble with that idea was that Gobbin Good could just as easily shift his aim and shoot him in the chest—

Besides, Measle's frying pan was shaking like a leaf in a gale.

The grimling lowered his crossbow, threw back his head, and laughed at the ceiling.

'Stupid boy—put that down, before I kill you!'

The crossbow was coming back up. There was only one thing left for Measle to do—and he did it. He threw the heavy frying pan with all his might straight at Gobbin Good's head.

Gobbin Good saw the pan flying towards him and, with amazing agility for one so misshapen, neatly sidestepped. The frying pan zipped past the grimling's head and crashed to the floor behind him.

Gobbin Good lowered his crossbow again, grinned, and spat.

'Missed!' he snarled. 'What are you going to do now?'

Measle didn't know what he was going to do now. There wasn't anything he *could* do. But Iggy, half-hidden behind Measle—and feeling a little brave—had an idea. Mumps might not have anything left to throw, but *he* did. Iggy lifted his old dustpan and brush and hurled them past Measle's shoulder at the hulking grimling.

Once again, Gobbin Good stepped smartly to one side and the dustpan and brush clattered harmlessly to the floor.

Gobbin Good spat. 'Got anything else you wanna throw?' he growled. Then, when neither Measle nor Iggy replied, he slowly raised the crossbow again and took steady aim at Measle's head. Then he paused.

'You know what I reckon?' said the grimling, cocking his small head to one side. 'I reckon that if I get you three lined up nice and proper, I could get you all with just one arrow! Yeah—I reckon that would work!'

Gobbin Good took a small sideways step and sighted down his crossbow, this time aiming for Measle's chest. Then he nodded to himself and muttered, 'Perfect!'

His finger started to tighten on the crossbow trigger.

Measle winced, waiting for the impact of an arrow stabbing through his ribcage, an impact he knew was only a fraction of a second away—

Then, everything seemed to happen very s-l-o-w-l-y.

Something fluid zipped over Measle's shoulder. It glittered in the dim light of the storeroom as it sailed past his eyes—a clear liquid that splashed over the crossbow and its arrow—

A familiar chemical smell hung in the air.

Nobody moved or said anything for five seconds, while Gobbin Good stared down at his crossbow, a puzzled frown creasing his lumpy green forehead.

Measle stared too—and watched in astonishment as the massive crossbow started to melt. The arrow dissolved first, then the string and then the actual body of the crossbow itself, all flowing together in a mess of different colours. The gooey stuff dripped down on to the floor at Gobbin Good's enormous feet, until all that was left of the crossbow was a stump of black wood in the grimling's right hand.

Gobbin Good was looking a little nervous.

'What—what's happened to my crossbow?' he said, in an injured tone of voice.

Measle pointed to the puddle at Gobbin Good's feet. 'It's on the floor,' he said, politely.

The chemical stink that Measle was smelling explained what had happened—but what Measle didn't yet understand was how the chemical smell had got there in the first place. He turned round and saw that Matilda, still in Iggy's arms, was wide awake and staring crossly at Gobbin Good. In one little hand she held an empty glass—

Iggy had his shoulders pressed against the back wall, right by the side of a wide shelf. On the shelf were the remains of Iggy's first attempt at breakfast—the plates of dusty bricks, the glasses and bowls of—

Of turpentine.

Then Measle understood. Matilda had seen the ugly creature. She'd seen him threaten her brother with his crossbow. She had watched first Measle and then her wet friend throw things at the nasty man. They had both missed. Now it was her turn. And she wouldn't miss. Matilda had reached for the nearest object, which just happened to be her brother's breakfast glass, still filled to the brim with turpentine. Then she had hurled the contents of the glass at the grimling.

The turpentine had fallen a little short, splashing not over the grimling as Matilda had intended, but across the creature's crossbow instead. And the turpentine had thinned and softened and weakened the paint that made up the crossbow, dissolving it all until it was nothing more than a little chemical puddle on the floor.

Gobbin Good snarled in fury and threw the useless stump of wood to one side. Then he glared at Measle with his yellow eyes and said, with a sneer, 'Well, it don't matter. I don't need no crossbow to kill you all. I can kill you just as good with these!'

Gobbin Good raised both of his huge, gnarled hands and stepped towards Measle—and Measle tried to take a step backwards. But he was already pressed so close to Iggy that he found himself forced to step sideways instead and it was this sideways movement that brought him within reaching distance of the shelf.

The grimling's huge, bony green claws were reaching towards Measle's throat.

Measle stretched out a hand towards the shelf.

His fingers closed over the rim of a dog bowl. The tips of his fingers dipped into an oily liquid—

In one smooth movement, Measle dragged the bowl off the shelf and threw the contents at Gobbin Good.

It wasn't a very good throw. Instead of hitting the grimling full in the face, the splash of turpentine struck Gobbin Good across the knees and then dripped down his shins, forming a puddle on the floor.

For a moment, the grimling simply looked a little surprised. Then the realization of what was happening to him struck him like a blow to the head. He looked down at his feet—

They were no longer there. They had dissolved in the turpentine and Gobbin Good himself now appeared to be steadily sinking into the puddle as, slowly but surely, the turpentine softened and dissolved the paint of his ankles, then his calves, then his thighs, then his middle—and now the grimling was no taller than Measle, because all that was left of him was his upper half.

To Measle's great relief, Gobbin Good didn't seem to be experiencing any pain. The only expression on his face was one of horrified surprise.

'I—I—I got a horrible sinking feeling!' he exclaimed. 'What have you done to me?'

'I'm very sorry,' said Measle, 'but you shouldn't go around killing people. Not when you're made of paint and there's turpentine around, you shouldn't.'

Gobbin Good had now sunk into the turpentine puddle right up to his chin, so all that remained was his little pointed head.

'Hah!' screamed Gobbin Good's head. 'Never mind! I don't need legs to kill you! Or arms, come to that! I can *bite* you to death!'

Gobbin Good bared his cracked, painted mouth, revealing his stained and jagged teeth. But then, a moment later, those teeth were gone as well and now all that was left was a pair of startled and angry yellow eyes. Then they too sank down into the turpentine puddle—followed by the lumpy green forehead—and lastly the wisps of greasy hair that grew from the very top of the pointed head. The strands of hair floated for a few seconds on the surface of the oily liquid and then dissolved into nothing.

There was a deep hush in the little storeroom for several moments. Finally, Iggy broke the silence.

'Coo. Dat is ssstrong ssstuff, dat purplepine.'

'It certainly is,' said Measle. 'And, in case there are any more of those things, I think we need a plan.'

THE IRON MAN

The plan they came up with was this: it was agreed that, with its door in splinters, the kitchen was no longer a safe place for them to be. Measle suggested they go back to the bedroom and hole up there—the bedroom door had looked pretty solid and there was a big iron bolt up near the top and, assuming there were no more grimlings or bulls roaming the passages of Caltrop Castle, the combination of bolt and door was probably stout enough to keep out pretty much anything else. Iggy produced three bottles of turpentine, in case they met any more paintings that had come to life, and also a box of cereal for Matilda—'In case it gets 'ungry and makes de 'orrible noise, Mumps.'

Measle retrieved the battered frying pan from

the floor of the storeroom. He liked the heavy feel of it in his hand and—well—it seemed as good a weapon as anything else.

The next problem was finding their way back to the bedroom, but Measle solved it by getting Tinker to lead them first to the little garden. Once there, Measle hoped that, by carefully backtracking the route they had taken earlier they'd be able to get back to the relative safety of the bedroom. With the loss of the pushchair, Iggy had taken the responsibility of carrying Matilda, which was lucky for Measle, because Iggy was much stronger than he was. Iggy didn't *look* particularly strong, with his weedy little body and skinny little arms—but there were real, wiry muscles under Iggy's damp black coat and he never seemed to get tired. In fact, even if Iggy *was* tired, Measle doubted that he would have stopped carrying Matilda. Iggy appeared to like carrying Matilda as much as Matilda liked being carried by Iggy and, every time Measle turned and looked at them both, Matilda— now wide awake—had given Iggy yet another wild and wonderful hairdo.

They were about halfway to the bedroom when a sound reached their ears. It was a strange combination of noises and it seemed to be coming from several corridors away, back in the direction of the kitchen. First, there was the distant sound of cracking, splintering, smashing wood. This was followed immediately by a series of desperate mooing noises and, a moment later, by the bellow from a furious bull. A very *large* and furious bull.

'Wossat, Mumps?' whispered Iggy, clutching nervously at Measle's arm.

'I think it's the cows, Iggy. And the bull. I think they're back to their full size again.'

'Wot about all dat noise of de wood breakin'?'

'I think that was them bursting out from behind the panelling.'

They hurried on and slowly the sounds of the herd diminished behind them. As they walked down the endless passages Measle was thinking hard. *Tilly made the cows small—now they're big again. And she couldn't have done an enlarging spell, because she's still wide awake and busy playing with Iggy's hair. Which means—which means Tilly's first spell must have worn off! Maybe . . . maybe they all wear off after a little time?*

Measle had one of his ideas.

'Iggy, show me your teeth!'

'You wot?'

'I want to see your teeth!'

'Why?'

'Because . . . because . . . because I really like them, Iggy! I wish I had teeth like yours! Especially the pointed ones! Please, Iggy—show me your teeth!'

Flattery worked wonders with Iggy. Looking pleased with himself, he opened his mouth and bared his teeth at Measle—and Measle saw in an instant that Iggy's teeth were no longer that attractive pearly-white colour that Matilda had turned them. Iggy's teeth were back to their ugly shade of yellow.

So, it looks as if Tilly's spells do *wear off—*

At last they reached the bedroom. Once inside, with the door bolted firmly shut, Measle felt more secure. Iggy put Matilda down on the floor, where she crawled about, chasing Tinker's tail. Outside the tall window it was getting dark. The distant trees of the park were shrouded in shadows, the lake was a sheet of blackness, and the wide, sweeping lawn had lost its colour and was now a dull and gloomy grey.

Night was falling. There was the question of where Iggy was to sleep. Measle suggested one of the armchairs, but Iggy shook his head firmly.

'No, Mumps—I can't do dat.'

'Why not, Iggy?'

'I can't go in dose sssquashy chairs. After I been in dem for a bit, dey sssmell all funny.'

Iggy found the perfect place all by himself. He dragged Measle into the bathroom and pointed excitedly at the big gleaming bath.

'Dere, Mumps! I could sssleep in dere! Sssee— dere's even a little hole where de water can go down!'

It was a good idea—and then Measle had one of his own. He went into the bedroom and pulled open the big wardrobe. The bottom half of the wardrobe was made up of three large drawers. They were all empty. Measle dragged the top drawer wide open—and then went on pulling at it until the whole thing slid free from its runners. Then he half carried, half dragged the empty drawer into the bathroom and laid it upside down, across one end of the bath, making a sort of roof.

'There, Iggy,' said Measle. 'That's nearly as good as your box, isn't it?'

Iggy squeaked with delight and crawled into the bath and under the drawer—and, to Measle's satisfaction, the little rain cloud stayed outside the makeshift shelter and dribbled its drops down onto the underside of the drawer, leaving Iggy in relative dryness inside.

'Dat is *better* dan my box, Mumps,' said Iggy from inside his shelter—and his voice sounded happier than Measle had ever heard it sound before.

Measle left Iggy in his new shelter and went back into the bedroom. There was nothing to do, other than watch Matilda play with Tinker—and Measle found his mind wandering down paths that grew more and more miserable with every passing thought. He missed his mum and dad terribly. Where were they? What had happened to them? Would he ever see them again? And how long was he going to be stuck here in this weird place, where a silly little wrathmonk was in charge, where the geography changed at will, and where pictures came horribly to life? And how could he look after Matilda, all by himself? Where was Nanny Flannel when you really needed her? What to do? How to get home? *What to do?*

Measle's increasingly despondent thoughts were interrupted by a chomping sound in his right ear. He turned round—Iggy was there. Iggy was chewing something. His jaws were going up and down and he had a look of rapture on his face.

Iggy swallowed—then he brought up his hand and Measle saw, to his horror, that Iggy was holding the little plastic bag of jelly beans.

'Where did you get those, Iggy?' said Measle.

'Out of your pocket, Mumps,' said Iggy, carelessly. He reached into the bag, took out another jelly bean and popped it into his mouth.

'My *pocket?*' said Measle, incredulously. 'When?'

'When we was in de ssstoreroom,' said Iggy, chewing greedily. 'When you was busy killing dat nasty green fing.'

'How?'

'How, Mumps? *How?* I jussst reached in your pocket and took dem, dat's how.'

'But I never felt you do it, Iggy.'

Iggy smiled a superior smile. 'Well, you wouldn't *feel* it, Mumps,' he said, proudly. 'You wouldn't feel it because I am not jussst a brilliant burglarider. I am *also* a brilliant pickle-pocket. I am one of de bessst pickle-pockets you will ever meet. Dere isn't a pocket I can't pickle.'

'You mean you're a *pick-pocket* too, Iggy?'

'Dat's what I *said*, Mumps,' said Iggy, rolling his eyes with impatience. 'A *pickle-pocket.*'

'But—but why, Iggy? Why did you pick my pocket?'

'Coz I *like* dese fings, dat's why. Dey is very nice, dese sssweeties.'

Measle frowned at Iggy, trying to look fierce. 'But they don't belong to you, Iggy. They're mine, not yours. And I thought we were friends. Friends don't do that, Iggy—they don't pick each other's pockets.'

A look of wonder swept across Iggy's face. 'Dey don't?' he said, in a surprised tone.

'No, Iggy. They don't. Now can I have my bag back, please?'

Measle held out his hand and glared firmly at Iggy—and Iggy sighed and slowly passed the bag over. 'I only eated a few of dem, Mumps,' he muttered.

Measle took the bag. It felt very light. He looked inside it and saw that there were very few jelly beans left. Frantically, he poked a forefinger into the bag and stirred the few remaining beans— There! Right at the bottom—two lonely little yellow ones!

'I like de yellow ones bessst, Mumps,' said Iggy.

'Really?' said Measle, sourly. 'I'd never have guessed.'

A thought crossed Measle's mind. Without appearing to be too interested in the answer, he said, 'What's your *least* favourite jelly bean, Iggy?'

'De green ones, Mumps. I don't like dem at *all.*'

'And . . . er . . . what happened when you ate a green one, Iggy?'

'I *didn't* eat a green one, Mumps,' said Iggy, rolling his eyes with impatience at Measle's stupidity. 'I told you—I don't *like* de green ones.'

Measle wondered whether he should ask—if Iggy hadn't actually eaten a green jelly bean—how he knew he didn't like them, but then Iggy distracted him by rummaging in one of the pockets of his damp and shabby old coat. He pulled out Measle's toothbrush. He held it up in front of Measle's face and said, 'Wot's dis, Mumps?'

'That's my toothbrush, Iggy. And I wish you wouldn't take my things.'

Iggy sniffed contemptuously. 'Dat's a funny lookin' toof brush, if you ask me, Mumps.'

'That's because it's electric, Iggy.'

Iggy's wide, fishy eyes grew even wider and fishier. ''Lectric?' he said. 'Wossat?'

Measle reached out and pressed the on switch on the toothbrush's handle and, when it started vibrating in his hand, Iggy almost dropped the thing.

'Coo!' he whispered, staring now with admiration at the toothbrush. 'Dat is *fantassstic*, dat is!' Then a crafty look came over Iggy's face. 'Er . . . Mumps,' he said, in a wheedling voice. 'Er . . . if I can't have dose sssweetie fings—can I have dis?'

'What do you want it for, Iggy?' said Measle, pretty sure that Iggy wasn't going to use it to clean his teeth.

Iggy had absolutely no idea what he was going to do with the toothbrush. All he knew was that he wanted it desperately. It looked so new and it did such interesting things—

'I could—I could—I could use it as a *weapon*, Mumps!' said Iggy, voicing the first thing that came into his head. 'A *sssuper* weapon! I could beat all my enemies wiv dis sssuper weapon! Coz it's *'lectric*, sssee?'

Measle was about to say that an electric toothbrush wasn't any better than an ordinary one when it came to weapons—and, anyway, Iggy really ought to stop taking other people's belongings—when he heard a sound from beyond the closed bedroom door. It was a distant sound, at least two or three corridors away—and it reminded Measle of the noise that Matilda sometimes made when she was allowed to bang her cereal spoon against one of Lee's saucepans—

Clang. Clang. Clang.

Measle turned away from Iggy, crossed over to the door, unbolted it, and carefully cracked it open.

There was still nothing to be seen in the passage but now the sound was just a little louder—

And it seemed to be getting closer, too.

Clang. Clang. Clang.

'Wossat noise, Mumps?'

Iggy pressed against him and stuck his face out into the corridor—and Measle felt the little drops of rain from Iggy's cloud spatter against the top of his head.

'I don't know, Iggy,' he muttered. 'But I don't think it's the cows.'

Clang. Clang. Clang.

Whatever it was, it was definitely getting closer because now Measle could hear another sound—

A measured, heavy tread, that was getting nearer and nearer—

Clang. Thump. Clang. Thump. Clang. Thump—

'Iggy,' said Measle nervously. 'Maybe we ought to shut the door.'

'Hah!' said Iggy, scornfully. 'Don't worry, Mumps. I got my weapons. Wotever dat fing is, I will sssave you—again!'

Measle was about to object to this latest bit of nonsense, and point out that Iggy hadn't saved him *once* yet—while he, Measle, had actually saved Iggy several times already—but Iggy had turned back and disappeared into the bedroom again and anyway, the clangs and the thumps were now getting so loud that Measle realized he was going to have to *shout* his objections over the now almost deafening sounds—

CLANG! THUMP! CLANG! THUMP!

And then Measle saw what was making all these deafening sounds and he realized, in an instant that was filled with horror, that he and Iggy and Matilda and Tinker were suddenly in a world of trouble.

A world of *terrible* trouble—because here, rounding the corner of the passage, came a figure out of a nightmare. At first, Measle wasn't sure what the thing was, other than it was huge. It seemed to fill the passage—a great, massive, hulking black shape, that swayed from side to side as it approached—

And then the thing came into a pool of light— one of the pools of light that was thrown regularly on to the floor and walls by the succession of dim light bulbs that hung from the ceiling—and Measle saw what the thing was.

It was the huge, jet-black suit of armour.

Next to Gobbin Good, it was one of the most awful things that Measle had ever seen—and *heard*, too. The deafening clanging sound the suit of armour was making was caused by the great swinging sword. Whatever was inside the armour seemed intent on making as much noise as possible as, with every lurching step, the sword was being swung from side to side in great sweeps. Measle thought he could hear the sound of the wind whistling as the blade sliced through the

air—and each sweep of the sword brought the gleaming blade into shattering contact with the walls on either side—

CLANG! CLANG! CLANG! CLANG!

And then Iggy was suddenly back at his side.

'Oo-er,' muttered Iggy—and Measle could hear the sudden uncertainty in the little wrathmonk's voice. 'Coo—dat is big, innit? But dat don't matter, coz I got my weapons! Ssstand back, Mumps! I—Mr Ignatius Niggle—will sssave you!'

Iggy elbowed Measle aside and stood in front of him, facing the approaching horror. In his left hand he held the electric toothbrush. Two bottles of turpentine were tucked under his arm—and he held the third bottle in his right hand.

'Take dat, you 'orrible fing!' screamed Iggy—and, at the same moment, he hurled the bottle of turpentine directly at the lurching suit of armour.

The bottle sailed through the air and smashed against the iron chest. Shards of glass flew everywhere and the turpentine splashed and dribbled down the breastplate—and the iron thing took no notice at all and simply continued on its swaying, lurching way—

Clang! Clang! Clang! Clang!

Iggy screamed, 'Ho—you want anuvver one, do you?' and he hurled a second bottle. It too struck the armour—this time on the crest of its enormous black helmet. There was another splintering crash as the bottle exploded—the turpentine splashed across the thing's lowered visor, and it had no more effect on the iron creature than if a fly had landed on it.

'It's not meltin', Mumps!' yelped Iggy over his shoulder. 'Why ain't it meltin'?'

'Because it's not made of *paint*, Iggy!' shouted Measle over the deafening clanging of the thing's huge sword. Measle grabbed at Iggy's shoulder and tried to pull him backwards—but Iggy didn't budge. Instead, he threw the third bottle, which smashed against the armour's knees. The turpentine did no more to the approaching monster than the other two bottles of the stuff had done, so Iggy, as a last resort, held the toothbrush out in front of him and pressed the button on the handle. The toothbrush started buzzing and Iggy waved it frantically at the lumbering iron monster, which was now only a few metres away and approaching fast.

'Run away, monsssster!' screamed Iggy. 'Run away, while you ssstill can! You can't beat my sssuper weapon, you 'orrible fing, you!'

Measle had seen enough. He grabbed Iggy with both hands and pulled with all his strength and Iggy lost his balance. He frantically back-pedalled his feet to stop himself from falling and, in doing so, allowed Measle to drag him quickly back into the bedroom.

Measle slammed the door shut, then reached up and smacked the bolt hard—and it slid, with a grating sound of metal on metal, into the hasp that was screwed to the frame of the door.

Tinker was where he always was whenever there was any danger—standing by Measle's side, growling very softly deep in his throat. It was an uncertain sort of growling, because Tinker was uncertain about what, exactly, he was growling at. He'd caught a whiff of the noisy thing just before Measle had slammed the door in its face. It had smelt of metal—in fact, it smelt exactly like the iron poker that stood by the fireplace in the living room of Merlin Manor. And that was fine—except Tinker couldn't remember a time when the iron poker had ever—well—had ever *moved*.

Measle only just made it in time. The moment

the bolt slid home, the entire door began to shake under a furious, thudding attack. Measle guessed that whatever was inside the suit of armour was using its great, iron-gauntleted fists to pound against the panels and Measle backed away slowly, wondering how long the door would stand, before giving way under this heavy assault.

He didn't have to wonder for long.

The thudding sound suddenly stopped. There was a moment of silence—and then the attack started again. But, this time, the sounds were quite different. The thuds were replaced by a series of deafening clashes and clangs which seemed to shake the door even more—and then there was the dreadful sound of splintering wood and Measle watched in horror as the tip of the great black sword suddenly stabbed its way through one of the door panels. There was a wrenching noise and the tip disappeared—then, a moment later, another splintering crash and the whole blade was thrust through the heavy oak, right up to its hilt. The blade twisted violently from side to side, slicing through the splintered wood and widening the hole it had made by several centimetres, so that Measle suddenly caught—through the section of shattered wood—a glimpse of the massive iron fist that was wielding the sword.

In growing panic, he turned away from the door,

his eyes searching the room for some other way out—

There was only the window.

Measle ran across the room. He knew that the window didn't open so he didn't even try—instead, he grabbed his battered frying pan from where he'd dropped it on the bed and swung it hard against the glass. Some of the diamond panes shattered and the lead strips holding them bent outwards—

Measle swung again—

And again—

'Wot is you *doin'*, Mumps?' screamed Iggy—and Measle turned away from the smashed window and saw that Iggy was crouching on the floor next to Matilda and they were both staring at him with horror plastered all over their faces.

'We've got to get out, Iggy!' yelled Measle, turning back to the job of breaking a hole big enough for them all to get through. It was easier said than done. The trouble wasn't with the glass panes. Those closest to Measle were now all smashed to smithereens. The trouble was with the lead strips, which bent but didn't break and, try as he might, Measle hadn't been able to do anything other than make them bulge to the outside.

'You mustn't break de window, Mumps!' screamed Iggy. 'Mr Jugg will get fuming mad! *Ssstop* it! Ssstop it dis *instant*!'

All this noise was too much for Matilda. There

was a nasty noise from the door, and a nasty noise from the window, and nasty yelling noises from her brother and from her new wet friend—so Matilda did what all babies do when they're upset. She screwed up her face and began to scream at the top of her voice. For a moment, Iggy looked at her in horrified amazement—the sounds she was making were hurting his ears.

'It's 'ungry, Mumps!' yelled Iggy, diving for the box of cereal. He ripped it open, plunged one claw-like little hand inside, scooped up a fistful of dry flakes and pushed them under Matilda's nose. ''Ere!' he shouted. 'Eat dis, baby!'

Matilda screamed louder and batted his hand away. The last thing she wanted at that moment was a handful of cereal. What she wanted was the noise to go away.

The worst noise was coming from the door. She looked over towards it and saw that the door was breaking—

Matilda didn't like things being broken.

So Matilda waved her hands and *mended* the door.

One second the panels were a splintered mess; the next, the hole filled itself in, replacing the jagged splinters with a smooth panel of unbroken wood.

The sudden halting of the sounds of splintering door made Measle turn away from his efforts with the window. He stared in amazement at the mended door—then threw a quick glance over to where Matilda was gulping back her tears. But then, a moment later, the attack from the great two-handed sword started up once more and the door began to shake again under a second wave of heavy blows.

Measle didn't waste any more time. He went for the window, using all the power in his arms to smash away at the lead strips. One wild whack of his frying pan succeeded in ripping a strip out of the corner of the window's stone frame and, with that single piece free and dangling, his next three blows tore out a man-sized hole.

Once again, the sounds of splintering wood made Measle whip his head round. Once again, there was a sizeable hole in the door. This time, Measle saw a huge iron fist come through the ragged fissure. The massive fingers opened and the hand grasped the edge of the broken panel and gave it a great wrench—and a section of oak broke off, as if it was no stronger than a biscuit.

The fist dragged the section back through the hole and was about to push its way back in order to break off more of the door, when the hole once again filled itself in, making the door as solid as it ever was. Measle transferred his gaze to Matilda and saw her head beginning to droop in sleep— and he knew immediately what that meant. Her two mending spells had exhausted her utterly and this brief moment was the last breathing space they were likely to get—

And, to confirm that fear, the thundering, crashing, smashing attack began again on the other side of the door—only, this time, the blows seemed even more furious and desperate than before. There wasn't going to be much time—

Measle turned and yelled, 'Tink! Come here!' and the dog instantly scampered across the floor to Measle's side. Measle didn't hesitate. He scooped Tinker up and pushed him through the ragged hole—and Tinker fell the short distance to the ground outside, landing with a rattling of leaves and twigs right in the middle of a small bush that grew below the window.

Measle turned back—

Iggy had disappeared.

No—there, poking out from under the hanging ruffle of the bed frame—a foot! Measle ran to the bed, bent down, grabbed Iggy's foot and pulled hard—and the wrathmonk slid out from under the bed, both hands pressed tightly over his ears.

Measle dragged Iggy to his feet. He could feel Iggy's thin, damp frame quivering with terror and he could see Iggy's fishy eyes swivelling madly in their sockets, so he didn't bother with trying to reason with him. There was no time for reasoning. Measle simply grabbed Iggy by one hand and pulled him across the room to the smashed

window. Once there, he shoved Iggy's head into the opening and then, ignoring Iggy's wails of terror, he bent down, grabbed both of Iggy's skinny ankles and heaved him bodily out of the window.

There was a short scream, followed instantly by a solid sounding thump, as Iggy landed on the ground outside.

Measle raced to Matilda's side. Her eyes were closed and she was slowly slipping over sideways, into another deep sleep. Measle grabbed her as gently as he could, lifted her up off the floor and carried her to the window.

'Iggy!' he yelled, through the gaping hole in the lead strips. 'Iggy! I'm going to drop Tilly down to you! You've got to catch her, Iggy!'

There was no reply, so Measle poked his head through the opening and saw Iggy staring up at him with fear-filled eyes.

'Do you understand, Iggy? I want you to catch her! OK?'

Iggy nodded dumbly and extended his arms and Measle gently pushed the sleeping Matilda over the threshold of the window—held her there for a moment—and then let go.

There was a sudden grinding, grating, tearing sound from the other side of the room. Measle turned and saw that the iron man had managed to push his way through the broken door and was now standing inside the bedroom, with the entire remains of the door—still in its frame—hung round his enormous black metal body, like a necklace.

For a moment, nobody moved—nobody spoke—nothing happened.

'Who are you?' whispered Measle, his voice shaking with fear.

Very slowly, the iron man raised one huge fist. When the fist reached the visor of the helmet, the iron man extended a forefinger. He touched the tip of his finger to the peak of the visor—and then, very slowly, he pushed the visor up—

Revealing—

Nothing.

There was no face inside the helmet.

There was nothing but blackness there.

The suit of armour was—empty.

Then the visor dropped shut with a clang and the iron monster raised its great sword and, with a thump that shook the room, stepped forward.

THE
PARK

When the iron monster stepped forward, Measle stepped backwards, until he felt the rough stonework of the window frame against his shoulder blades.

He watched in dread as the suit of armour tramped towards him. He could feel the floor shaking under the huge weight—and then the iron creature began to sweep its great black sword from side to side, the blade whistling as it cut through the air.

It was time to go.

With a quick, twisting movement—like a fish suddenly changing direction in a stream—Measle turned and dived through the opening in the bent and broken lead strips. It was so dark outside the window that, for Measle, it seemed as if he was diving into a bottomless abyss—except that the abyss wasn't bottomless because he was in the air, and falling, for only about a second before he landed, with a bone-shaking thump, on the hard ground. For a moment he lay there, gathering his breath. Then he felt Tinker push his cold nose against his cheek and then a spattering of raindrops splashed against his face.

'You pushed me out of de window!' said Iggy's voice, in an accusing tone. 'You didn't ought to do dat, Mumps—dat's not very polite, pushing people out of windows.'

Measle looked up. He could see, dimly in the darkness, Iggy's form looming over him. Measle was relieved to see the little lump that was Matilda nestled safely in Iggy's arms—and he could just make out the fuzzy shape of Tinker, who was standing by his side. A little light filtered out of the bedroom—it was just enough to see by, once his eyes had adjusted to the gloom.

And then the light dimmed and, from above his head, there came the sound of something huge and metallic grating against stone. Measle struggled to his feet and looked up at the tall window—

There, filling the whole space—and blocking the small amount of light from the room beyond—was the outline of the iron man. The thing seemed to be trying to push its way through the remains of the window and Measle heard the sounds of glass cracking and lead strips popping apart—

'Come on—quick!' shouted Measle. 'It's coming through the window!'

Iggy shrieked and, clutching tight to Matilda, put his head down and started to run—and Measle and Tinker were close behind him. They pounded across the gravel drive, their feet crunching on the stones. It was very dark and Measle was finding it difficult to see where they were going—

Then, directly in front of Measle there was a sudden thud, followed by a sharp squeal of pain—and, a second later, Measle himself ran hard into something that was soft and damp, and smelt strongly of wet clothes and mildew.

'Owww!' squealed Iggy again. Measle felt the little wrathmonk slide to the ground at his feet, so he too squatted down in the near pitch darkness, straining his eyes to see what had happened.

Iggy was rubbing the top of his head with his free hand. 'Oooh—dat hurts, Mumps!' he moaned.

'What's the matter, Iggy?' whispered Measle.

'Wot's de matter? Wot's de *matter*? I'll tell you wot's de matter, Mumps—a big bump on de head, *dat's* what de matter is!'

Measle peered past Iggy, trying to see what it was that he had bumped into. There didn't seem to be anything there. The park stretched out in front of him: a sweeping lawn, leading the eye down to a dark lake, a line of trees beyond it—

And then, as his eyes grew more accustomed to

the dark, Measle saw for himself what it was that Iggy had bumped into.

It was a wall.

And not just any wall. It was very high and very wide. Quite *how* wide and high it was, Measle couldn't make out—but it was huge, because its extremities disappeared into the darkness above and to both sides.

The other extraordinary thing about the wall was—it was only a wall in *close-up*. From a few metres away, it looked as if there was nothing there—just the sweeping lawn and the distant lake, with its line of trees—but, when you were no more than a few centimetres away, it was then possible to see that what you *thought* was a sweeping lawn, a distant lake, and a line of trees was, in fact, the most brilliantly realistic of paintings—

A vast painting, almost photographic in its realism, that stretched up and out as far as the eye could see.

A painting of a park.

'It's a wall, Iggy,' whispered Measle. 'You ran into a wall.'

'Wot?' said Iggy, irritably. 'Wot is you talking about, Mumps?'

'You're leaning against it, Iggy. Turn round and look.'

Iggy sighed—one of those long, impatient sighs people give when they think somebody has said something really stupid—and then he turned his head and stared at the wall he'd been leaning against.

Iggy stared for quite a long time, blinking slowly at the smooth, solid surface only a few centimetres from his nose. Then, without any warning, he burst into floods of tears.

Behind them, from the direction of the castle, there was the sound of what might have been a clap of thunder—or perhaps a small landslide. Measle's head whipped round and saw that the part of the stone frame that surrounded the remains of the window was now smashed to pieces and the fragments were lying in a heap on the ground below—and now the opening was that much bigger—

The iron man was making one more attempt to squeeze through it. There was a noise of metal grating and screeching against the stone—then, like a cork coming out of a champagne bottle, the iron man was clear. He was so tall that he didn't have to jump from the window to the ground below, he simply stepped down, his huge iron boots crushing the broken glass underfoot. Then, raising his great black sword, the iron man began to stride across the gravel drive towards them.

Measle turned and grabbed Iggy's trembling shoulders.

'Come on, Iggy!' he yelled into the little wrathmonk's tear-stained face. 'Get up!'

Measle struggled to his feet and, using all his strength, he dragged Iggy upright. Iggy's legs were wobbling—but his arms didn't move from their tight hold on Matilda's little body. Together, Measle, Iggy, and Matilda started a kind of staggering run along the bottom of the wall. Tinker gave a couple of aggressive little barks in the direction of the iron man—*just to show him who's the boss*—and then, tail tucked tightly between his legs, he ran to join Measle and Iggy.

The further they ran, the darker it became, until Measle—fearful of running into something—was forced to trot along with one hand touching the wall. Tinker—whose eyes were better equipped for seeing in the dark—ran just ahead and it was his little white outline, glimmering like a small canine ghost, that Measle was following.

Behind them they could hear the clumping, crunching sound as the iron man pounded along the gravel driveway in pursuit. From the slow and steady pace of the creature's footsteps, Measle guessed that the iron man wasn't running. Maybe running was something a suit of armour simply couldn't do? So perhaps, as long as they kept up this sort of pace, they could stay ahead of the thing?

But where were they going? It was now very dark but Measle had a sense that, by following the wall, they were travelling in a steady curve. It was as if the wall surrounded Caltrop Castle in a perfect circle of stone—which meant that, sooner or later, they were going to arrive back where they started from—

But there, ahead—a little gleam of light!

It was quite high off the ground and it seemed to Measle that it must be coming from a window in the castle's wall. Measle decided that, instead of running endlessly in this great circle, they should head for it. So he veered away from the curving wall and hurried towards the faint gleam, with Tinker's ghostly little form scurrying just ahead of him.

'Where is we goin', Mumps?' gasped Iggy, stumbling at his side.

Measle didn't reply. Dragging Iggy along was exhausting work and he didn't have enough breath in his body for an answer—even if he'd known what the answer *was*, which he didn't. All he knew was that a light—any light—was better than this darkness.

As they drew nearer, the point of light turned into the small rectangle of a window, lit from inside. Measle put on an extra burst of speed and he, Iggy, and Tinker arrived at the base of the castle walls, beneath the window, their breaths coming ragged and exhausted. Only Matilda's breathing was slow and steady—she was now deeply asleep on Iggy's shoulder.

Measle looked up at the window. It was about four metres above his head and the walls that surrounded it were heavy with ivy. In this darkness, the leaves looked as black as night. The ivy grew from a bed right at Measle's feet and he saw that the trunk and the branches that supported the ivy were thick and strong.

'Quick, Iggy!' he said. 'We're going to climb up there! You first!'

'You want me to climb up dere?' said Iggy, staring up at the window.

'Yes, Iggy! And you'll still have to carry Tilly, too. Can you do it?'

Iggy turned and glared at Measle. 'Of *courssse* I can do it,' he said, grandly. 'I was a burglarider, wasn't I? All burglariders can climb—*and* dey can carry a big heavy bag of ssswag at de same time! I am an extremely *fantassstic* climber—'

'Good, Iggy,' said Measle. 'Please do it—*now*!'— and he pushed the little wrathmonk firmly towards the wall because there, in the distance, he heard the steady Clump! Crunch! Clump! Crunch! as the iron man drew closer and closer.

Iggy did as he was told. He jumped up and grabbed a handhold in the ivy branches—and then Measle watched as he scrambled upwards like a monkey, heading fast towards the window. Measle bent and grabbed Tinker and stuffed him down the front of his leather jacket. Then he seized hold of a rough branch of ivy and began to climb. He wasn't as fast as Iggy but he managed to haul himself upwards at a steady pace and was soon high enough off the ground to worry about falling.

Don't look down! Just keep climbing! Like you did on the Ferris wheel on the Isle of Smiles! Reach up with your hand, then find a new foothold, then pull and push, up and up and up—

But then the clumping, crunching, clattering sounds became very loud and close by and Measle was forced to take a quick glance downwards—

There, emerging from the gloom, came the huge suit of armour. The iron monster paused for a moment at the foot of the wall, its great helmeted head turning this way and that. Measle heard the squeak of metal on metal. Then, slowly, the helmet tilted backwards and whatever it was using as its eyes seemed to peer upwards, straight at Measle. Then, to Measle's horror, it stepped forward and thrust its gauntleted hands deep into the ivy and began to pull itself off the ground.

Panic gave Measle some much needed strength and energy. He turned back and, grabbing fistfuls of the dusty branches, began to scramble upwards towards the window.

Then, beneath him, the ivy shook.

Under Measle's grasping hands, the branch of ivy to which he was clinging suddenly started to pull away from the ancient stones with the sound of tearing cotton. Measle felt the angle of his body change as the branch sagged off the wall—the ivy shook and bent some more and, a moment later, Measle felt his feet slip away and dangle in mid-air. Now he was hanging from a branch which was sticking at right angles away from the wall—and the branch was bending in a frightening way, the gnarled wood making ominous groaning, creaking, cracking sounds. Measle's fingers began to lose their grip—

A moment later he felt a hand on the top of his head. The hand grasped a fistful of his hair and then it started to pull him skywards.

'I got you, Mumps!' hissed Iggy's voice, and he pulled harder, making Measle's scalp feel as if it was being dragged off his head. Measle's eyes began to water from the pain and he yelled, 'It's all right, Iggy—I can manage!'—but Iggy took no notice and just went on trying to drag Measle upwards as if he was a sack of potatoes.

Measle risked a quick glance downwards. He couldn't move his head because of Iggy's tight grasp on his hair but he was just able to swivel his eyes down enough to see what was happening below. The suit of armour was now halfway up the ivy, dragging its great weight slowly but steadily upwards—and it was the great weight of the iron creature that was pulling the mass of ivy away from the wall.

The branch to which Measle was clinging bent some more. Then it gave a sudden lurch, as more of it was pulled away from the wall—

And then it broke.

But Measle didn't fall.

Instead, the pain from where his hair was joined to his head increased a hundred times as Iggy's iron grip took the entire weight of Measle's—and Tinker's—bodies.

'Oooowwwww!' yelled Measle. He felt himself being lifted upwards, as if he was on the end of a powerful crane. Beneath him he heard a ripping, tearing, crackling sound, as the entire section of ivy was dragged off the stone wall of the castle. Then, a moment later, there was a great crashing, clanging, smashing sound—like a car running into a concrete wall.

The pain on his scalp was becoming unbearable and Measle screwed his eyes tight shut and opened his mouth to let out a really loud yell—but then he felt himself being swung sideways and, a second later, the grip on his hair was released and he was dropped heavily onto a wooden floor.

When Measle opened his eyes, tears spilled out of them and dripped down his cheeks. Measle never cried and he wasn't really crying this time either. The tears in his eyes weren't tears of hurt or misery—they were just a natural reaction to having his hair pulled. Everybody's eyes water when they have their hair pulled—

'Why is you cryin', Mumps?' hissed Iggy's voice, close to his ear. 'I ressscued you, didn't I?'

Measle glared up at Iggy through blurry eyes.

'Thank you, Iggy,' he muttered. 'And I'm *not* crying.' Measle blinked the tears away. The pain from his scalp was just beginning to die down—

Tinker poked his head out from the folds of Measle's jacket and swiped his tongue over Measle's face.

'Stop it, Tink,' muttered Measle, wiping his cheeks with the back of his hand. Then he opened the zip of his leather jacket and pushed Tinker gently out on the floor.

Iggy, with Matilda still in his arms, was leaning on the narrow windowsill and staring down towards the distant ground. Measle scrambled to his feet and joined him.

There, far below, lay the iron man. The creature was flat on its back and covered by a great heap of ivy, so that all that could be seen of it were its outstretched arms and legs. Measle and Iggy watched as the suit of armour struggled to sit up but the combined weight of its own iron shell— and the pile of leaves and twigs and branches that entwined its huge body—was too much for it and all it could do was writhe and squirm and wriggle in a horrible way, making the mound of ivy that lay over it shift and shake and shudder, just as if it were alive.

'I did dat, Mumps,' said Iggy, proudly. 'I resscued you—*again*—and den I made all de leaves and ssstuff fall down on top of de fing and now it can't get up and I did dat too.'

'Well done, Iggy,' said Measle, gratefully. The fact was, Iggy really *had* rescued him this time, even if his scalp did still sting like crazy.

Measle looked around. They were in a strange little five-sided room, bare of any furniture and with only the single window and, opposite the window, a single door. A dusty bare light bulb hung from a cord in the middle of the ceiling and it was the light from this that had guided Measle to the window. Measle tiptoed to the door and cracked it open—and, almost immediately, he closed it again, careful not to make a sound as he did so—

He'd heard voices.

Measle turned and put his finger to his lips. 'We've got to be very quiet, Iggy,' he whispered. 'There are people out there.'

Iggy nodded seriously and took an extra firm grip on Matilda. Measle scooped Tinker up and pushed him back down into the front of his jacket.

Oh, here we go again, thought Tinker, wriggling a little to get himself comfortable against Measle's chest. *The smelly kid always thinks his two legs are better than my four—*

Measle reached out and flicked the brass light switch by the door and the room was plunged into darkness. Then Measle carefully turned the doorknob, eased the door open a fraction and put one eye to the narrow gap.

The room he was looking at was enormous and Measle's position in it seemed, at first, to be a little peculiar. It was partly the shadows that confused him—shadows that danced and flickered in the light of an unseen fire—but also the fact that he seemed to be somewhere up near the roof of the room, because there, only a couple of metres over his head, he could just make out the dim shapes of massive oak rafters that stretched out across the huge space, their extremities lost in the gloom.

But then, as his eyes grew accustomed to the lack of light, he saw where he was. He was in one corner of a minstrel's gallery that was built round all four sides of the great room—the great room that was therefore well *below* him, its floor probably at ground level. In the opposite corner of the gallery, Measle saw that a spiral staircase, made of iron, circled its way down to the lower level. The voices were coming from down there, so Measle opened the door a little wider, just enough to let him squeeze through. He shifted Tinker's body to one side and then lay flat on the floor and crawled, slowly and silently, forward—across the dusty wooden boards, towards the balustrade that ringed the minstrel's gallery.

It was dark up there near the ceiling—the only light seemed to be coming from below and that was a dim, orange, flickering affair, which still allowed much of the great room to be in relative darkness—and this made Measle fairly confident that he was unlikely to be seen by any of the owners of the voices. All the same, he was extra careful as he got near the banisters and he moved forward centimetre by centimetre, until at last his face was very near the wooden uprights. Now, for the first time, Measle could see a part of the floor of the great room. There, below him, was a huge stone fireplace, with flames dancing around a great pile of logs. At first glance, Measle thought that these flames were the only illumination in the room but then he saw the candlesticks on the mantelpiece—a whole row of them—and each held a lit candle, their little flames steady in the still air.

And now, at this range, Measle could hear everything quite clearly.

There, sitting in a large leather armchair that was set by the fireside, was the long, thin figure of Sir Peregrine Spine. Opposite him, in a matching armchair, hunched Ermintrude Bacon, her pink, piggy face shiny in the light from the fire.

What are these two doing at Caltrop Castle?

Measle inched forward a little more.

Another pair of armchairs came into view. In one chair sat Dorian Fescue, his yellow face made even yellower in the candlelight. Opposite him was Tully Telford, who was polishing his pebble glasses on a handkerchief. Even in this reduced glow, Measle could see the dark stains on Tully's ear tips.

The Advisory Committee! All of them—except for that boring looking one—what was his name?

A moment later, Measle realized that every single member was present and correct, because here, drifting out of the shadows at one side, came the dull figure of the government minister—*the one whose face your eyes didn't want to stay on, simply because it was so incredibly dreary to look at—what was his name?*

The man held two glasses of red wine and, as he passed one to Sir Peregrine Spine, the question of the minister's name was resolved for Measle, because Sir Peregrine said, 'Ah, my dear Underwood, thank you—you're too kind.'

Underwood! Quentin Underwood!

Tinker was feeling a little crushed in the confines of the leather jacket and he let out a tiny growl of displeasure—and, immediately, Measle wrapped his fingers round Tinker's muzzle and whispered, 'Shhh, Tink!' into a fuzzy ear. A moment later, Measle felt movement on his other side and he turned his head and saw that Iggy, holding carefully to the sleeping Matilda, had crawled up next to him. Measle held a finger to his lips and looked at Iggy with a desperate, pleading look— and Iggy scowled and bent his damp head next to Measle and whispered, 'If dere's one fing burglariders know about, Mumps, dat's being quiet, all right?'

'All right, Iggy,' whispered Measle. 'Sorry.'

'Now den,' muttered Iggy, his smelly breath drifting into Measle's nostrils, 'who is dese people and wot is dey doing 'ere, traipse-passin' in my castle?'

'I don't know, Iggy. Let's just be very, very quiet, so we can listen and find out.'

Iggy nodded his agreement and then he, Measle, and Tinker, straining their ears, settled down to hear the conversation far below.

Sir Peregrine was twirling the stem of his wine glass and staring into the dark red liquid. He sniffed delicately at the wine. Then he lifted his noble head and said, 'You asked us here in order to allow us to express our concerns, Prime Magus—'

Prime Magus! That means that Justin Bucket is down there too! Well, that made sense, of course— if the Prime Magus's Advisory Committee is here, then the Prime Magus should be as well—

Measle inched himself forward another few centimetres, trying to get a better angle of view but most of the floor of the great room was still hidden from him, so he assumed that Justin was somewhere just out of his line of sight.

Sir Peregrine went on, '—so perhaps we should voice our concerns, one by one—and then you can address them in turn. Would that be agreeable?'

There was no reply, but Sir Peregrine inclined his silver-maned head in what looked to Measle like a grateful way—so perhaps Justin had simply nodded, inviting Sir Peregrine to continue.

'Thank you, Prime Magus,' said Sir Peregrine. 'Perhaps I shall start? My main concern is just how long we are going to be able to keep the Stubbs family under lock and key, before some serious questions will be asked?'

Tully Telford looked up from polishing his glasses. 'I agree with Sir Peregrine, Prime Magus,' he squeaked. 'As a lawyer, I must remind you that—by the rules of the Court of Magistri—charges must be brought sooner or later. If they are not, then the Stubbs family will have to be released. We cannot hold them without accusing them of something, you understand.'

Ermintrude Bacon looked towards the middle part of the room. 'And then there is the matter of this Mallockee creature, Prime Magus. What exactly are we going to do about her? The dear little poppet!'

Dorian Fescue turned his yellow face away from the fireplace and said, 'Personally, Prime Magus, I feel that the Stubbs family was far too powerful even *before* the appearance of this Mallockee. With this all-powerful child joining the family, I don't see how we can possibly allow any of them to go free.'

Quentin Underwood had been leaning against the mantelpiece, but the fire was evidently getting a little too hot for him, because he moved away from it, perching himself on the arm of Ermintrude's chair. His flat, dreary, colourless face turned in the same direction in which the rest of his colleagues were all looking, and he said, in a dull and monotonous drone, 'And then of course there is the boy, Prime Magus. Our original target. What have you learned about him? Does he in fact possess the powers of which he is suspected?'

There was a pause, while the Advisory Committee all stared towards the centre of the room, obviously waiting for some sort of response. Measle heard the sound of measured footsteps as the Prime Magus walked slowly towards the fireplace, his back to Measle.

When the Prime Magus reached the fireplace, he turned around.

It wasn't Justin Bucket.

It was Toby Jugg.

TOBY JUGG

It felt to Measle as if his blood had turned, suddenly and without warning, into iced water. The shock of seeing Toby Jugg down there—Toby Jugg, his friend and rescuer—Toby Jugg, a man his mum had said was 'very nice'—Toby Jugg, with a warm and affable smile on his rugged face, and that same smile being directed at each and every member of the Advisory Committee, not one of whose members could ever be called a friend of the Stubbs family—well, all that was enough to freeze Measle into a sort of paralysis, and the only thing he could do was simply stare down at the dreadful scene below him, his eyes wide and his jaw gaping open.

Measle felt a sudden movement at his side and

he turned his head just in time to see Iggy take a deep breath and open his mouth—and somehow Measle knew that Iggy was about to shout some sort of welcome down to his master—

Measle reached over and clamped his hand over Iggy's lips and Iggy, his fishy eyes glaring, huffed and spluttered wetly through Measle's fingers.

'Ssshhhh! Iggy!' Measle whispered, as fiercely as he could without raising the volume.

'Mmmmfff?' mumbled Iggy, now shaking his head from side to side, in an attempt to rid his face of Measle's hand. Measle felt the raindrops spatter his cheeks.

'We've got to be quiet, Iggy! We've got to find out what's going on! We can say hello to Mr Jugg later—all right?'

Iggy's head stopped shaking and so did the huffing and sputtering under Measle's clamping hand. Iggy's fishy eyes stopped glaring and a trace of understanding flitted across them. Then Iggy nodded slowly—and Measle felt it was safe enough to take his hand off Iggy's mouth. Once he was free, Iggy bent his head close to Measle's and whispered into his ear. 'We can sssay hello later, Mumps?'

'Yes, Iggy. Later. Right now, we've got to be like little mice, OK?'

Iggy grinned, showing his yellow teeth. Then he turned his head away and concentrated on listening to what was being said down below—and Measle, breathing a silent sigh of relief, did the same.

Toby was standing casually in front of the fireplace, his shoulder blades resting comfortably against the mantelpiece, his legs crossed and his hands thrust deep in his pockets. He looked into the face of each member of the Advisory Committee, a small smile on his lips. Then, after a long pause, he took a deep breath and said, 'Well, I'm glad you all feel the need to express these "concerns" of yours—and I shall be happy to address each one in a minute. But first, I must ask you all to stop calling me "Prime Magus".'

'But you *are* the Prime Magus, Toby,' said Sir Peregrine. 'You won the election in a landslide!'

What? thought Measle. *Surely Justin Bucket won the election?*

Toby laughed. It was a rich, easy-going, friendly sort of laugh—the sort of laugh that would make you like such a person immediately and, for a moment, Measle felt his suspicions begin to drain away. *Surely, somebody like Toby Jugg couldn't be a bad chap—not with a laugh like that? Or a face like that? Or a smile like that? And Mum said he was very nice—surely Mum couldn't be wrong? Could she?*

Toby stopped laughing but he kept a broad, amiable smile on his face. He said, 'The fact that I won, Peregrine, is neither here nor there. The point is, we agreed that Bucket should believe that he'd won the election and was therefore the new Prime Magus of the Wizards' Guild.'

'In name only, Toby,' murmured Sir Peregrine Spine.

'Of *course* in name only, Peregrine,' said Toby. 'The poor idiot certainly couldn't manage the job for real. But you will remember that we also agreed to conceal the fact that I had won, in case my true identity should somehow be discovered.'

Measle's mind was in a whirl. *His true identity? Toby Jugg's got a true identity? So—if he's not Toby Jugg, then who is he?*

'Well, but my dear Prime Magus,' said Ermintrude Bacon, in a very oily and humble little voice, 'I cannot see the harm in addressing you with your proper title when we are in private, the way we are at the present moment. After all, you deserve it, you really do! I mean to say—your plan to separate the boy from his family, in order to study him closely, was brilliant! As, indeed, was the carrying out of that plan. *Brilliant!'*

'Thank you, Trudy,' said Toby. 'Now, to get back to—'

Ermintrude wasn't going to be stopped so easily. Here was her chance to really suck up to the Prime Magus! 'And then, *dear* Prime Magus—your *brilliant* decision to seize the Mallockee child as well, during all the confusion—well, it was nothing short of *brilliant*!'

Toby bowed his head in Ermintrude's direction. 'You're very kind, Trudy,' he said. 'But, nevertheless, I must insist that you stop calling me Prime Magus. If you all continue to do that in *private*, then there's the possibility that your tongues might slip and you could—quite by mistake—do the same when we're in *public*. If the secret got out that I was the real Prime Magus of the Wizards' Guild—well, that could be disastrous for us all and for our intended sweeping programme of rule changes. Therefore, I must ask you all to call me by my name—and not by my title—at all times. Is that agreed?'

There was a moment or two of mumbling and murmuring, during which Measle was unable to catch any of what was being said, and then Sir Peregrine lifted his noble head and said, 'Agreed, Prime Mag—or, rather, *Toby*, I should say.'

'Indeed you should, Peregrine,' said Toby, smiling so broadly that Measle could see, quite clearly, his flashing white teeth.

There was a little polite laughter and then Toby

raised his hand and, when the laughter had died away, he said, 'Now—to your various concerns. Peregrine, I believe you wanted to know how long we can hold the Stubbs family? My reply? Not long at all. Quite soon questions will indeed begin to be asked, for which we have no adequate answers. Therefore, the problem of the Stubbs family will have to be—*disposed* of. You also asked about the boy and whether or not I have learned anything about his possible magic powers. Well—yes, I have.'

Toby paused, smiling pleasantly down at his audience. *He looks so relaxed*, thought Measle, who was feeling about as un-relaxed as it's possible to feel, without cracking from the strain.

Toby pushed his shoulders away from the mantelpiece and began to pace up and down in front of the fireplace.

'I've been watching him carefully for several hours now and I've learned that the boy possesses no magical powers whatsoever,' he said, quietly. 'None at all. The Mallockee, on the other hand, is everything that Octavo said she was. An extraordinary creature. At the moment she tires too easily, but as she grows older that weakness will disappear, I think. As for young Measle, he has experienced some very dangerous situations down here and never, at any time, has he resorted to magic to get out of any of them. What he *has* shown, however, is remarkable courage, an active imagination, and some splendid examples of resourcefulness.'

'It rather sounds, Toby,' said Dorian Fescue, his thin voice dripping with scorn, 'as though you *admire* the beastly little fellow.'

Toby stared at Dorian and, for the first time that night, Measle saw Toby's smile disappear.

'Oh, but I *do* admire him, Dorian,' said Toby, in a steely tone. 'And for good reason. When your enemy is a dolt, you can sneer at him. But when your enemy is brave and resourceful and clever, then it's stupid *not* to admire him. Even if he is only twelve years old.'

'It is a little hard to believe,' squeaked Tully, 'that a boy so young has managed to overcome so many dangers without the use of magic. Are you quite, *quite* sure, Toby, that he's powerless?'

'I didn't say he was powerless, Tully,' said Toby, stopping in his tracks. He rested one elbow on the mantelpiece and grinned amiably. 'For a start, he's had the Mallockee with him all this time. Mind you, not everything she has done was entirely helpful. However, as for Measle—I can assure you he has no magical abilities whatsoever. And yet, what he has accomplished *without* them is nothing short of miraculous. I've been watching him closely— and I've also been throwing a number of obstacles in his way. As you all know, this vast labyrinth of chambers down here is steeped in natural mana— and I'm sure you also know that this free form of magic is programmed to fulfil the wishes of the current Prime Magus. As the actual current Prime Magus, I have been able to direct the power down here to accomplish certain results, all of them extremely unpleasant for young Measle to experience. Several of them were in fact downright dangerous, too. And yet he has survived them all. As I say, quite miraculous, really. And here's another interesting fact about young Measle Stubbs—and, in itself, something of a miracle, as well: the boy and the Mallockee are, at this precise moment, a mere six metres away from us and, while she is mercifully asleep, he has managed to overhear almost everything that we've been saying. And if that isn't an extraordinary feat, I don't know what is.'

DiSCOVERED!

Measle froze.

So, apparently, did Toby Jugg's audience because, for several long seconds, nothing happened at all. Toby Jugg, one elbow resting easily on the mantelpiece, the other hand thrust deep in his pocket, continued to smile his friendly smile— but there was no movement and no sound at all from any of his listeners, until suddenly Dorian Fescue jumped to his feet, his head whipping wildly from side to side as he searched the shadows of the great room.

'Here, Toby? *Where?* Where are they?'

Toby didn't reply. All he did was grin more broadly—then, slowly, he took his right hand out of his pocket and, extending his forefinger, he pointed up to the exact spot in the dark, shadowy minstrel's gallery, where Measle, Iggy, Matilda, and Tinker were lying.

'Up *there*?' demanded Dorian, his yellow face lifting towards the ceiling.

'You can't see them, Dorian,' said Toby. 'They're in the shadows. But I think we all would *like* to see them—yes? Very well, then.'

Toby lifted his head. Now he wasn't smiling. He called out, 'Officers! Go up to the gallery and bring our eavesdropping guests down here! Quickly now—before they decide to go to another party instead!'

There was a clatter of heavy boots and two black-uniformed men emerged from the shadows. They ran fast up the spiral staircase, round the gallery, and were at Measle's side before he could think of anything to do. With a hard yank, one of the men pulled Measle to his feet and then he began to walk purposefully back to the iron staircase, dragging Measle behind him. Measle twisted in the man's grip and managed to look behind him. He saw the second man put his hand on the scruff of Iggy's neck, lift him up bodily, and then push him roughly after them.

Measle's captor clumped down the iron steps and Measle half-walked, half-fell with him, until they reached the bottom. Then the man dragged Measle towards the fireplace and into the middle of the circle of armchairs, depositing him on the floor at Toby Jugg's feet. A moment later, the second man brought Iggy and Matilda into the circle, pushing Iggy down into an awkward squat on the floor.

'Thank you, officers,' said Toby. 'That will do.'

The two men nodded and then marched out of the circle, disappearing once again back into the gloom.

'Niggle,' said Toby firmly, 'you will remain perfectly still. You will keep hold of the Mallockee and you will not—I repeat, you will *not*—allow her to wake up. Is that clearly understood, Niggle?'

Iggy gulped, nodded nervously, and muttered, 'Yessss, Missster Jugg, sssir.'

Toby switched his gaze to Measle and smiled broadly. 'Well, Measle old son,' he said, in his cheerful, friendly voice. 'How nice to see you again.'

Slowly and warily, Measle sat up. He held tight to Tinker, pulling his leather jacket round the little dog's body. He looked around at his audience. Their faces were lit by the candles and the flickering firelight—and they didn't look at all friendly.

Sir Peregrine Spine and Ermintrude Bacon were closest to him, both sunk deep in their armchairs. A little further out were the other two armchairs, containing Dorian Fescue and Tully Telford—and beyond them, and half-obscured by shadows, was the standing figure of Quentin Underwood.

Measle felt the five pairs of eyes boring into him. *It's a bit like being in a forest at night and being watched by a pack of wolves,* he thought. *In this light, their eyes look sort of shiny—and red.*

'May I ask what is going on, Toby?' said Sir Peregrine, suddenly. 'What are the boy and the Mallockee doing, running free in these quarters?'

'Well, Peregrine,' said Toby, in a casual voice, 'it would appear that they have escaped from *their* section, only to be recaptured in *ours*.'

'But—but *how* did they escape?' said Dorian, angrily.

'By being brave and resourceful and clever, of course,' said Toby—and Measle felt Toby's hand patting his shoulder, as if the man was trying to show his approval of Measle's actions to his audience. Then Toby's hand stopped patting and settled on his shoulder and Measle could feel the steely muscles in Toby's firm hand, and he knew that—whatever Toby had in store for him—this time he certainly wasn't going to let Measle out of his grasp.

There was a long silence, while the five warlocks simply stared at Measle. Then Toby took his hand off Measle's shoulder and walked to a spot directly in front of him. He looked down at Measle, smiling warmly. Then he said, 'Is there anything you want to ask us, Measle old son? I'm sure you're bursting with questions. I know *I'd* be. If so—fire away.'

Measle sat there for a moment, his mind buzzing. It was true—there were a lot of questions—but which were the important ones?

'Are you really the Prime Magus?' he blurted, staring up into Toby's friendly eyes.

'Yes, I really am,' said Toby.

'Why has it got to be a secret? Why can't you tell anybody?'

'Well, old son—because of who I am, you see.'

'You mean—you're not really Toby Jugg?'

Toby laughed—a rich, careless sort of laugh—the sort of laugh people do when they haven't a care in the world.

'Oh, I'm Toby Jugg, all right,' he boomed. 'At least, I was the last time I looked.'

There was an appreciative little laugh from the five warlocks and Ermintrude, in her oily voice, muttered, '"The last time he *looked*"—so clever.'

'But—you said it was because of who you *were*,' said Measle, slowly. 'Doesn't that mean you're really somebody else?'

Toby shook his head. 'Not so much some*body* else, old son. More like some*thing* else. Here—I'll show you.'

And then Toby squatted down in front of Measle. He raised both his hands and once again Measle instinctively reared back—but Toby's hands weren't going for Measle. Toby's hands were reaching towards his own head—

Reaching for the long, wavy locks of greying hair that hung on either side of Toby's face—

Curling the strong brown fingers around the locks of hair—

Pulling the locks back from his face—

And revealing—to Measle's astonished eyes—Toby's ears.

THE
PLOT

Toby's ears were almost completely black.

The Gloomstains were at their blackest at the tips of Toby's ears, fading down to a dark grey by the time they reached the lobes. Measle stared at them in horror, because he knew exactly what they meant: Toby Jugg wasn't a wizard at all—he was a warlock, and a very powerful one at that. Far more powerful than Tully Telford, for example, whose ears were only black at the tips—

'Surprised?' said Toby, grinning cheerfully into Measle's face.

Measle didn't answer. His mind was clicking furiously from gear to gear while he tried to find an explanation for the fact that, a mere twenty-four hours ago, Toby's ears had been as pink as his own—

And then Measle's agile brain found exactly the right gear.

Click.

'You wear make-up,' said Measle, quietly. 'You wear make-up on your ears.'

Toby raised his eyebrows and turned and looked over his shoulder at the rest of the warlocks. 'You see?' he said. 'You see what I mean? The boy isn't just brave and resourceful—he's got a quick mind too.'

Toby turned back and looked at Measle thoughtfully. Then he said, 'Indeed I do, Measle—at least, when I want people to think I'm just a simple wizard. Down here I needn't bother, of course. But I'm curious—how did you find that out, old son?'

'I saw the make-up in your bathroom. I thought it belonged to a woman. I never guessed it might belong to you.'

Toby nodded. 'I see. Well—now you know what I am, any more questions?'

Measle thought hard. There were lots of questions he wanted to ask—but there was one question that stood head and shoulders above the rest.

'Why?'

'Why what?'

'Why—*everything*?'

Toby laughed. Then he thought for a moment—shrugged—and then he pulled himself out of his squat and up to his full height.

'You want to know everything, do you?' he said, smiling down at Measle. 'Well, why not?'

Tully Telford leaned forward again and raised a warning finger. 'Ah—Toby—as your legal adviser, I must caution you against saying anything that might incriminate you.' Tully glanced round at his fellow warlocks and added, quickly, 'And *us*, for that matter.'

Toby laughed again. 'It won't matter,' he said.

'It won't?' said Sir Peregrine Spine, raising both eyebrows as high as they could go.

'No, it won't,' said Toby, easily. 'What we say here in this room, to this boy, won't matter in the least. I hope you all take my meaning?'

There was a long silence. Then, one by one, Measle saw the warlocks nod. The only warlock whose head didn't move at all was Sir Peregrine Spine. Measle saw that Sir Peregrine was biting his lip in a nervous way and twitching his bushy silver eyebrows.

'Toby—my dear fellow,' said Sir Peregrine, 'do please forgive me—but am I to understand—'

'Yes, Peregrine,' said Toby, firmly. 'You are.'

Understand what? thought Measle, looking uneasily into the face of each warlock. Then Toby Jugg started speaking again.

'Well, what all this is about, Measle old son, is this: there are going to be some changes made. Some big changes, starting with the Wizards' Guild. Now, I'm a warlock and I'm the Prime

Magus of the Wizards' Guild—and that's not allowed, you see. So, first we have to change that rule. The new rule will be that *only* a warlock can be Prime Magus. Once that's done, I can reveal what I really am, you see? Meanwhile, we have to pretend that Justin is the Prime Magus and not me. Now, the point of being the Prime Magus is to have power—and that's something that none of the previous Prime Maguses have ever really understood. Well, how could they? They were just simple wizards, weren't they? However, now that a warlock has become the Prime Magus—even if it is a big secret still—all that's going to change.'

'H-how?' stammered Measle.

'The Wizards' Guild is going to have a lot more say in how the world is run, old son. It's always avoided interfering in human affairs—but not any more. Not with us warlocks managing things. And there's lots to do. All those silly little countries, with their silly little leaders, all arguing with each other. But not for much longer, old son. Once we get rid of the whole ridiculous lot of them, we warlocks will be able to make the world so much more—*efficient.*'

Toby grinned down at Measle and Measle realized that Toby was enjoying himself. And then Measle felt himself getting rather cold—and a clammy sweat broke out on his forehead—because Measle began to understand what it was that everybody else in the great room already understood: the only reason Toby was telling him all this was because Toby had no fear that it would ever be repeated to anybody—which meant that, quite soon after Toby had *finished* telling him everything, there was a strong probability that Measle's life was going to come to an abrupt and maybe sticky end—

'What's the matter, Measle?' said Toby, in a concerned voice. 'You look a little peaky all of a sudden.'

'N-nothing,' muttered Measle, staring hard at the floor. *I've got to keep him talking!* 'W-what other things are you going to change?'

'Ah—well, one of the first things we shall do is begin a world-wide hunt for more Manafounts. There are sure to be a few out there—besides your mother, I mean—that haven't yet been discovered— and, when we find them, we'll bring them back here and we'll have a lovely mass wedding.'

There was an appreciative little laugh from the other warlocks and Ermintrude Bacon said, in her coy little baby voice, 'I'm *so* looking forward to finding a husband! Now, be sure to find me a really *handsome* manafount, Toby! I want one at least as attractive as yours, mind!'

Toby bowed in Ermintrude's direction. 'I shall do my best for you, Trudy,' he said. Then he turned back to Measle and said, 'You see, Measle old son, if we each have a manafount at our side—well, hand in hand, we can do pretty much as we like, can't we?'

'But—but what if they don't *want* to marry any of you?' said Measle, thinking that nobody in their right mind would ever want to marry Ermintrude Bacon—or Tully Telford, come to that—and frankly, Dorian Fescue and his yellow face was hardly a very attractive proposition either, and nor was Quentin Underwood, with his dull and pointless personality—and Sir Peregrine was a bit old to be getting married—

'Oh, that won't be a problem, Measle,' said Toby, genially. 'You'd be amazed at all the pills and potions that we've got in our alchemy labs. Half of them seem to have something to do with getting people to fall in love with you, and the other half seem to be about getting people to do exactly what you want—so persuading a few manafounts to marry us is not going to be all that hard, I promise.'

'Besides,' cooed Ermintrude, 'who *wouldn't* want to marry us? The most powerful group of warlocks the world has ever seen! I'm sure that silly girl would far rather be married to Toby Jugg than to that ridiculous wizard!'

'What silly girl?' blurted Measle. 'What wizard?'

Toby cleared his throat loudly and shot an angry look at Ermintrude Bacon—and, immediately, Ermintrude's piggy face turned a little pink and she lowered her eyes to the floor. There was a short, uncomfortable silence. Then Toby shrugged his shoulders and said, 'Well, I suppose it can't hurt to tell him now, can it?'

'Tell me what?' said Measle.

Dorian Fescue got up out of his armchair and poured himself another glass of wine. Then he turned and faced Measle, his yellow face distorted by a broad smirk of pleasure.

'Toby won't have to search the outside world for *his* manafount, boy,' he said, each word dripping with venom. 'Toby already *has* his manafount, ready and waiting. Her name, boy—her name is Lee Stubbs.'

If Measle had felt cold and clammy before, now it seemed as though he was packed in ice. He stared up at Dorian Fescue's cruel face, his mind racing with all the reasons why there was no way that his mother would ever—could ever—marry Toby Jugg—

'My mum's got a husband already,' said Measle.

Dorian Fescue let loose a short laugh. Then he sipped his wine and said, 'Not for much longer, boy. Not for much longer.'

'What do you mean?' said Measle—although he was pretty sure he knew *exactly* what Dorian Fescue meant.

'I mean, boy, that if your father is—how shall I put it?—if your father is "out of the way", then your mother *won't* have a husband any more—and that means she'll be free to marry Mr Jugg.'

Sir Peregrine Spine shifted uncomfortably in his armchair. 'This is nothing personal against you, young man,' he said, smoothly. 'I do hope you understand that?'

'No, indeed not,' said Toby, shaking his head sadly. 'Sir Peregrine's right—we've got nothing against you, Measle old son. It's just that, to achieve our ends, certain unpleasant things are going to have to occur. One of them is the elimination of your dad, I'm afraid.'

So—there it is. The truth at last . . . Measle felt his heart beating very fast. It also seemed to be twice as heavy as usual and a strange little lump was rising in his throat.

'And what about my sister?' he said, his voice a little quivery now. 'What are you going to do with her?'

'Oh, we're going to keep her, old son,' said Toby, in the sort of over-cheerful tone people use when they've just delivered a piece of gloomy news and are then very relieved when they can deliver a happy one immediately after. 'Yes, she's far too interesting to throw away. Her powers will, no doubt, develop splendidly—and, since I'll be her stepfather, I'll be controlling her. Yes, it'll be very interesting having a Mallockee in the family.'

Good luck with that, thought Measle, *with controlling Matilda. I'm the only one who can do that!*

'And—and, what about me?' said Measle.

'*You*, old son?'

'Y-yes. What are you going to do with me?'

'Oh, don't you worry about that,' said Toby. 'We're just going to keep you safe, while we see what's what. But there'll be no more wandering around the place, I'm afraid. Officers! Come here, please!'

Measle watched as the two uniformed men emerged from the shadows in the far corner of the room and marched into the circle of light.

'Officers, you will escort us all down to the Detention Centre.'

'The D-Detention Centre?' said Measle, trying hard to keep the sound of fear from his voice. 'W-what's that?'

'Oh, don't worry, old son. It's just a secure place where we can keep you safe. Safe and sound, eh?'

Ermintrude coughed a little ladylike cough and said, 'And what about this nasty wrathmonk, Toby? What shall we do with him?'

'A good question, Trudy,' said Toby, staring coldly down at Iggy, who was now crouching on the floor and trembling like a whipped dog. Toby sighed, irritably. 'I've often wondered, what is the *point* of you, Niggle? I've never understood that.

As a servant you're a waste of time. In fact, why aren't you in the Detention Centre with all the other wrathmonks, eh?'

'I was ricky-bended leaningsea,' Iggy muttered, almost under his breath.

'What?' said Toby, clenching both hands into fists and frowning angrily.

'Ricky-bended leaningsea,' repeated Iggy, a little louder this time.

Tully Telford leaned forward, an amused little smile on his lips. 'I think what the creature is trying to say is that he was "*recommended leniency*", Toby. It means that the arresting wizard obviously suggested that—since the crime was not too wicked—the punishment should not be too severe.'

Oh, thought Measle, *so that's what 'ricky-bended leaningsea' means!*

'I know what it means, Tully!' barked Toby. Then he pointed a finger at Iggy and said, in a stern and commanding voice, 'And who, Niggle, was this wizard who recommended leniency?'

'It was Missster Sssam Ssstubbs,' said Iggy, smiling nervously up at Measle.

'*Was* it now?' said Toby slowly. 'How very interesting.' He seemed deep in thought for a moment. Then he said, 'You will come with us, Niggle. You will carry the Mallockee. You will carry her very carefully—and you will not wake her up. Understood?'

'Yess, Missster Jugg, sssir,' said Iggy, nodding wildly and scattering raindrops in a wide circle.

'Good!' said Toby. 'Well, then—shall we go?'

Toby clapped his hand onto Measle's shoulder. To anybody watching, it looked like a friendly gesture; but Measle felt once again the steel in Toby's grip—

The other warlocks were getting to their feet. Iggy positioned himself next to Measle and, with the two uniformed men leading the way, they all set off—a little procession, with Measle, carrying Tinker, and Iggy, carrying Matilda, in the middle.

THE DETENTION CENTRE

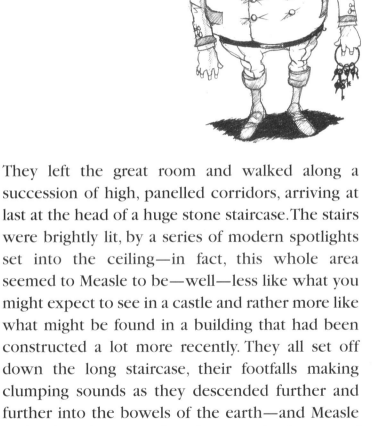

They left the great room and walked along a succession of high, panelled corridors, arriving at last at the head of a huge stone staircase. The stairs were brightly lit, by a series of modern spotlights set into the ceiling—in fact, this whole area seemed to Measle to be—well—less like what you might expect to see in a castle and rather more like what might be found in a building that had been constructed a lot more recently. They all set off down the long staircase, their footfalls making clumping sounds as they descended further and further into the bowels of the earth—and Measle realized, with a start, that this was the first set of stairs that he'd seen in Caltrop Castle. Through all the exploration of the place—and, later, during the frantic chases—he'd never come across a single staircase in the entire place! Where were the ones that should, logically, lead to upper floors? What sort of castle had only a ground floor and a deep, deep basement?

After what seemed an age, they arrived at the bottom. There was a single, heavy, iron door that was set into the wall in front of them. Toby tapped Tully Telford on the shoulder and said, 'Your department, Tully,' and Tully nodded and pressed a small button on a speaker on the wall by the door and, a moment later, a tinny, gruff voice came out of the speaker. The voice said, 'Officer Offal on duty—kindly state your business.'

Tully Telford raised his head and spoke, in his squeaky voice, in the direction of the loudspeaker. 'Attorney Tully Telford here, Offal. Open up, if you please. We have a . . . um . . . a "*guest*" for the Detention Centre.'

'Yes, sir. Right away, sir,' said the voice—and, a moment later, there was a click and the heavy door swung open.

Measle found himself in a brightly-lit, circular hallway. Several doors led off this hallway and a stout, uniformed man was emerging from one of them. He nodded respectfully at the group of warlocks and then beckoned them towards a second door on the far side. He took a heavy keyring from a hook on his belt, picked out a key, pushed it into the lock and turned it—and then threw the door wide open and stood aside to let the warlocks through.

'Thank you, Officer Offal,' said Tully, stepping through the opening. The rest of the procession followed him into a small, bare office. There was a steel desk in the room, with a swivel chair behind it. On the desk was a big, old-fashioned silver microphone on a short stand and, next to the microphone, what looked like a sort of intercom, with switches on it. Around the walls were several filing cabinets, painted a dark green and, in one corner, a door that looked to be even heavier and more strongly barred than the one through which they had just entered. Next to this door was a panel with a pair of large round buttons on it. One button was black. The other was a dull green and had the number 20 painted on it.

Officer Offal came and stood behind the desk. He was big and heavy-looking, with a fat belly that hung over his belt. His face was pink and puffy and his red hair was cut very short, so that his scalp gleamed through the bristles.

'A new tenant for you, Offal,' said Tully—and the other warlocks stepped aside, revealing Measle and Iggy and Tinker in their midst.

Officer Offal nodded efficiently—but it wasn't Measle he was staring at. His eyes were locked grimly on Iggy.

'I see he's already got his wrathring on, sir,' he said, stepping out from behind the desk. 'That makes my job a lot easier, I don't mind telling you.' Offal marched up to Iggy and said, sternly, 'Come along then, my lad—and gimme your dolly—you can't take that with you where you're going, you know.'

'Wha'?' said Iggy, nervously looking about him.

Toby laughed. 'That's not a doll, officer,' he said, cheerfully. 'That's a rather precious little creature who happens to be asleep at the moment. I'd be obliged if you didn't wake her up, too—so please keep your voice down.'

'Ah—right you are, sir,' whispered Offal, peering shortsightedly at Matilda. 'Er . . . what do you want me to do with the little thing, sir?'

'Leave her where she is, officer,' said Toby. 'You see, it's not Mr Niggle whom we want you to keep down here. It's this boy here—and his dog. We need to put them somewhere safe for a while— somewhere very, *very* safe, you understand?'

Officer Offal looked doubtful. 'Er . . . right, sir. Yes. The only thing is, sir—well, I understood that the Detention Centre is reserved for wrathies—I mean wrathmonks, sir.'

Tully Telford nodded impatiently. 'Indeed, indeed,' he squeaked. 'However, this is a matter of some urgency, Officer Offal, and we—the Advisory Committee to the Prime Magus—are ordering you to carry out our wishes. Kindly do so without further delay.'

Officer Offal's face went even redder than it was

before and he stood up very straight and saluted smartly. 'Yessir!' he whispered. 'Right away, sir!'

Offal stepped towards Measle and Toby said, 'And gently, officer, if you please. Young Measle Stubbs is our guest, not our prisoner.'

'Right, sir.'

Officer Offal stared at Measle for a moment, as if unsure how to treat a guest. Then he turned on his heel and went to the heavy door on the far side of the room. He pulled it open and stepped through, calling back over his shoulder, 'This way, young feller.'

Measle felt the pressure of Toby's hand on his shoulder and he led the small procession through the door and into a broad corridor. There were series of cells on either side of the corridor. Measle saw that, while the doors to the cells were made of very solid-looking studded iron, the outer walls of the cells were of thick heavy glass, with wire embedded in it, so that it was practically unbreakable. These glass walls allowed you to see into the cells, which meant that the occupants had no privacy whatsoever.

Iggy Niggle nudged Measle. Measle glanced at Iggy and saw that the little wrathmonk was looking frightened.

'What's the matter, Iggy?' whispered Measle.

Iggy bent his head close to Measle's ear and muttered, 'Dis is de *uvver place*, Mumps! Where all de really *bad* wraffmonks go!'

As they all walked down the wide corridor, following the massive figure of Officer Offal, Measle peered into each cell as he passed it. Most were occupied by wrathmonks, of all shapes and sizes. They were dressed in white, one-piece jumpsuits—which was, Measle realized, in sharp contrast to the black clothes that wrathmonks always wore when out in the world. Each had a dull grey steel wrathring round their necks.

Measle didn't recognize any of them.

No—wait! There, in that cell—a huge, bulking figure, sitting on the edge of his bunk and staring curiously out at the passing procession! It's Mr Cudgel! Buford Cudgel!

Buford Cudgel's face changed the moment the giant wrathmonk caught sight of his old enemy, Measle Stubbs. His eyes narrowed, a frown appeared in the middle of his narrow forehead, his nostrils flared like a racehorse—and then Cudgel jumped up from his bunk and began to beat both huge hands against the glass. He opened his mouth and roared with rage.

'Somebody you know, old son?' said Toby.

'That's Mr Cudgel,' said Measle.

'Ah, yes. From your adventure with the Dragodon. He looks quite pleased to see you. Perhaps you'll find a few other old friends down here.'

And Measle did.

In the neighbouring cell, Frognell Flabbit was sitting moodily on his bunk, scratching at his red and lumpy face. Next to him, Judge Cedric Hardscrabble, one hand pressed to his long jaw, was pretending to read a book (Measle noticed that the book was *upside down*)—and, next to *him*, in a cell that seemed a little cleaner and tidier than all the others, stood the small round figure of Griswold Gristle, the bank manager.

As the procession passed by, each of the remaining three wrathmonks caught sight of Measle and each had a different reaction. Where Buford Cudgel had become enraged, Frognell Flabbit simply stared for a moment, an angry look in his little red eyes. Then he shrugged his shoulders and went back to scratching his face. Judge Cedric Hardscrabble looked up from his book, saw Measle and waved, a vague smile of recognition hovering on his thin lips.

Griswold Gristle's reaction was the most disturbing: he simply stood and stared, his snub nose pressed flat against the glass wall in front of him. His round white face was completely expressionless and the only movement was in the pair of tiny black eyes that followed Measle fixedly as he walked by.

'Seems like a friendly crowd,' said Toby.

'Can—can they get out?' asked Measle, nervously.

'*Can* they get out, Officer Offal?' called Toby.

Offal stopped in his tracks and turned round. 'Not unless I let 'em out, sir,' he said. 'That happens once a day. They get an hour of mixing together, out here in the corridor. Then I give them their marching orders over the microphone in the office and they all 'ave to go back to their cells. And they do it pretty smartish too, I don't mind telling you. The wrathies do as I tell 'em, 'cause they know what'll 'appen if they don't, see?'

'What will happen?' said Measle, using his most innocent voice. (Measle had discovered that, if you wanted the answer to a difficult question, putting on an innocent-sounding voice often got it for you.)

Officer Offal looked down at him and winked. 'Let's just say that the wrathies don't like me, and I don't like them—but they know who's the boss, see?'

'Why are the walls made of glass?' said Measle, who wanted to find out as much as he could before anybody thought to tell him to be quiet.

'Because we like to see what they're doing, young feller,' said Officer Offal. 'They got the wrathrings on, see? Well, those are fine for stopping their major spells, but they don't do nothing for their breath. Nothing stops that. Disgusting, that's what it is. 'Ave you ever smelt a wrathmonk's breath, young feller?'

'Yes,' said Measle, remembering the terrible stink of Basil Tramplebone's breath.

'Well, then you'll understand why we 'ave the glass walls then. We want to see them, but we certainly don't want to smell 'em, do we? And some of their breathing magic is very nasty indeed.'

'Mine is *'orrible*!' announced Iggy, proudly.

Officer Offal took a step away from Iggy and frowned. 'Well, you'd better not use it down 'ere, chummy. Not if you know what's good for you.'

They had reached the end of the broad corridor. The last cell on the left was empty and open, its door pushed back against the wall. There was a number painted on the cell door—the number 20.

'There you go, young feller,' said Offal. 'You'll be all right in there.'

Measle felt the pressure of Toby's hand on his shoulder, pushing him gently but firmly towards the open door. There was nothing he could do, so he said, 'Come on, Tink,' and, together, he and Tinker entered the cell.

'He'll be quite safe here, will he, Officer Offal?' asked Toby, leaning carelessly against the door frame and smiling in at Measle.

'Oh, yes, sir,' said Officer Offal. 'See, what 'appens is this: when it's time to let the wrathies out—

that'll be in a couple of hours now—I push the big black button in the office and that unlocks all the cell doors, see? We're all very up-to-date down here, sir. All electronic, see? I can talk to them, too, and hear 'em as well—every cell has got a two-way communication system in it. Mind you, I keep that turned off most of the time—wrathies' conversations aren't my cup of tea at all. Oh yes, we're all very high-tech, sir. Now, as to the young feller being safe—I can isolate *this* cell, see, so that it don't get unlocked when I push the black button. This number 20 cell is operated independently, see? That's what the *green* button back in the office is for, see? The green button just locks and unlocks *this* cell. That's why I'm putting the young feller and his little doggie into it, see? It's a special cell, where we put the ones we 'ave to keep separated from the rest, 'cause you see, sir, some wrathies really hate each other, and, when that 'appens, well, we 'ave to keep 'em apart.'

'I understand,' said Toby, thoughtfully. He seemed to think for a moment—then his face cleared and a small smile twitched at the corners of his mouth. 'Excellent!' he boomed. Then he turned to Iggy and said, quite casually, 'Let me have the Mallockee, Niggle.'

There was a pause, while Iggy thought about this. It was a request he quite obviously was reluctant to grant, because his face muscles started to twitch and to writhe, so that it looked as if he had a whole mass of wriggling worms just under his skin. Toby Jugg waited for Iggy to make a decision—and, when it didn't seem likely that Iggy was going to come to one any time soon, he barked, 'The Mallockee, Niggle! *GIVE HER TO ME!*'

There was something harsh and commanding in Toby's voice. Iggy shuddered with sudden terror and then, mutely, he disentangled Matilda's arms from round his neck and held out her sleeping form—and Toby scooped the little girl gently into his own arms.

Measle's mind seem to freeze, so that he was, for an instant, incapable of thought. He wanted to shout out that Toby must give her back! That he couldn't take her away! That he wanted Matilda here with him! But, before he could do so, Toby shot out his free hand and grabbed Iggy by his collar. Without a word, Toby dragged Iggy to the door and pushed him with great force into the cell, making Iggy totter out of control across the cell floor and then crash against the far wall.

'Oooowwww!' wailed Iggy, sliding down the wall and slumping into a heap on the floor.

Toby's voice hissed, 'Once a wrathmonk, always a wrathmonk! We are withdrawing the recommended leniency! Welcome to your new home, Niggle!'

Then, before Measle could react to all this, the door was swung shut with a clang! and there was the sound of a heavy bolt slamming home.

'Oooh!' cried Iggy, bursting into a flood of tears.

'Wot did he do dat for? Why did he take my little fing away? Oooh!'

Measle went to the glass wall and stared out. Officer Offal was standing several metres down the corridor, separated from the warlocks and possibly out of their earshot. The warlocks themselves were clustered tightly around Toby Jugg. Toby's head was bent towards them and he seemed to be whispering hurriedly. There were a lot of glances thrown back towards Measle's cell, and then what looked like a furious whispered discussion between them all. Then, finally, there was a collective nodding of heads. Measle watched as Toby beckoned to Officer Offal. The big man immediately hurried over to the group of warlocks. Toby spoke to him and Measle saw Officer Offal's eyes widen in shock—then Officer Offal stared hard in the direction of Measle's cell—Toby did some more talking—Officer Offal shook his head firmly—then Measle saw Toby reach into his pocket and pull out a great wad of money. Measle had never seen so much money in his life. He watched as the money was pushed into Officer Offal's beefy hand—more talk—and now Officer Offal was nodding slowly and, one by one, he and the warlocks each glanced back at Measle's cell— and Measle saw that each one had a small, satisfied smile on their lips. Toby patted Officer Offal on his shoulder in a very friendly manner and then the whole group walked away down the broad corridor. Measle watched them, his mind a whirl, until they all disappeared through the door at the far end.

Iggy was whimpering piteously to himself, so Measle went to his side and sat down next to him, leaning his back against the cold stone wall.Tinker, guessing that the smelly kid wasn't going to want him to go anywhere in a hurry, lay down and closed his eyes and was soon asleep.

Measle's quick mind was in desperate overdrive. His main concern was for his sister. *Where were they taking her? What would they do to her?* And, when no immediate answers sprang into his mind, Measle shifted gears and concentrated on something else. *What was all that whispering about? Why did Toby give Officer Offal all that money? Why did the warlocks smile those awful little smiles when they looked back at this cell? Why did Toby shove poor Iggy in here with me? What are they going to do with me?*

It was that last question that stuck in Measle's mind—*what are they going to do with me? Toby had said they're going to keep Mum and Matilda alive—they're going to get rid of Dad—and what about me?*

Slowly, a sick realization began to seep into Measle's mind—and then he knew exactly what was going to happen to him. It was all linked to that wad of money—and the wad of money was linked to Officer Offal—and Officer Offal was linked to the opening of all the wrathmonks' cell doors—

all except this one, if Officer Offal so decided. And Officer Offal had shaken his head at something Toby had said, but when Toby had given him the money, Officer Offal had nodded—and all the warlocks had looked back at him and grinned their horrible grins—

Officer Offal wasn't going to keep Measle's cell door locked!

Officer Offal was going to open the door to Measle's cell—so, when it was time for the wrathmonks to mingle in the corridor, there was going to be nothing to stop Griswold Gristle, Buford Cudgel, Frognell Flabbit, and Judge Cedric Hardscrabble from marching up to Measle's cell and walking in and—

And breathing on him.

And Measle remembered what those four wrathmonk exhalation enchantments did to a person. The first two were nasty and very painful. Judge Cedric's breath gave you horrible, painful red boils all over your face and body and Frognell Flabbit's caused the most terrible, agonizing toothache. But the breaths of the other two wrathmonks were deadly. Buford Cudgel's made all the microscopic organisms on your body grow to the size of beetles; and Griswold Gristle's dried up all the moisture in your body—all the sweat and the tears and, most importantly, all the *blood*—until you were nothing more than a little, dried up, shrivelled corpse.

A very *dead* little shrivelled corpse.

And, this time, there was no Dad or Mum or Nanny Flannel to help him out. This time, there was no Matilda to do a helpful spell. This time, there was only Tinker—and Mr Ignatius Niggle. And Mr Ignatius Niggle was a wrathmonk himself! Measle looked at Iggy, who was still snivelling—*he won't be any use*, thought Measle, *not against those wrathmonks. And why should Iggy even try—he's one of them!*

Measle got up abruptly and went to the cell door and pushed against it. It was a pointless thing to do but it's something everybody does if they've been locked in somewhere. Needless to say, the door didn't budge.

Two hours! thought Measle. *That's what Officer Offal had said—he'd be opening, the cell doors in two hours! So, I've got two hours to get me and Tinker and Iggy out of here!*

But how? How to open a massive, electronically-operated cell door?

iGGy GOES TO WORK

Measle had discovered that, if he sat down and thought about a problem—*really* thought about a problem—then more often than not the solution would simply pop into his brain like a shaft of sunlight. In the past, some of these solutions had come to him very quickly, simply because they *had* to come to him quickly, or else he would certainly have died—but, this time, Measle had a little longer to come up with one of his brilliant ideas, so he went and sat down on the bunk and started to think.

How to open a door?

Iggy. Iggy said he could open things with his one and only spell—so perhaps Iggy could open this massive door and let them out?

But Iggy was wearing a wrathring—and a wrathring stopped all magic, except for a wrathmonk's exhalation enchantment, and Iggy's exhalation enchantment did nothing more spectacular than kill a few insects.

But without *the wrathring—*

Click—Click—Click went Measle's brain—and here was a shaft of sunlight!

Measle crossed the cell and sat down again at the little wrathmonk's side. Iggy turned his tear-stained face and stared mournfully at Measle through his fishy eyes.

'Why did Missster Jugg do dat?' he said, sadly. 'Why did he push me in 'ere? Why did he take my little fing away from me? I was a good wraffmonk, I was. I didn't do no harm to nobody.'

'I know you didn't, Iggy,' said Measle, in his friendliest and most consoling voice. Measle let a few seconds tick by, because he wanted to change the subject. Then he said, 'Iggy—you know when you were a burglar—I mean, a *burglarider*—did you ever want to open something *without* using your magic spell?'

'I don't do de burglariding no more, Mumps,' hissed Iggy, looking fearfully towards the cell door. 'I'm a *good* wraffmonk, I am.'

'I *know* you are, Iggy. But, when you *weren't*, did you ever open something without using your spell?'

Iggy thought for a moment, his face twisting with the effort. Then he nodded, cautiously.

'What did you open, Iggy?'

'Locks.'

Measle frowned. 'But—but I thought you used your spell for locks?'

'I *did*, Mumps,' said Iggy, in that patient sort of voice that people use when they're trying to explain something to somebody who's not all that bright. 'I *did* use my ssspell to open locks—but only de *difficult* ones. Sssee, you can only do a big ssspell like dat once a day.'

'I know that, Iggy.'

'Well den—I didn't do my big ssspell on de *easy* ones.'

'So how did you open the easy ones, Iggy?'

Iggy's eyes narrowed suspiciously. 'Why do you want to know dat, Mumps?' he said. 'Dat's a sssecret. Only burglariders know dat—and you're not a burglarider.'

Measle thought furiously. How could he get Iggy to tell him? Wrathmonks weren't too bright—and Iggy Niggle was one of the dimmest.

Flattery. I could try flattery—

'Well, the thing is, Iggy—I really, really, *really* want to *be* a burglarider! I want to be the best burglarider in the whole wide world—just like you! You're so clever and brave—look at all the times you've rescued me! You're wonderful, Iggy! And, if that's what being a burglarider means— then I want to be one too! I want to learn how to be one, Iggy—will you teach me?'

Iggy's face transformed. It went from sad and hurt and suspicious to pleased, confident, and even a little boastful.

'Ho, Mumps—I will be *happy* to teach you how to be a burglarider. And you will be learning from de bessst, too! Coz I was de bessst burglarider in de whole wide world! I was de bessst roof-climber, I was de bessst window-breaker, I was de bessst night-creeper, I was de bessst pickle-pocket, I was de bessst—'

'I know you were, Iggy! And you know what I want to learn first?'

'What, Mumps?'

'I want to start at the beginning. I want to learn how to open *little* locks. Can you teach me how to do that?'

'Course I can, Mumps. Dat's not difficult at all! What you do is, you get a little bit of metal—'bout ssso long—' (and Iggy held up his hand and measured a distance of about two centimetres between his thumb and his forefinger) '—and den you put de little bit of metal into de lock and you go twisty-twisty one way, den you go twisty-twisty de *uvver* way, den you go wiggle-wiggle-wiggle *very* fassst and den, if you're good at it, de lock opens! I was very good at it! I had de bessst little bit of metal, too! I was de bessst *little* lock-opener, I was de bessst *medium* lock-opener, and I was de bessst *big* lock-opener.'

'Have you still got your bit of metal, Iggy?' said

Measle, quite slowly and carefully, because that was the most important question of all and he wanted to be sure that Iggy understood it.

Iggy's face fell. 'Not any more, Mumps. Dey took it away from me when your dad ricky-bended leaningsea.'

Measle's heart sank—then, a moment later, he pushed his hands, one by one, into each pocket in his clothes, searching for something—anything— which might fit the description of 'a little bit of metal'. All Measle found was the small plastic bag of jelly beans—

The jelly beans! He'd forgotten all about them. Everything that had happened at Caltrop Castle had been so weird and unexpected, he'd never thought to use the jelly beans—and now, with the knowledge of just how useful they could be, finding a little bit of metal for Iggy seemed even more urgent.

Measle looked round the bare cell. There was nothing there that even looked like it might do—

Think, Measle! There must be something—

—and there was!

'Iggy, have you still got my toothbrush?'

Iggy reached into the pocket of his mildewy old coat and pulled out Measle's toothbrush.

'Can I borrow it for a moment, Iggy?'

Iggy's eyes narrowed. 'You will give it back, Mumps?'

'Yes, Iggy.'

Reluctantly, Iggy handed Measle the toothbrush

and Measle, without hesitation, instantly pulled the brush section away from the handle.

'Aaaaah!' screamed Iggy. 'You've *broked* it! You've broked my super weapon!'

'I haven't broken it, Iggy!' said Measle, quickly, because Iggy was reaching for the handle. 'Look— see? It goes back together again! See?'

Iggy watched dubiously as Measle slipped the brush section back onto the handle, his face relaxing as Measle pulled it off again and then slipped it back on, each time fitting it precisely over the slender spike of metal, a slender spike of metal that was about two centimetres long—

Once again, Measle pulled the brush section off and, this time, he kept it off. He held up the handle of the toothbrush, right in front of Iggy's staring eyes, forcing Iggy to look at the metal spike that protruded from the handle.

'Is this like the sort of bit of metal that you used, Iggy?'

Iggy shook his head. 'No, dat's not like it at all, Mumps,' he said, dismissively. 'Dat's got a handle on it. My little bit of metal didn't have no handle on it.'

'Yes, but—but would this one *work*, Iggy?'

'I sss'pose ssso,' said Iggy.

'Good,' said Measle. 'Now—will you show me how to open a lock, Iggy?'

'What lock, Mumps?'

Measle extended his left hand and touched Iggy's wrathring with his forefinger.

'That one, Iggy,' he said, softly.

Iggy pulled away from Measle's finger, a look of shock on his face. 'Open my wraffring? Dat would be wrong, Mumps!' he hissed. 'Missster Jugg wouldn't like dat at all!'

'But Mr Jugg doesn't *like* you, Iggy!' said Measle, urgently. 'He threw you into this cell with me and Tink! He took Tilly away from you! So you don't have to do what Mr Jugg says any more!'

'Don't I, Mumps?' said Iggy, looking unconvinced.

'No, Iggy! So, please—show me how to open the lock!'

Measle pushed the toothbrush handle at Iggy but Iggy shook his head and said, 'I can't do it, Mumps.'

'Why not? Is it a difficult lock?'

Iggy snorted contemptuously. 'Nah, it's not difficult, Mumps. It's a dead easy one. But I can't open it 'cause I can't *sssee* it, Mumps. I got to be able to sssee it.'

Iggy demonstrated by tilting his head so that it was bent over as far as it would go. He squinted his fishy eyes downwards and Measle could see that it was true—there was no way that Iggy could look directly at the wrathring that was round his scrawny neck.

'Well, maybe I could do it, Iggy, if you just tell me what to do?'

'I already *told* you, Mumps. You twisty-twisty

one way, den you twisty-twisty de uvver way, den you wiggle-wiggle-wiggle it very fassst and den, if you is lucky, de lock opens. Dey always opened when *I* did it.'

'Can I try, Iggy?'

'You can *try*, Mumps,' said Iggy, smugly. 'But you won't be able to *do* it. 'Cause you isn't a burglarider, see?'

Iggy lifted his chin, exposing the dull grey wrathring. Measle saw that there was what looked like a simple lock, in the front, that fastened the two halves together. Very carefully, he pushed the metal spike into the small keyhole. He twisted the handle one way. Then he twisted the handle the other way. Then he wiggled the handle backwards and forwards—

Nothing happened.

'You have to do de wiggly-wiggly fassster dan dat,' said Iggy scornfully, staring up at the ceiling.

Measle was concentrating so hard—and clutching the toothbrush handle so tightly—that he let one finger slip over the toothbrush switch. Instantly he felt a buzzing sensation in his hand as the little metal spike started to vibrate back and forth—

'Oooh,' said Iggy, a trace of admiration in his voice. 'Dat is *very* fassst wiggly-wiggly. Dat is nearly as fassst as *my* wiggle-wiggly. You is quite a good learner, Mumps, but you have to do it jussst a little bit fassster dan dat if you want de lock to open—'

And then, without Measle doing anything more, the wrathring made a sort of *doingggg!* sound— and the two halves suddenly sprang apart.

Iggy lowered his chin, a look of astonishment on his face. He reached up and took hold of the wrathring and slipped it off his neck. Then he grinned, showing his pointed yellow teeth.

'Dere! Sssee, Mumps? Dat's how to do it! Oooh—how clever I am!'

Measle took the wrathring from Iggy's hands and threw it into a corner of the cell. Iggy went on prattling about how incredibly clever he was when it came to opening locks, until Measle took hold of his damp shoulders and gave him a little shake.

'Iggy! Listen! Now you haven't got your wrathring on—do you think you could use your spell and open the door?'

Iggy stopped prattling. He looked at the heavy iron door and then curled up the corner of one lip in a sneer.

'Pooh—I can open de mossst compri-clated

sssafes in de world wiv my ssspell! Dat old door is easy-peasy!'

'Well—go on then, Iggy. Use your spell on it.'

Iggy turned and stared at Measle, his eyebrows raised as high as they would go. 'Open it, Mumps? But—dat would make Missster Jugg really, *really* cross, dat would! I mean, breakin' open de wraffring is bad enough, but—'

Measle lost his patience. He grabbed Iggy's shoulders again and, this time, gave the little wrathmonk a really hard shaking, so that Iggy's head flew back and forth on the end of his scrawny neck and several drops of rain spattered against Measle's face.

'Iggy! You've got to understand—Mr Jugg is our enemy now! He locked us in, Iggy! He took Tilly away! He's going to kill my dad! My dad, who ricky-bended leaningsea for you! And then Mr Jugg is going to kill *us*! Don't you see that, Iggy? *Don't you see?*'

Measle stopped shaking Iggy—and Iggy's head stopped wobbling about on his neck. Then Iggy's face started going through its twisting, grimacing sequence, while Iggy's little brain tried to deal with all this new and frightening information. Then, the muscles in his face settled down and Iggy simply stared solemnly into Measle's eyes. He said, quite simply, 'All right, Mumps. I'll do it. Just don't do dat shaky-shaky fing no more. And give me back my sssuper weapon, too.'

Measle put the brush section back on the handle and then handed over the toothbrush. Iggy stroked it tenderly and then stuck it back in his pocket. Then he turned his head and faced the cell door. He took a deep breath and said, '*Unkassssbhhriek gorgogasssshhh plurgholips!*' — and, at the same moment, a pair of bright lavender-coloured beams shot from his eyes and sizzled their way at lightning speed across the cell. The beams struck the lock with the sound of bacon frying—and then, a second later, Measle heard, quite clearly, a heavy, metallic *thonk!*

The twin beams disappeared and Iggy stood there, looking pleased with himself.

'Did—did you do it, Iggy?' said Measle, staring at the door, which hadn't moved at all.

'*Course* I did it, Mumps,' said Iggy. He strode across the cell, put his hands flat against the heavy iron door and pushed—and, silently, the door swung open on its oiled hinges.

'Oh, well done, Iggy!' whispered Measle. He went to the open door and carefully stuck his head out into the corridor. He looked down its length, towards the far end—and then his heart sank. He'd forgotten about the *other* iron door—the one that led to Officer Offal's office. That door was sure to be locked as well—and, almost certainly, was openable only from the other side—

For a moment, it seemed to Measle that using Iggy's spell had accomplished nothing useful at all—they were still locked down tight into the Detention Centre, with a heavy iron door and a heavy fat guard between them and freedom.

Measle started to use his brain to its fullest capacity. And then the idea came. It was, like so many of Measle's ideas in the past, a terribly risky idea, but it was the only thing he could come up with at the moment—and time was running out.

Measle hurried to Iggy's side and began to explain the idea. It took six explanations before he thought that Iggy might perhaps just about understand what they were going to do—so, just to be on the safe side, Measle explained the idea another three times and, at the end of it, Iggy nodded solemnly and said, 'Right, Mumps. I got it.'

I hope you have, Iggy, thought Measle. Then he turned to Tinker who, ever since he'd been woken by the sound of the wrathring clanging into the corner of the cell, had been watching the proceedings with some interest.

Tinker was doing his best to like the nasty little damp thingy, if only because the smelly kid seemed to get on with it all right. In fact, the smelly kid had been doing an awful lot of the talky-talky business, right in the nasty little damp thingy's ear, and the smelly kid didn't do that unless he *liked* doing it, so Tinker was doing his best not to show his teeth every time the nasty, damp little thingy came near him.

'Tink! Sit! Sit and stay, Tink! *Stay!*'

Tinker knew what '*sit and stay*' meant. *It meant don't move from this spot until the smelly kid says you can—but not for too long, mind, 'cause a little dog's only got so much patience—*

Tinker sat down on the cell floor, his stubby tail flipping to and fro. He watched as Measle and Iggy backed slowly away, towards the open door. Then, they were gone.

Measle and Iggy hurried down the corridor. Measle sensed movement in the cells as they passed them—he saw, out of the corner of his eye, several wrathmonks approaching the glass walls of their cells and staring at them with wonder as they hurried by—Buford Cudgel's face twisted with fury and Judge Cedric screwed up his face into a look of deep bewilderment—but there was no time to linger, so Measle averted his eyes and hurried Iggy along, until they reached the heavy iron door that led to Officer Offal's office.

Very gently, Measle tested the door. It was locked fast as he guessed it would be. Then, standing close to the wall next to the door, Measle turned to Iggy and put one arm tight round the little wrathmonk's skinny waist.

'Ready?' he whispered.

'Ready, Mumps.'

'And you know what's going to happen, Iggy?'

'*Yesss*, Mumps! You told me a *sssquillion* times!'

'All right. Here we go.'

Measle reached into his pocket and took out the

bag of jelly beans. He poked around until he found one of the two remaining yellow ones. He took the yellow jelly bean between his finger and thumb and held it close to his mouth—

And then he waited.

It wasn't long before Tinker got bored with '*staying*'. He never could do it for very long before deciding that enough was enough.

It's a bit much, expectin' a little dog just to sit here, for ever and ever—and perhaps the smelly kid's gone and forgotten all about me—forgotten all about a poor little doggie, wot's been sittin' here for a hundred years at least—perhaps it's time to remind the smelly kid that I'm here—

And Tinker—as Measle knew he eventually would—raised his nose in the air and started to howl at the top of his voice.

Measle clutched Iggy tightly and waited. This was the one part of the plan that had a big element of doubt about it—what if Officer Offal was deaf? What if the door was so thick that not even the loudest sounds could get through it? What if Tinker decided to stop howling and simply leave his post and come after them instead? What if all three '*what ifs*' happened?

Then, a moment later, his doubts were answered. There was a *clunk!* from the door by his side and it began to swing open—and, as it did so, Measle popped the jelly bean into his mouth and bit down hard on it.

He and Iggy vanished.

Iggy gasped and Measle could hear the sudden terror in the sound. Measle had explained to Iggy—nine times in fact—exactly what would happen when he bit down on the jelly bean, but Iggy was so easily frightened—and Measle knew that terror like Iggy's could easily lead next to a loud, Iggy-type shriek—so Measle reached up and clamped an invisible hand over Iggy's invisible mouth, cutting off the sounds of fear.

The door swung wide and Officer Offal's heavy body stepped into view. Measle watched as Offal's eyes took in the sight: the long corridor—the open cell door at the far end—the howls coming from the open cell—

'What the—?' muttered Offal. Then the big man set off at a shambling run towards the end of the corridor. Measle let him get about halfway down the passage then he let go of Iggy and, pushing him towards the open door, hissed, 'Go, Iggy! *Go!*'

The moment Iggy was released from Measle's clutching arm, he reappeared. Measle saw Iggy react with delight to the sight of his own hands materializing in front of his face—and then Measle's heart almost stopped beating, because Iggy wasn't going through the open door! Iggy was just standing there, staring down at himself—

'*Iggy!*' hissed Measle. 'Don't just stand there! Go *on!*'

Iggy's skinny body jerked at the sound and he

seemed to remember what he was supposed to be doing, because he suddenly scuttled like a black spider through the open door and into Offal's office. The moment he had disappeared around the corner of the door, Measle began to sprint after Officer Offal. He ran as silently as he could, hoping that Tinker's howls would cover any sound he made. He saw Officer Offal reach the open door of the cell and peer inside—then Offal walked into the cell—

Only a few more metres to go! Measle put on an extra burst of speed and reached the open door.

He threw himself against it as hard as he could and, immediately, the massive door began to swing on its oiled hinges—

'Tink!' screamed Measle. 'Tink! Come on, boy! Come on, Tink!'

The moment Tinker heard the urgent sounds coming from the smelly kid outside, he stopped howling. He jumped to his feet and darted—like a fuzzy white bullet—through the legs of the big man with the red face and fat belly, who had been staring at him with a look of utter bewilderment on his face—*almost like he'd never seen a little howlin' doggie before—well, excuse me, no time to explain, gotta dash—*

And Tinker burst out of the cell, just as Measle was closing the last few centimetres of the gap—

The door thudded against the frame and Measle turned his head and yelled, at the top of his voice, 'Now, Iggy! *Now!*'

It should have worked. Iggy's job in this operation was such a simple one. All Iggy had to do was stand by the panel with the two big buttons and, when Measle shouted 'Now, Iggy!' his only duty was to push the green button with the number 20 painted on it.

But, in the short time between Iggy getting his orders and Iggy actually carrying them out, Iggy had forgotten what it was he was supposed to do. *Sssumfing about pushing buttons, wasn't it? Dere's two of dem 'ere—a black one and a green one—*

From down the corridor came Measle's panicking voice. 'Iggy! Push the button! Push the *button!*'

All right, Mumps! I'll push it! De only fing is— which one?

And then Iggy, doing what only a small, confused, and very silly little wrathmonk would do, extended an index finger on each hand and pushed both the black and the green button at exactly the same moment.

SURROUNDED!

When Iggy pushed both buttons, simultaneously, the first thing that Measle was aware of was a wonderful sound—a heavy *thunk!*—as the electronically-driven bolt in the door of cell 20 slammed home into its slot.

Measle heaved a sigh of relief. It had worked! Officer Offal was securely locked into cell number 20—and, in fact, Measle could see the big man staring towards the door with a puzzled look on his pink face. Measle watched through the glass wall as Offal marched to the door and gave it a great shove—but the door was locked fast and nothing short of another press on the green button back in the office was going to budge it.

Officer Offal stared furiously out through the

glass wall, his pink eyes swivelling in every direction. At first, all he could see was the little white dog—but then, like swirling grey smoke, the boy suddenly materialized on the other side of the wall. For a moment, Offal could only gape—but then his fury overcame his wonder. He shook his fist, opened his mouth and—his voice muffled from behind the thick glass—he yelled, 'Let me out, boy! You let me out this instant!'

And then Measle heard something else.

'Well, well, well,' said an oily voice from close behind Measle—an oily voice that wasn't muffled at all. 'Ssso, we meet again, Massster Ssstubbs.'

Measle whirled round—

There, standing only a few feet away, stood little, round, bald-as-a-billiard-ball, Griswold Gristle. Griswold was smiling unpleasantly, showing his two sets of pointed yellow teeth—and, behind him, Measle saw that the door to the cell that Griswold had been occupying was wide open—

And, beyond Griswold's cell, other doors were slowly swinging open and wrathmonks—*lots* of wrathmonks—were cautiously stepping out into the corridor.

Measle felt himself rooted to the spot, unable to move and almost unable to breathe. *What's happened? How are they all getting out?*

And then Measle found the answer. *Iggy! Iggy must have pressed both buttons!*

'Cedric! Missster Cudgel! Missster Flabbit! *Do*

come and sssee who's here!' Griswold's smile was even broader than before and he was rubbing his podgy little hands together in glee.

The enormous figure of Buford Cudgel emerged from his cell. The huge wrathmonk looked strange without his motorcycle helmet and his black leather jacket—and somehow, to Measle, Buford Cudgel—in his white prison clothes—appeared larger and even scarier than he had back at the Isle of Smiles.

Frognell Flabbit stuck his head out of his cell. He had lost a little more of his precious hair and now his greasy comb-over looked even more ridiculous than before. Flabbit's face was still red and lumpy from Judge Cedric's old boil spell and the redness was made even worse because Flabbit had been scratching at the sore patches for a very long time—ever since he and his fellow wrathmonks had been locked up in the Detention Centre, in fact. Flabbit came out of the cell and strolled to Griswold's side.

'Well, well—look who it is,' said Flabbit, smoothing his greasy hank of hair over his shiny head. 'I've been hoping for thisss day, I don't mind telling you.'

Buford Cudgel stood behind Flabbit and Griswold, towering over them both. His great fists were clenching and unclenching and a dark frown creased his narrow forehead.

'I should have sssquashed you before, boy, like a beetle,' he rumbled, his voice like distant thunder. 'Well, I shan't miss the opportunity again.'

Griswold turned his round head and looked back over his shoulder.

'Cedric!' he called. 'Cedric—come and sssee!'

The frizzy, white-haired head of Judge Cedric Hardscrabble poked nervously out of his cell. One hand was pressed against his jaw. He was obviously still in some pain from Flabbit's old toothache spell.

'What is it, Griswold?' he asked, his vacant eyes staring vaguely round the corridor. 'Surely it's not yet time for our exercise?'

'Oh, but it is, Cedric!' said Griswold, excitedly. 'And sssuch exercise we shall have! Sssee—young Measle Ssstubbs is here, at our mercy—and, oh, what fun we shall have with him!'

Judge Cedric tottered up the corridor on his ancient legs and, when he got near enough, he stopped and peered short-sightedly at Measle.

'Goodness gracious me!' he exclaimed. 'It's that boy—but surely he was eaten by a dragon, wasn't he?'

'No, Cedric,' said Griswold, patiently. 'He escaped the dragon—more's the pity. However, this time, he won't escape *usss*!' Griswold turned to Measle and said, quite loud enough for Judge Cedric to hear, 'Poor Cedric! Ever sssince he's been in here, his memory has been getting worse and worse. And you are to blame for that, boy! You are to blame for all our misfortunes! And now, we have you! We have you at our mercy! And thisss time, there is no father to protect you! And no mother to help your father! And no Nanny to ssstand between us! Jussst *you*, Measle Ssstubbs, on whom to wreak our revenge! Jussst you—you and your beassstly little dog, I sssee!'

Griswold was staring down at a spot on the floor by Measle's feet and Measle looked down and saw that Tinker was standing at his side, all the wiry hair on his back sticking up, from his neck to his tail, in a line of bristles. Tinker's lips were curled back and he was showing all his teeth at the wrathmonks—and the beginning of a growl were starting deep down in his throat.

Measle instinctively bent down and scooped up Tinker into his protective arms. As he did so, Measle felt a small pressure in one of his pockets—the action of bending and lifting was pressing a lumpy object against his thigh—

The jelly beans! They were his only hope now! But there was only one yellow bean left in the bag—if he simply reached in and pulled one out, what were the chances that it would be the right one? And if he took the whole bag out, wouldn't the wrathmonks become suspicious?

What to do? What to do?

Click—click—click—

All these thoughts took only a fraction of a second and, in that short time, Griswold Gristle had obviously done some thinking of his own.

'Ssso, young Measle Ssstubbs!' he exclaimed, cheerfully. 'How shall we start to wreak our revenge, eh? Both Missster Cudgel's and my exhalation enchantments end in ghastly death, ssso we shall leave them for later—but to whom of my other colleagues shall go the honour of ssstarting, eh? Shall we let Judge Cedric give you sssome horrible, painful boils? Or shall we have Missster Flabbit breathe his agonizing toothache onto you? Either way, it will be mossst entertaining for all the ressst of usss!'

Griswold made a sort of sweeping gesture and

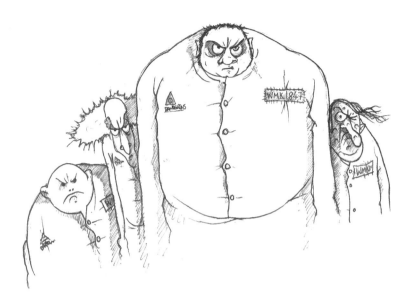

Measle saw that a small crowd of curious wrathmonks had now gathered behind his four arch-enemies. They were all peering over the shoulders of Griswold Gristle, Frognell Flabbit, and Judge Cedric Hardscrabble—but they were all peering round the *sides* of Buford Cudgel, whose shoulders were far too high to peer over.

'Fellow wrathmonks!' shouted Griswold in his squeaky, oily little voice. 'This horrid boy is the ssson of the notorious wrathmonk hunter, Sssam Ssstubbs! Sssam Ssstubbs, of the infamous Ssstubbs family!'

There was a sudden hissing from the collected wrathmonks as they all spoke the name of Sam Stubbs—and Measle could hear the hatred in their voices.

Griswold Gristle held up his fat little hands. 'And that's not all, fellow wrathmonks! Thisss Ssstubbs child was the one ressssponsssible for capturing myself and my friends! It was through his actions that we were brought to this terrible place! It was he who—'

Griswold tailed off, because he became aware that this latest piece of news was being greeted by several of the wrathmonks as something of a joke.

'Aaah—poor old Grissstle!' called out a young, skinny wrathmonk, who was standing at the front of the crowd. He had bright ginger hair and pointed ears that stuck out of his head like jug handles. 'Did 'e get 'imself caught by an itty-bitty kiddy-wink, then?'

Buford Cudgel turned his massive head and glowered down at the young, skinny wrathmonk. 'Shut your ssstupid mouth,' he growled—and instantly the young wrathmonk shrank away from him, a look of pure terror on his face.

At that exact moment, every wrathmonk eye was looking in either Buford Cudgel's direction, or towards the ginger-haired wrathmonk who was cowering under Cudgel's angry glare—and it was in that moment that Measle saw his opportunity. He dived his free hand into his pocket and then into the plastic bag, closing his fingers around as many jelly beans as he could hold. Quickly, he pulled his fist back out of his pocket and, holding his hand close by his side, he darted a glance down at it. There were about ten jelly beans in the palm of his hand—

And not a single yellow one among them.

'What's that you have there, dear boy?' said Griswold, who had turned back just in time to see the look of despair that crossed over Measle's face.

'Nothing,' muttered Measle, closing his fist round the useless jelly beans.

'Oh, I don't think it's nothing, dear boy,' said Griswold. 'And we've had thisss sssort of trouble with you before, haven't we? Hiding little magical things on your perssson? Oh yesss. Missster Cudgel, kindly show usss what is in the boy's hand?'

Buford Cudgel turned away from the frightened little wrathmonk and lurched like a small mountain towards Measle.

'Open your hand, boy,' he rumbled.

Measle thought very fast. There was only one thing he could think of and he wasn't at all sure that it would work—but it was the only chance he had—

'Anybody like a jelly bean?' he said, loudly and cheerfully, as if they were all at a party and he was the host, offering his guests a slice of cake. At the same moment, he brought his hand up and threw the handful of jelly beans as hard as he could, over the heads of the crowd of wrathmonks. He even managed to get the jelly beans to sail over Buford Cudgel's head—and Buford Cudgel's head almost scraped the ceiling.

The effect was immediate.

Measle knew quite a lot about wrathmonks—after all, he'd lived with his horrible old wrathmonk guardian, Basil Tramplebone, for several years. One of the things he knew about wrathmonks was that they liked sweet things; when Basil had played with his train set up in the attic of the horrible house, he always used to eat a plateful of glazed doughnuts—and drink a whole jug of pink lemonade—while he was doing it. And Iggy had almost eaten his way through the whole bag of jelly beans—

The other thing Measle knew about wrathmonks was that, on the whole, they weren't very bright.

The head of every wrathmonk—including those of Gristle, Flabbit, Judge Cedric, and Cudgel—turned to see the little brightly-coloured ovals as they landed—and then scattered—across the stone floor behind them.

'Oooh! Sssweeties! Lovely sssweeeeties!' screamed the wrathmonks—and even Griswold Gristle took a couple of steps towards the mob, who were now scrabbling about on the floor and grabbing every jelly bean they could find and stuffing them into their mouths.

In that moment—and given that second chance—Measle reached back into his pocket and pulled out the plastic bag. There weren't many jelly beans left now—but there! nestled among them—was the single remaining yellow one! Measle poured all the jelly beans into his open palm and then put his thumb firmly over the yellow one. Then he threw the rest into the scrambling mob.

Griswold Gristle—whose brain was a little sharper than others of his kind—turned back towards Measle just in time to have his suspicions confirmed. *Why is he throwing sssweets all over the place? And what is under his thumb? The boy is up to sssomething!*

'Missster Cudgel! Missster Cudgel! Please come here and deal with thisss boy!'

Measle swiftly brought his hand up to his face and popped the yellow bean into his mouth. He bit down on it, tasting the familiar sugary lemon taste—

'Aaaaarrrgh!' screamed Griswold, his piggy little eyes swivelling madly around in the direction where he'd last seen Measle. 'He has gone! The boy has gone! But he is ssstill here! Quickly, all of you—feel for him! *Feel* for him!'

Griswold, Cudgel, and Flabbit immediately stretched out their arms and started to feel the air with their fingers. Judge Cedric, with a look of extreme puzzlement on his face, started patting his own body, as if Measle might perhaps be in one of his pockets. But the rest of the wrathmonks were still too busy gathering up the scattered jelly beans to take any notice of a fat little wrathmonk who was screaming about a boy disappearing into thin air—*as if a human boy could do that!*

It wasn't just Measle's brain that was quick. His legs could go pretty fast too. He tucked his head down and, clutching tightly to an invisible Tinker, started to scurry down the corridor, towards the open door that led to Offal's office. He darted round Flabbit, ducked under Cudgel's waving, searching fingers—each one was the size of a banana!—and slipped past Judge Cedric as if he was made of smoke.

The corridor ahead was clear, apart from a couple of wrathmonks still grubbing about on their knees. Measle jumped over them, like a hurdler in a race—and behind him, he could hear Griswold's impassioned screams—

'You fools! Don't let him get away again! *Don't let him get away again!*'

And then Measle was through the doorway— and there was Iggy, still staring at the two buttons on the panel and looking a little bewildered—and Measle had never been so glad to see a wrathmonk in his entire life—

But there was no time for any of this! Any second now, Griswold and the others would guess that Measle was now safely past their searching hands, which must mean that he was inside Offal's office— and the door to Offal's office was wide open—

Measle looked back over his shoulder and saw, to his horror, that Buford Cudgel was charging, head down like a rhinoceros, at full speed towards him. Measle threw a quick glance at his hands—or where his hands would have been, if they hadn't been invisible—*no, he still can't see me—but he can see this open door! I've got to get it shut!*

Measle put his shoulder against the massive door and shoved as hard as he could—and the great iron door swung smoothly to and, a moment later, slammed shut. There was an audible click as the latch fell into place—then, a moment later, a thunderous *thump!* against the outer surface of the door as the full weight of Buford Cudgel slammed against it. Measle felt the door shudder under the impact—but even Buford Cudgel's great mass could never break through a door like this.

'Dat door jussst closed all by itsssself,' muttered Iggy to himself. 'And den dere was a big bump! And where is Mumps? And de little dog? Where is dey, I wonder?'

'Here I am, Iggy,' said Measle, watching his fingers change from wispy grey smoke to their usual, solid pinkness (although, by now, what with all his adventures in the last few hours, his hands were pretty dirty). 'We're both here.'

Iggy blinked a couple of times and then stared in fascination as Measle and Tinker solidified in front of him. Then Iggy seemed to forget all about the wonder of the magic, because he said, 'I pushed de buttons, Mumps! I pushed dem like you told me—and I sssaved you! I sssaved you—again!'

'Yes, Iggy, you did,' said Measle. He put Tinker

down on the floor. 'And thank you very much—again.'

'Dat's all right, Mumps,' said Iggy, grandly. 'Any time.'

And—what to do now? thought Measle, listening with half an ear to the steady thumping sounds against the door. Obviously Buford Cudgel wasn't going to give up that easily. *Meanwhile—where to go? How to get Matilda back from the warlocks? How to get out of this castle? How to get back to the city and find Mum and Dad—*

And then something occurred to Measle that he hadn't thought of before. If all the wrathmonks who were caught were imprisoned here in Caltrop Castle—was it possible that his mum and dad were imprisoned here too? It seemed that a lot of things went on at Caltrop Castle—

There was only one way to find out.

Measle went to the desk and sat down in the swivel chair. He reached forward and pulled the big silver microphone towards him. He looked down at the intercom panel next to it—there was a row of switches, numbered 1-20. Measle flipped the switch with the number 20—

He listened.

There was the sound of heavy breathing.

'Officer Offal?' said Measle, into the microphone.

'What? Who's that?' Officer Offal's voice sounded tinny and distant, coming out of the intercom loudspeaker.

'It's me, Officer Offal. Measle Stubbs.'

There was a long pause. All Measle could hear was the sound of Offal's lungs, going like a pair of wheezy old bellows. Then—

'You're in a lot of trouble, young feller me lad. A *lot* of trouble! Best thing you can do is go and tell the gentlemen—and the lady—who brought you down here what you've gone and done. It's very *bad*, what you've gone and done, see? But if you make a clean breast of it, young feller—maybe they won't be too angry, eh? What do you say, eh?'

Measle felt a little strange. He'd never had a grown-up in his power before—not *completely* in his power, like Officer Offal was right now. Half the feeling was rather exciting—the other half was rather frightening. But this wasn't the moment to be frightened.

'Do you know where my mum and dad are, Officer Offal?'

There was another pause, filled with Offal's breathing. Then the gruff voice came again. 'Never you mind about that, boy. You just go and—'

'No. Not until you tell me if you know where they are.'

'Now look 'ere, boy—'

'Do you know where my mum and dad and sister are?'

'Yes, I do, boy—but I'm not going to tell you! Now, don't make things worse for yourself, eh? Just go and get—'

'Where are they, Officer Offal?'

'I told you—I'm not going to tell you!'

Measle leaned close to the microphone and spoke into it. He used a quiet, calm voice, and he spoke very slowly, carefully picking out each syllable, so that there would be no doubt at all in Officer Offal's mind that he meant every word.

'Officer Offal, if you don't tell me where my mum and dad are—I'm going to push the green button.'

This time, the pause went on for a very long time—and Officer Offal's breathing was twice as heavy as before. To Measle's ears, it sounded a little—well, a little *nervous*.

Then—

'Now, you don't want to go and do a thing like that, young feller,' said Officer Offal's tinny voice. This time there was a tone of great friendliness in the voice, of great reasonableness—but the voice also held a faint trace of trembling—

Officer Offal was *scared*.

Measle leaned into the microphone again and whispered. 'Officer Offal—when I've finished talking to you, I'm going to get up and go over to the door and I'm going to push the green button. And then the door to cell number 20 is going to open. That's *your* cell, Officer Offal. The only trouble is, all the wrathmonks are out of *their* cells—you can probably see them, can't you? And they don't like you, do they, Officer Offal? And you won't be able to stop them getting at you, will you? Now, I'm going to ask you again—where's my dad and my mum?'

The breathing was now very heavy—but Officer Offal said nothing.

'All right, then,' said Measle. 'I'm getting up now—'

Measle pushed with his legs, making the feet of the swivel chair scrape loudly against the stone floor of the office—and instantly the intercom burst out with sound. A very panicky, pleading sound—

'All right, all right! No need for that, young feller! I'll tell you! *I'll tell you!* Just don't you go near that green button, all right?'

Wow! thought Measle, *the wrathmonks must really hate Officer Offal!*

'They're in the next section but one, young feller. Right out of the door, take the second door on the left—they're in High Security.'

Measle's heart jumped into his throat. *They're just around the corner!*

'Is there another guard there, Officer Offal?'

'No, I'm alone down 'ere at the moment. The

other guard doesn't come on duty for another four hours. Now then, young feller, seeing as how I've told you what you wanted to know—how about getting me out of here, eh? I mean, without touching that green button of course!'

But Measle never heard those last words from Officer Offal, because the moment Offal had said the word 'No', Measle had whistled once at Tinker, grabbed Iggy by the arm, and had started to run out of the office.

With Tinker scurrying at their heels, Measle and Iggy ran out into the circular hallway. Measle headed towards the second door on the left. He realized that, by an incredible stroke of luck, it was the one that Offal had first emerged from to greet the Advisory Committee—and, in his nervousness at dealing with such important persons, Offal hadn't closed it completely behind him.

Measle heaved open the door and ran inside, to an office that seemed almost identical to the one they had just left. Another steel desk, another row of filing cabinets, another silver microphone with an intercom next to it—the only difference in this office that Measle could see was the panel by the inner door. There were only four numbered buttons on this panel—and all were coloured bright red.

Measle's first instinct was to run to the inner door, yank it open, and then press all those four red buttons, releasing—

Releasing what? Perhaps his mum and dad and sister weren't here at all? Perhaps it had been a trick on Officer Offal's part? Well, there was one way to find out.

Measle hurried to the desk, leaned towards the microphone and flipped the first switch.

'Mum? Dad? Are you there?'

There was nothing but a faint electronic hiss of static from the intercom. Measle was about to try another switch, when he heard it—

A faint and horrible throaty, choking, gurgling sound—as if somebody was being sick, a long way away.

Measle didn't like the sound at all. There was something very *different* about it, as if it was coming from something not at all human—in fact, something terribly, terribly alien.

Measle hurriedly let go of the switch and tried the second one.

'Mum? Dad?'

This time, there was no silence, no pause—

'Measle?' came the voice of his mother from the intercom. 'Measle—is that you?'

'Yes, Mum, it's me!'

'But—but where are you, darling?'

'I'm right here, Mum! I'm in the office! I'm going to let you out!'

'Oh, Measle—we've been so worried about you! And now you're safe! Oh, thank goodness!'

'Where's Dad, Mum?'

'Dad's in the third cell. Now, darling—can you get us out?'

'All right, Mum—I'm going to open all the doors now—'

Lee's voice changed suddenly. It changed from a sort of joyful astonishment at hearing that Measle was safe and coming to the rescue to a sudden, panic-stricken scream—

'No, Measle! Don't open all the doors! NO!'

Measle at Large!

'But—'

Lee obviously took charge of her terror and managed to bring her voice back under control, because the next thing Measle heard was his mother saying calmly but very firmly, 'Measle, my darling, be very, *very* careful. Whatever you do, don't open the door of the first cell. Understand? Not Cell Number One, whatever you do. If you open the door to Cell Number One, *you might kill us all*. Only open number two and number three, and please, *please*—don't touch the button that opens number one. Understand, darling?'

Usually, Measle's mind was one that liked to question things as startling as this—but he knew, from the tone of his mother's voice, that this was not the time to start asking her anything. Instead, he said, 'Right, Mum—I've got it. Not number one. OK, hang on a sec.'

Measle left the desk and crossed over to the panel by the inner door. Very carefully avoiding the button marked 1, he pressed the buttons marked 2 and 3. Then, he grasped the big iron lever on the door and twisted it, and the door clicked open. Measle heaved and it swung wide. He stepped into a short, dark corridor. There were no glass walls here, just solid stonework, with four massive doors set into its surface. Two of the doors were open wide—

A pair of arms threw themselves round his neck and he felt himself being pressed against something warm and soft and very familiar. Measle looked up at his mother's face and saw that tears were streaming down her cheeks, but she was smiling and laughing at the same time—and there was a dull silver ring around her neck—

And then, a moment later, another pair of arms was around him as well, and *these* arms were hard and strong and were hugging him with enormous power—and Measle looked sideways and saw his father, his face a little pale and a little drawn, beaming down at him—and Sam too had a dull silver ring round his neck.

Then a very small pair of arms went round Measle's right leg and clutched him fiercely and Measle looked down—and there was Matilda sitting at his feet and grinning up at him and showing off all her six teeth—and round her chubby little neck was yet another silver ring—

'Are all dese people hurtin' you, Mumps?' said Iggy, peering anxiously round the doorframe. 'And, if dey are—do you want me to ressscue you—*again*?'

Measle's reply was a little muffled, because both his parents had their arms wrapped so tightly around him that he was having slight difficulty in breathing—but he managed to gasp out, 'No, Iggy—look, it's my mum and dad! And Tilly, too!'

Iggy came slowly into the corridor. When he saw Matilda sitting on the floor, a great beaming smile split his face in two—and, when Matilda caught sight of Iggy, she stopped hugging Measle's leg and held out her arms in Iggy's direction and started to kick her legs furiously against the stone floor.

'Cubba doogy *wump*!' she yelled—and Iggy darted forward and scooped Matilda off the floor and into his arms.

'Where you bin den, you naughty fing, you?' he crooned into Matilda's face—and Matilda wrinkled her nose at the smell of Iggy's breath and waved her hands to make it go away—but this time, the nasty smell didn't go away at all. Then Matilda tried to change Iggy's teeth—but they stayed as yellow as ever. So Matilda gave up trying to do her special things, because obviously they weren't going to work this time, and played with Iggy's wet hair instead.

Measle felt the iron bands that were his father's arms drop away from him. Then Sam said, 'I don't believe it! Mr Niggle? Is that you?'

When Iggy saw Sam, he became so excited that he could hardly speak. All he could do was cling tightly to Matilda and dance about on the spot and grin so widely that all six of his pointed yellow teeth were exposed.

'Ricky-b-b-bended leaningsea!' he stuttered. 'You ricky-b-b-bended leaningsea!'

'I did, didn't I?' said Sam, smiling a little uncertainly at the wrathmonk. 'And I just hope I was right to do so.'

Lee stepped forward, a very worried look on her face. She said, 'But I'm afraid I don't trust you with my daughter, Mr Niggle. Please give her back immediately.'

Measle grabbed his mother's hand. 'It's all right, Mum,' he said. 'Iggy's been carrying her everywhere. They're friends. Tilly really likes him—see what she's doing to his hair? And Iggy's rescued us lots of times, Dad—really he has!'

Sam looked a little doubtful at this. He leaned down and whispered into Measle's ear. 'I didn't think he was all that bright, son. Are you sure it wasn't the other way round?'

'Well—mostly yes, Dad,' whispered Measle back into his father's ear. 'But once he really did rescue me. He pulled my hair and it hurt really bad but that didn't matter because the suit of armour was about to grab me and he pulled me up so it couldn't reach me any more—'

'Don't you know it's very rude to *whipser*?' said Iggy, who had got over his initial excitement and was now looking at them all with a slightly hurt expression on his thin little face.

'I'm so sorry, Mr Niggle,' said Sam, straightening up. 'Measle was telling me all about how very helpful you've been to him and to Matilda and I'd like to say a very big thank you.'

'Oh,' said Iggy, his face brightening. 'All right. Go on den.'

'Go on?' said Sam. 'Go on—what?'

'Sssay a very big fank you.'

'Thank you, Mr Niggle,' said Sam. He stepped forward and shook Iggy's hand. 'Thank you very much indeed. Now—perhaps you'd like to give Matilda back to us?'

Reluctantly, Iggy held Matilda out to Sam, but Matilda, sensing what was about to happen—and determined not to be wrenched away from her wet friend again—screamed 'Cubba doogy *wump*!' and wrapped her arms tightly around Iggy's scrawny neck.

Sam smiled a little ruefully and said, 'Or . . . er . . . or you can hang on to her if you like, Mr Niggle.'

Iggy nodded seriously and tightened his grip on

Matilda—and Sam and Lee glanced at each other and, smiling, shrugged their shoulders.

Measle pointed at Matilda's wrathring and said, 'When did Tilly get that ring put on her?'

'I don't know, darling,' said Lee. 'Wasn't it on her all the time?'

'No, Mum. It's new.'

'Oh. Well, all I know is that my cell door opened a few minutes ago and Toby Jugg was there. I couldn't believe it! He had Tilly in his arms. He handed her to me and she had the wrathring on then.'

'Did he say anything, Mum?'

'Well, it was rather odd, darling. He smiled in a really weird and nasty sort of way and then he said, "A little present for you, Lee. The first of many, I hope." Then, before I could say anything, he slammed the door and went away. I didn't care—I was just so happy to see Tilly. And then, a few minutes later, here you are too! It's like a sort of miracle—'

Lee broke off because, suddenly, something thudded against the closed door of cell number 1. It was a soft, squelchy sort of thud, as if somebody had thrown a sack full of jelly against the door. A very large sack of jelly—

At the same moment, a wisp of what looked like yellow smoke drifted out from under the door—and a dreadful, disgusting, revolting stink seeped out into the corridor. It was so strong that it made them all choke—even Iggy, who Measle thought should be quite used to that sort of thing.

'Let's get out of here,' muttered Sam, holding his hand against his nose.

They all hurried back into the outer office and Sam closed the heavy door with a clang—and, instantly, the stink subsided and Matilda stopped wailing and went back to styling Iggy's hair.

'Wh-what is that thing?' asked Measle nervously.

'Some sort of manifestation,' said Sam. 'They say it was conjured up by a crazy warlock, many, many years ago. Apart from that, all we know about it is that it's horribly dangerous. That's why it can never be let out of there. Talking of which—what have you been up to?'

For the next ten minutes, Measle told them everything that had happened to him and Matilda and Tinker ever since Toby Jugg had brought them to Caltrop Castle. Because Iggy was right next to him, Measle exaggerated just a little when he described Iggy's part in the adventure, making out the little wrathmonk to be more of a hero than he really was—and Iggy listened to the story with rapt attention, as if he was hearing about the events for the very first time. When Measle finished, there was a long silence. Then Sam said, 'Right,' in a firm voice and Measle saw that his father's face was dark with anger.

'First things first,' said Sam. 'Mr Niggle—do you think you could let go of my daughter for a moment and use your ... er ... your super weapon and get us out of these wrathrings?'

Iggy was so eager to do something—anything!—for Sam that he happily handed Matilda over to Lee and then rushed forward to Sam's side, pulling the brush section away from the toothbrush handle as he did so. Sam shook his head.

'My wife first, please, Mr Niggle.'

Iggy dealt quickly with Lee's wrathring and it took only a few seconds before the two halves clicked apart. Lee ripped it off her neck and threw it into a corner of the office.

'That's wonderful, Mr Niggle!' cried Lee, and Sam said, 'What a talent!'

Next, after a few quick twists of the toothbrush handle, Matilda's wrathring fell away from around her neck and clattered onto the floor.

Measle picked it up and stared at the thing.

'Why are they so easy to open, Dad?' said Measle, wondering (not for the first time) why such an effective magical device seemed to be so easy to break open.

'I guess it's because they're anti-magic, Measle,' said Sam. 'They neutralize any magic their wearers try to conjure. So the locks *themselves* can't be magical—they wouldn't work, you see. The lock part *has* to be mechanical. And we wizards aren't all that good at making mechanical objects. So, for somebody as good at picking locks as Mr Niggle, they don't seem to present much of a problem.'

Iggy came shyly up to Sam, who tilted his head back to let Iggy get to work. Iggy carefully pushed the spike into the keyhole, turned the toothbrush handle this way, then that—he wiggled it—turned it again backwards and forwards—

'Sssumfing's wrong,' he muttered.

'Try pressing the button, Iggy,' said Measle. 'That worked for me.'

Iggy pressed the button on the handle and the toothbrush began to buzz in his hand. Iggy gritted his teeth and went back to work—twisting, wiggling, twisting again—

Nothing happened.

'Dere's sssumfing wrong wiv de lock,' announced Iggy, pulling the spike out of the keyhole and turning off the toothbrush's vibrations. 'Sssomebody's been messin' about wiv it. It's all jammed up inssside.'

'That was probably me, Mr Niggle,' said Sam. 'I've been pulling on it with all my strength—maybe I've damaged it.'

Iggy put a look on his face that reminded Measle

of the expression that one of his teachers at school had used when she'd caught him passing a note to a friend.

'Dat wasn't very clever, Missster Ssstubbs, sssir,' he said, disapprovingly. 'You've broked it—and dat means I can't open it, not even wiv my sssuper weapon.'

'Hmm,' said Sam, thoughtfully. 'That gives us a bit of a problem, doesn't it? If I can't use my magic—'

'We won't be able to get out of here without it!' blurted Measle. 'How are we going to get past the guards—or the warlocks?'

'A hacksaw, that's what we need,' said Sam. 'I've got a terrific one back at home.'

'But—how are we going to *get* home, Dad?' said Measle. 'It's miles away! And how are we going to get out of *here* in the first place?'

Measle's voice trailed away. He felt very small and very useless. The last time he'd felt as small and as useless as this was back on the table top of the great train set in Basil Tramplebone's attic, when Basil had shrunk him down to the size of a paperclip.

But even now that he was his full size, he was still too small to do much about protecting them all. If only he was as big as his dad—then he could really do something! But Sam himself couldn't do much at the moment, not with that wrathring stuck round his neck.

What they needed right now—to get them out

of this place—was something so big and powerful that even guards and warlocks might think twice about interfering with it—

Then, with a sort of thud, a new idea popped into Measle's mind. Like so many of Measle's ideas, it was pretty wild and crazy—but it was the only one he could think of.

Measle went to Matilda and put his face close to his sister's.

'Tilly!' he whispered, putting a sort of fun and excited tone into his voice. 'Tilly—make me big, Tilly! Make me really, *really* big, Tilly!'

Matilda listened with interest. She'd always wanted a big brother. Measle was wonderful and fantastic and brilliant and funny and handsome—Matilda especially loved his sticky-up hair—but there was no way he could be described as 'big'. Measle was small and rather skinny and not particularly strong—

And now he was saying he wanted to be big.

Well, that was easy.

Matilda waved her hands.

And for Measle, quite suddenly, everything around him seemed to be getting smaller.

Sam and Lee and Iggy and Matilda and Tinker all seemed to be moving away from him, moving *downwards*, in fact—as if Measle was in a lift and the lift was going swiftly *upwards*—

Measle looked around him. The office was shrinking, the floor was getting further away, the walls diminishing, the desk becoming the size of a matchbox—

Measle felt his head brush against the ceiling.

'All right, Tilly,' said Measle. 'That's enough now.'

'Grubble?' said Matilda, smiling up at the giant in front of her.

'Yes, Tilly! Grubble!'

Matilda stared up at Measle, admiring her handiwork. She wasn't at all sure that she was going to 'grubble'. Perhaps he ought to be just a bit bigger—

Measle's head was now being bent sideways by the ceiling and he could feel his shoulders pressing against one of the fluorescent lamps. It was all getting rather painful—

'Ow, Tilly! That hurts!'

Matilda saw that her really, *really* big brother was getting squashed—and it was all because the room wasn't big enough. Well, that was easy to change—

Matilda waved her arms and the room got bigger. Much, much bigger. And Measle got bigger with it. Up and up and up he grew, his head getting further and further away from the floor, but no closer to the ceiling because the ceiling grew taller with him—now Measle was four metres tall, then five metres, then six metres, seven, eight—

'All right, Tilly! Stop it! Stop it right now!'

Measle's voice was now just a little bit fierce, so Matilda decided that she'd done enough. She

waved her chubby fists and, instantly, Measle felt
the upward movement of his head come to a halt.
He looked down at his tiny family, clustered round
his feet. They looked no bigger than plastic action
figures.

'Good girl, Tilly,' he said, his enormous voice
booming round the office. Matilda hardly heard
him. She was already dropping into a deep sleep.

'Interesting,' said Sam, edging carefully away
from Measle's giant sneakered foot. 'But what was
the point of it, son?'

'I thought—well, in case we meet some guards,
Dad,' said Measle, lamely.

'Yes, fine,' said Sam. 'But what if we meet some *warlocks*, eh? You could be the size of Mount Everest and it wouldn't do you any good. Not against them—and I can't help you at the moment.'

Measle looked down at his tiny father. Sam's head now came to just above Measle's ankle. Sam was doing what he always did when he was thinking hard about something—he was frowning and tapping the front of his teeth with the nail of his index finger. Lee was still staring up at her giant son with wonder and Tinker was busy sniffing curiously at Measle's left foot and making up his mind that, since this mountain in front of him *smelt* like the smelly kid, then that's what this mountain *was*: just the smelly kid and therefore nothing to worry about.

Sam seemed to come to some sort of decision because suddenly he stopped tapping his teeth. He looked up at Measle and said, 'Well, under the circumstances, Measle, I think it's probably the best idea any of us could have had. Well done. At least it'll give them something to think about, won't it?'

'I hope so, Dad,' said Measle. Then a thought occurred to him. 'One other thing, Dad—I don't think Tilly's spells last very long. I think I'm only going to be this size for a few minutes, so we ought to get going. The trouble is—I don't know the way.'

'I do,' said Sam, firmly. 'So let's make a start.'

Then he pointed to the office door and said, 'Do you think you can squeeze through the door to the hall out there?'

'I think so,' said Measle, wondering how, exactly, Sam could be so sure about knowing the way out of the labyrinth that was Caltrop Castle.

Measle shuffled his enormous body round, lay down flat on the floor and started to edge through the doorway. He had to turn his shoulders sideways to wriggle through the opening and, when he got as far as his hips it suddenly became a very tight squeeze indeed but he worked the rest of his body through the opening centimetre by centimetre until—with a *pop!*—all of him was at last in the outer hall.

He felt something in his hand—a little circle of metal. He looked down and saw Matilda's wrathring nestling in his palm. It was big enough to have been fastened round Matilda's neck but now it looked tiny.

Small enough to fit round his little finger—

Measle sat up. A moment later, Sam, Lee, Iggy, Matilda, and Tinker came out of the office and joined him in the circular hallway.

'Well done, son,' said Sam. 'Now then—let's get out of here, shall we? Squeeze yourself through that next door and I think you'll be fine after that. Once we're clear of the Detention Centre, the rest of this section has fairly high ceilings and it shouldn't be too much of a squash for you.'

Measle lay down and wriggled his body through the outer door. Once on the other side, he found he was able to stand up. His head brushed the high ceiling and the walls of the corridor came uncomfortably close to his sides—but there was just about room to move if he was careful.

'Right—let's be off, then,' said Sam. Then he appeared to get an idea, because his face brightened and he grinned widely.

'Put us in your pockets, Measle,' he said. 'You can move a lot faster than we can and it'll save time. Mum and I up front, so I can tell you which way to go. Perhaps Mr Niggle won't mind being in one of the side pockets—and Tilly and Tinker can go in the other. Quickly now!'

Very carefully Measle picked up the members of his family and distributed them in his jacket pockets. He put Sam and Lee in his top pocket, which was shallow enough to allow their heads to poke out of the top. He slipped Matilda and Tinker into one side pocket. Matilda was fast asleep now and Measle knew that nothing short of an earthquake would wake her for a long while. Once Tinker found himself in the warm darkness of the pocket, he curled up next to Matilda and went to sleep himself.

Iggy, alone in the other pocket, initially felt a bit resentful that the little doggie had got Matilda for company and not him. But he soon forgot all about that because, for a start, there was no room for his rain cloud in there, so Iggy was warm and dry for the first time in ages—but even better was the thing that Iggy found in there; it was a red jelly bean. It had slipped out of the plastic bag during one of Measle's fumblings. The jelly bean was now the size of Iggy's head and Iggy forgot all about everything that might be happening outside the pocket and settled down in the warm darkness of the pocket to eat his way through the enormous thing.

'Right,' said Sam, leaning forward against the front of Measle's top pocket, like the captain of a destroyer leaning on the bridge of his ship. 'Let's go, shall we?

FREEDOM!

This, thought Measle, *is fun!*

The long staircase, which had taken him and the warlocks a good two minutes to walk down, was climbed in a mere five giant steps. Next came the series of panelled corridors—they were tall and wide and Measle only had to duck his head a little bit to avoid bumping against the ceiling. Each corridor took only four or five of Measle's huge paces before he was at the end of it. Sam called out directions as they went along—'Left! Now right! Left again!'—and, quite soon, Measle realized that they were approaching the double doors to the great room where he'd been caught by the warlocks. Instinctively, he slowed down.

'What's up, son?' said Sam, staring up at Measle from the top of the pocket.

'That's where the warlocks found me,' said Measle, quietly. 'They might be in there now.'

'So—they're using the Grand Salon, are they?' said Sam, equally quietly.

This took Measle by surprise. *How does Dad know so much about Caltrop Castle? How does he know his way around the place?*

'How do you know about that room, Dad?' whispered Measle.

'I know a lot about this place, Measle,' muttered Sam. 'You'd be surprised. Come on—let's get past those doors, shall we? Quiet as we can, everybody—we don't want to meet any warlocks right now, not while I'm helpless.'

Measle moved forward, as cautiously and as quietly as his enormous bulk would allow. *It's lucky,* he thought, *that the floor here is stone. If it had been wooden floorboards, they'd have been sure to creak under my tremendous weight—*

Then, quite without warning, Iggy stuck his head out of Measle's pocket. His lips were smeared with red sugar. He cupped both hands round his mouth and yelled up at Measle at the top of his voice—

'OI! MUMPS! I CHANGED MY MIND, MUMPS! I DON'T LIKE DE YELLOW ONES BESSST NO MORE! I LIKE DE *RED* ONES BESSST NOW! GOT ANY MORE RED SSSWEETIES, MUMPS?'

For a small and skinny wrathmonk, Iggy's voice was extraordinarily loud. It echoed round the stone corridor, bouncing off the walls and the floor and the ceiling, with the effect that, to Measle's ears, it sounded louder than it really was.

'*Shhh, Iggy!*' hissed Measle. He put his finger on top of Iggy's tiny head and tried to push him gently back down into his pocket—but Iggy was having none of it.

'OI! DON'T PUSH, MUMPS! I'VE 'AD ENOUGH PUSHIN' TODAY, FANKS VERY MUCH! NOW DEN—'AVE YOU OR 'AVE YOU NOT GOT ANY MORE OF DOSE RED SSSWEEETIES?'

And then, any hope that Iggy's voice *hadn't* penetrated into the Grand Salon suddenly disappeared, because the two great double doors were flung wide open, revealing, to Measle's horrified eyes, the figures of Toby Jugg, Tully Telford, Ermintrude Bacon, Dorian Fescue, Quentin Underwood, and Sir Peregrine Spine.

The six warlocks stood in the open doorway, their jaws gaping with astonishment—and a certain amount of fear as well. For several seconds, nothing happened and nothing was said. Then Toby Jugg recovered himself. He stepped forward and stared up at Measle with a puzzled smile on his rugged face.

'Well, well, Measle old son,' he said. 'Look at you! Now, how on earth did you manage that, eh?'

Measle didn't reply. He simply stared down at

Toby, with what he hoped was a fierce and grim look on his face. He didn't know how successful he was being with that look—when you're twelve years old, it's pretty hard to look really grim and really fierce when faced with a brawny grown-up who also happens to be a very powerful warlock—and, somehow, the fact that Measle was about eight metres tall and was towering over Toby and the other warlocks didn't seem to make all that much of a difference right now.

'See what I mean?' said Toby, turning his head and looking back at the rest of the warlocks who were clustered behind him in the doorway. 'See what I mean about this boy? Brave and resourceful and imaginative! And now, somehow, he's grown to the height of a decent-sized tree! A worthy enemy indeed!'

Toby turned back to Measle and stared up at him—and Measle thought he detected a slight look of admiration in Toby's expression.

'I'm not going to ask you how you did this, old son,' said Toby. 'There'll be plenty of time for that later. I'm also not going to ask how you got out of the Detention Centre, when nobody and nothing has ever managed to do that before—but you obviously did and I congratulate you. However, right now, we must stop all this nonsense, you know. We need to cut you back down to size and put you somewhere secure—and somewhere obviously a bit more secure than the Detention

Centre, I think. So, I'm going to use a spell on you—a simple diminishing spell, which will reduce you to a more manageable size. Now, don't worry, this won't hurt—'

Toby broke off, because he suddenly caught sight of Sam and Lee's heads, sticking out of Measle's top pocket. A look of fear flooded Toby's face and he took a hurried step backwards.

'Oh—hello, Sam, old chap,' he said, smiling warily up at them. 'And there's the lovely Lee, too! What a pleasure to see you both!'

'Hello, Toby,' said Sam quietly. 'I won't say it's a pleasure to see *you*.' There was an edge of steel in Sam's voice and, to Measle, his dad sounded very, very dangerous.

Toby's eyes narrowed and he squinted up at Sam, staring hard at Sam's neck.

'Ah—I see you still have your wrathring on, old man,' he said, his voice relaxing and a cunning grin appearing on his face. 'Now, that's interesting. Sam Stubbs, with no magic. You know, old man—with all due respect, you're not much of a wizard at the best of times. In fact, without your lovely Lee, you're a bit of a nothing, aren't you? A few minor defensive spells is pretty much all you're good for—and, with a wrathring round your neck, you're not even good for *them*, are you? Poor old Sam—now I come to think of it, you really are the least admirable of the Stubbs family. The lovely Lee is magnificent and I have some very interesting plans for her. The baby Mallockee is a fascinating creature—and, as for young Measle, well, I think he's probably the best of the sorry bunch. But making him this ridiculous size! It won't help you, I'm afraid. Not without your magic to protect you, Sam. Now then, let's put a stop to this nonsense, shall we?'

Toby pointed his finger straight up at Measle and shouted, '*Reductiornus Bekswakwee Sagaftra!*'—and, instantly, twin beams of light—beams of light that appeared, to Measle's horrified eyes, to be *black* (*but how can light be black?*) shot from Toby's eyes at the speed of lightning and sizzled up towards Measle's head—

Instinctively, Measle threw up his hand to ward off the spell—and, even as he did so, he was thinking, *This won't do any good, you can't stop a spell just by putting your hand in front of it—*

And yet—

And yet—

That was *exactly* what happened.

What in fact happened was—well—*nothing* happened.

The twin beams of dark light splashed against Measle's hand, like two jets of black water. Where they hit, they exploded outwards, in two rippling circles of darkness—then the ripples became a small, fast-running stream of shiny blackness that trickled directly across Measle's palm and into—*into something that hadn't been there before.*

There was a long, frozen silence. Then Measle slowly turned his hand and stared at the palm in amazement. Apart from its hugeness, it looked the same as always—a bit grubby, with all the familiar lines and creases in all the right places—the only small difference was the dull silver ring round his little finger—

Matilda's wrathring.

Matilda's wrathring, which had been round his sister's neck but which now fitted snugly round Measle's little finger. He'd slipped it on back in the circular hallway, without giving the action a second thought.

Matilda's wrathring, which stopped her magic dead in its tracks—and which seemed to be stopping somebody *else's* magic dead in its tracks as well.

Sam was staring up at Measle's hand. 'Well, that's very interesting,' he muttered. 'I don't suppose a wrathring has ever been put on a non-magical person before. I mean—what would be the point? So, it looks to me that once the ring discovered it had no magic to absorb from *you*, it decided the only thing it could do was absorb magic from somewhere *else*.'

Toby whirled round and stared at his companions. His face was dark with fury and bewilderment. 'What are you all *waiting* for?' he bellowed. '*Do* something!'

Dorian Fescue stepped forward, raised his yellow

face and screamed, '*Reductiornus Bekswakwee Sagaftra!*'—and the twin beams that shot from his eyes were yellow too, just like his face—

Measle moved his hand. The yellow beams splashed against his palms and Measle noticed that, as with Toby's dark beams a moment before, he felt nothing other than a slight tickling sensation against his skin.

'*Fascinating,*' muttered Sam from Measle's top pocket.

'All of you!' shrieked Toby. 'All the rest of you—*together*!'

Ermintrude Bacon, Quentin Underwood, Tully Telford, and Sir Peregrine Spine all stepped forward and screamed the spell in unison. '*REDUCTIORNUS BEKSWAKWEE SAGAFTRA!*' The twin beams of light that shot from Ermintrude's eyes were a sickly pink; Sir Peregrine's were silver; Tully's were grey—and Quentin Underwood's were a dusty beige. All eight beams merged as they got near to Measle, their colours twisting together like a braided length of hair and, once again, Measle intercepted the beams with the palm of his enormous hand. There was a brief, tickling sensation as the spells splashed against his skin—

'Oh dear,' said Sam, leaning comfortably out of Measle's top pocket and grinning down at the group of warlocks. 'It looks like you've used up all your mana. So, what are you going to do now?'

Toby stared furiously up at Sam. 'Don't think you're going to get away with this, Sam!' he shouted. 'You're not! This escape attempt is illegal! You are committing a serious crime by breaking out of the Detention Centre! That's where you belong until your cases are brought up before the courts!'

Sam shook his head. 'But, Toby, our cases not *going* to be brought up, are they? Our cases are going to disappear from the books, aren't they? Because *we* are going to be made to disappear, aren't we? You see, Toby, we know everything.'

Toby suddenly pulled a small silver whistle from his pocket. He stuck it into his mouth, took a deep breath and blew a piercing blast. Then he screamed, 'Guards! GUARDS! *GUARDS!!!*'

From far down the dark corridor came the crash of a door being hurled open. Then, out of the gloom, a group of black-uniformed figures came running towards them. All of them wore shiny black helmets on their heads and all carried heavy truncheons—and their boots made a drumming sound on the stone floor as they raced along.

Measle turned his massive body to face them. As the guards drew nearer, they saw, for the first time, what was facing them—a human mountain that completely filled the great corridor. It had hands the size of coffee tables, feet the size of small cars—and suddenly, the guards' boots stopped drumming on the stone floor. All the guards slowed their pace down to a cautious walk and their leader—a huge man, who Measle thought looked very like the one who had chased Toby and himself up the spiral staircase on the night of the Inquiry—took several more paces forward and then stopped dead. The rest of the guards bunched up behind him. Measle could see their eyes glittering behind the visors of their helmets. The big guard in the front smacked his truncheon down into the palm of his hand several times, as if, by doing this, he could somehow give himself a little courage and authority.

'Guards, arrest these criminals!' yelled Toby. 'Do your duty and arrest them immediately!'

The leader of the guards stepped forward and stared a little fearfully up at Measle.

'You'd better come along with us, if you know what's good for you,' he said, his voice shaky with nerves.

'And if you know what's good for *you*,' said Sam, leaning forward out of Measle's front pocket and pointing his finger down at the guard, 'you'll get out of our way.'

The big guard took a step backwards, treading heavily on the toes of several guards who were huddling behind him.

'Now—look here, sir,' he said, feebly, 'we don't want no trouble.'

'Then move out of the way,' said Sam, firmly. 'And *stay* out of the way and you won't get hurt. Come on, Measle—let's go, shall we? Straight down the corridor—and try not to tread on anybody if you can possibly help it, all right?'

Measle looked down at the guards in front of him. Then he turned his huge head and looked down at the five warlocks standing in the open doorway. Suddenly, they all looked—well—very *small*.

Very small and very—*powerless*.

Measle took a lumbering step forward—and immediately the guards scattered in all directions. Some pressed themselves hard up against the walls, others simply turned and fled into the darkness. Only the leader stood his ground. He licked his lips nervously and held up his truncheon and quavered, 'Now then, y-young fellow—don't m-make me use this.'

Measle had been bullied enough. It was time to do a little bullying of his own.

Measle bent down, stretched out his huge right hand, picked up the guard between his finger and thumb and lifted him slowly upwards. As he was brought closer and closer to Measle's face, the expression on the guard's own face became more and more terrified. And then Measle parted his lips—and slowly he opened his enormous mouth. Centimetre by slow centimetre, he lifted the guard upwards, bring him steadily closer and closer—

'You're not going to eat that, are you, son?' said Sam, in a voice that sounded only mildly curious.

'Well, I thought I might, Dad,' said Measle, halting the slow movement of his hand for a moment.

'Oh, I wouldn't,' said Sam, easily. 'They taste horrible, you know. I thinks it's all that plastic they're wrapped up in.'

'Well, I'll just try a little bite,' said Measle—and once again, he started to bring the guard nearer and nearer to his gaping mouth.

The guard started to scream—a long string of panic-filled words, without a pause between them. '*Nononodon'teatmepleasedon'teatmepleasedon't eatme—*'

Measle grinned, revealing teeth the size of encyclopaedias.

The guard, petrified beyond anything he'd ever experienced, simply stopped screaming. His body went as stiff as a board in Measle's fingers, and all he could do was stare with utter horror up into the vast cave that was Measle's mouth. Measle could hear the guard's teeth chattering—he could feel the shivering muscles of the guard's rigid body in his fingers—

Perhaps it was time to stop being a bully.

Measle snapped his jaws together with a loud click—then he lowered his hand and placed the guard gently to one side of the passage. The guard was so terrified that, when Measle let go of him, his knees gave way under him and he slumped to the floor in a shapeless heap. Then the guard watched through frightened eyes as Measle lumbered slowly by.

'Stop them!' roared Toby. 'You *cowards*! Stop them!'

Measle ignored everything, except his father's directions. He began to move fast now, thundering down the long dark passage, the sounds of Toby's wild yells receding into the distance behind him.

'Good, Measle!' called Sam. 'Keep going, son—now turn right here—round to the right, then the second on the left—good—now all the way to the end—'

Measle followed Sam's directions blindly—and he moved as fast as his huge bulk allowed. Long passages were taken in five giant steps, shorter ones in two. Measle was moving so fast now that the wind he made as he rushed by rattled the doors in their frames.

Far behind him, Measle could hear faint sounds of pursuit, so he guessed that Toby had managed somehow to organize the remaining guards into some kind of order and had persuaded them to give chase—but that didn't worry him too much, not now that he was the size of an elephant! He remembered being picked up by Basil Tramplebone's enormous tweezers and being deposited on the coal heap in the dirty railway yard—and now the tables were turned and it was *his* turn to be huge—and if all the little people didn't want to be trampled to death, then they would simply have to get out of his way! *Only please let Tilly's spell last a little longer—*

They had just started down a corridor that was so long that the walls, the floor, and the ceiling came to a single point in the far distance. The corridor was lit by a series of harsh white fluorescent strips set in the ceiling and there were doors, hundreds of doors, set into each wall—

I've been here before, Measle said to himself.

Then—

'Hey, it's getting a bit tight in here!' called Sam.

'We're being squished!' shouted Lee.

Measle looked down and saw that his father and mother were now pressed uncomfortably close together—and they were getting a lot heavier, too.

Measle had hardly noticed their combined weight when he'd first lifted them into his top pocket—now it was bulging and pulling his whole leather jacket forward, making the collar cut into the back of his neck.

And there were other bulges too, in the pair of side pockets in the jacket—and the bulges were getting heavy, as well—and Matilda's wrathring suddenly slipped off Measle's little finger and clattered to the floor.

And the corridor was getting taller and wider—

'Quick!' yelled Sam. 'The spell's wearing off! Get us out of here before we all get squashed! Tilly first—get Tilly out first, Measle!'

Measle stopped and reached his shrinking hands into his shrinking pockets. He carefully pulled the still-sleeping Matilda out and laid her down on the floor. Tinker jumped out on his own and then watched with interest as the smelly kid extracted Iggy, his face now smeared with red sugar, from his other pocket.

Sam and Lee had taken matters into their own hands and had scrambled out of Measle's top pocket, hanging at first by their hands, their legs dangling in the air. But now the drop from the pocket to the floor was only a couple of metres, so Sam and Lee jumped for it, landing with two thumps on the hard floor. Then they all stepped back and watched as Measle swiftly returned to his proper size.

Measle, now looking *up* at his family, said, 'See?

Tilly's spells don't last very long. And doing them puts her fast asleep. She won't do another one until she wakes up.'

'Very interesting,' said Sam. 'Very interesting indeed. I wonder—'

Lee had hurried to Matilda's side and had lifted her into her arms. She suddenly turned her head and looked back down the long passage—then she cupped a hand behind one ear and listened hard.

'There's no time to be wondering about anything, Sam,' she said, quickly. 'They're heading this way—and this time, we're helpless! Come on, everybody—we've got to move fast!'

Sam led the way, running ahead of them down the long corridor. He went at a steady, easy pace, making sure that everybody could keep up with him—but, in doing so, he also allowed their pursuers gradually to close the gap. It wasn't long before Measle heard the distant sounds of heavy boots, pounding along far behind them and Sam threw a look over his shoulder and called, 'Come on, everybody! It's not too far now!'

Too far to where? thought Measle, as he trotted along behind his father. The corridor they were in seemed to be endless and featureless, apart from the regular succession of doors on either side.

On and on they ran—and steadily the sounds of thudding boots behind them got louder and louder—and now they could hear muffled shouts, that turned quickly into yells—

'Oi! You! Stop! Stop right there!'

And Sam did indeed appear to obey the distant command, because he suddenly skidded to a halt. In front of him was a pair of sliding doors, and next to them was a panel of buttons—

A lift!

But the doors were closed and Sam was frantically punching buttons and muttering, 'Come on! Come on!' under his breath. Measle, panting hard, looked fearfully back the way they had come—

There, in the distance, racing towards them, came the group of black-uniformed figures. Measle saw them all suddenly increase their pace as they realized that, now, there wasn't an eight metre boy-mountain confronting them any more; now there was just a small group of helpless-looking people clustered together in the distance, right by the closed doors of a lift—

A lift that wouldn't come!

'Come on! Come ON!' barked Sam, still wildly punching the buttons.

And then, quite suddenly and without warning, the lift doors hissed open.

'Quick! Inside, everybody!' yelled Sam—and they all piled in together, all except Iggy. Iggy was staring with more fear at the inside of the lift than he was at the approaching guards.

'Come on, Mr Niggle!' shouted Sam—but Iggy didn't move.

'Is dat one of dose fings wot goes whooshy-whooshy up and down?' said Iggy, suspiciously.

'Yes!' yelled Sam impatiently—and, immediately, Iggy took a step backwards and shook his head. 'I don't like dem fings,' he announced, firmly. 'You can't sssee where you is goin'.'

Measle stuck his head out of the lift and looked down the corridor. The guards were only twenty metres away—and they were fast closing the gap—

PUSH

'No, Iggy!' shouted Measle. 'It's just a box! A big box to keep the rain out! Come on!'

Iggy's face brightened and he took a step forward—and Sam shot out one brawny hand, grabbed Iggy by the front of his jacket, and yanked him into the lift. Sam stabbed his free hand against a red button—and the doors hissed shut at the very moment that the leading guard slammed his heavy body against them.

The lift began to shoot upwards.

Iggy sniffed loudly.

'Dat was a bad fibby-dib you jussst told, Mumps,' he said, sadly. 'Dis *is* a whooshy-whooshy fing. It's not a box to keep de rain out at all. I've ssstill got my rain cloud in 'ere wiv me, 'aven't I?'

There wasn't really anything that Measle could say about that because it was true. Iggy's fist-sized rain cloud was indeed still hovering over Iggy's head, dribbling gently down on the little wrathmonk. Iggy sniffed disapprovingly once again and then relapsed into a sulky silence.

The lift raced upwards.

Measle looked up at his father. Sam's face was grim—and so was Lee's.

'Dad—?' said Measle—but Sam held up a hand and shook his head.

'Not right now, son,' he said, quietly. 'There's one more obstacle before we're clear. Let's deal with that first, shall we?'

Ten seconds later, the lift hissed to a stop. The doors slid open and they all stepped out of the lift, with Sam leading the way.

Measle saw that they were in a big lobby, with a shiny marble floor. Ten metres away was a revolving glass door—and across the lobby, to the right, was a desk—

A big man stood behind the desk.

He had a red face and a droopy, walrus moustache.

The big man caught sight of the Stubbs family.
He stepped out from behind the desk.

'Hello, Fred,' said Sam.

Retracing Steps

Measle realized—with a shock that felt as if he'd jumped into an icy lake—why everything had looked so familiar for the last few minutes; that final, long corridor, those lines of wooden doors, the lift, this shiny marble lobby—

He'd been here before. Just yesterday, in fact—when he and Sam and Lee and Matilda and Nanny Flannel and Tinker had all trooped across this exact same floor, only *then* they'd been going in the opposite direction—*away* from the revolving door of the Wizards' Guild building and *towards* the lift in its lobby.

But—but this isn't possible! thought Measle, trying desperately to sort out all his whirling notions. Right now, his mind was a bit like a pile of damp clothes in a tumble dryer. All the ideas were jumbled together and were tumbling, multicoloured, round and round—*How can I be in Caltrop Castle one minute and in the lobby of the Wizards' Guild building the next? The two places are miles and miles apart—maybe even hundreds of miles apart—we drove forever, Toby and me, all through the long night—and besides, Caltrop Castle is in the country, and the Wizards' Guild is in the city! None of this makes any sense!*

Measle's wild thoughts were interrupted by the sudden pressure of Sam's hand on his shoulder. They were halfway across the lobby now, but the way ahead was barred by the stout figure of Fred the lobby guard.

Sam, with his hand resting lightly on Measle's shoulder, stopped—and the rest of them stopped as well. For a moment there was silence. Then Fred said, 'Hello, Mr Stubbs. Been keeping well, have you?'

'Quite well, thank you, Fred.'

'Good, good.' Fred nodded amiably. Then he frowned and said, 'I 'eard about some sort of aggravation down there in the lower quarters. I couldn't quite get the sense of it but somebody said that you were involved in it, sir. Something about you and Mrs Stubbs being held in the Detention Centre—is that right, sir?'

Measle heard something behind him. He turned and saw the lift doors sliding shut—then he heard the whine of the hydraulic mechanism starting up.

The lift was going back down—

'Dad—?' he said, tugging gently on Sam's sleeve.

Sam didn't take his eyes off Fred but he nodded and said, 'Yes, I know, son.'

Fred was looking uneasily at each member of the party. Iggy was trying to hide himself at the rear—but Fred caught sight of him and took a hurried step backwards.

'Here—is that a nasty little *wrathmonk* you've got there, Mr Stubbs?'

'Yes, Fred, it is,' said Sam, in a very calm and collected voice. 'Although it turns out that he's not really all *that* nasty—are you, Mr Niggle?'

At this difficult question, Iggy did his face-twisting act again. Then he said, hesitantly, 'I fink I'm *quite* nasty, actually.'

Fred took another step backwards.

'Sorry to mention this, Mr Stubbs, sir,' he said, 'but a wrathmonk's got no business here. Not up here in the lobby of the Wizards' Guild, he hasn't. He should be down in the Detention Centre, where he belongs.'

Sam stepped forward, moving closer to Fred. Then he put both hands on Fred's shoulders and looked the stout man straight in the eye.

'Fred, we haven't much time,' said Sam. His voice was quiet but firm. 'So, I'll be honest with you. We're on the run, my family and I. And Mr Niggle too. Any second now, a bunch of uniformed guards is going to burst out of that lift over there and they're going to arrest the lot of us. We haven't done anything wrong, Fred. Not even Mr Niggle. In fact, Mr Niggle has been very helpful to my family. But this Advisory Committee says we're to be arrested—and there's nothing we can do about it. Unless you help us by letting us go on our way, that is.'

Fred's eyes were wide with astonishment. He looked long and hard at Sam—then he switched his gaze to Lee, then to Measle. He glared fiercely at Iggy, who was busy picking his nose. He brought his look back to Sam—and then, at last, Fred nodded slowly.

'I've known you a long time, Mr Stubbs, sir—and you've always been straight with me. And Mrs Stubbs is a fine lady, I've always thought that.'

'Thank you, Fred,' said Lee.

'And what I've heard of young Measle—well, it's all been good. And we can't be letting anybody arrest a little baby, now can we? And I'll tell you another thing—I don't like this Advisory Committee and I *specially* don't like these clumsy new guards they've got. I dunno where they come from and I don't want to know—but they've got no business clod-hopping around in the Guild building, doing whatever they like.'

Fred talks too much! thought Measle. *The lift is going to get here any minute!* Measle started hopping anxiously from foot to foot, shooting desperate glances at Sam, hoping to catch his attention. Sam looked at him and then glanced over his shoulder towards the lift doors.

'Fred, if you're going to let us go, perhaps now might be a good time to do it. I think I hear the lift coming back up—and it's going to be chock-full of those clod-hopping guards we don't like.'

They all stood still, straining their ears—there was the distant whine of a lift ascending at great speed and the whine was getting louder and louder.

Fred abruptly turned on his heel and marched quickly back to his desk. At the same moment, Sam started to herd his family fast towards the revolving doors.

Out of the corner of his eye, Measle saw Fred reach under his desk. The big man appeared to be fiddling with something under there—a switch, perhaps, or a button—then Fred straightened up and, at the exact same moment, there was a hissing sound as the lift arrived.

But the lift doors didn't open.

Instead, after a short silence, there was a sudden hubbub of sound from inside. There were raised voices—then shouts—then the noise of heavy fists pounding against metal.

'Oh dear, Mr Stubbs!' shouted Fred. 'I'm terribly afraid something dreadful has happened! Oh dear, oh dear—whatever shall we do?'

Fred's voice sounded very odd to Measle. It was in a sort of over-loud, high-pitched sing-song tone—the sort of voice that a very bad actor might use on stage when he's talking about something awful that has just taken place.

Sam paused, his hand on the revolving door.

'What's the matter, Fred?' he said, loudly—and, to Measle's ears, Sam's voice sounded a little artificial as well, as if he was reciting lines he'd just learned.

Fred shook his head dramatically. 'A most unfortunate thing, Mr Stubbs!' he exclaimed, waggling his eyebrows and pointing wildly towards the lift. 'Most unfortunate indeed! It would appear that the lift is malfunctioning, sir!'

'Malfunctioning, Fred?'

'Yes, sir! It would appear that the lift doors are, in fact, stuck, sir! Oh dear, oh dear, oh dear! Whatever shall we do, sir? All those poor people—trapped in the lift, sir!'

Sam smiled. Then, in his normal voice, he said, 'Thank you, Fred. I won't forget this.'

'No, sir! Neither will I, sir!' shouted Fred at the top of his voice. 'A lift malfunction is not something one can easily forget, sir! All those poor, poor people! Now then, don't you worry about this—it's my problem, Mr Stubbs! You be on your way, sir!'

'Thanks, Fred,' Sam said. 'Goodnight!'

Sam gave the revolving door a great shove and set it turning—and one by one the Stubbs family spilled out onto the dark and empty street.

Once outside, Sam gathered them all together.

'Now then,' he said, urgently, 'we'd better get a move on. Those lift doors won't hold the guards for long. Come on!'

Sam led them in a fast run down the dark street. There was nobody around at this time of the night and few of the buildings that surrounded them showed any lights in their windows.

The Stubbs car was still where they had parked it. Sam yanked open the doors and everybody piled in—Measle and Sam and Tinker in front, Lee in the back holding tight to Matilda—

'Come on, Iggy!' yelled Measle. Iggy was still standing on the pavement. He was staring with admiration at the huge car, his fishy eyes wide with wonder.

'Iggy! Get in!'

Iggy shook his head. 'Can't,' he muttered.

'Why not, Iggy?'

'I'll make it all wet,' said Iggy, sadly. 'Dose nice seats—dey will smell all funny when I get off dem. Dey always do.'

Sam reached under the dashboard and pulled a short lever—and the lid of the boot clicked open and then swung upwards.

'How about in there, Mr Niggle?' Sam shouted. 'Nothing to spoil in there—and besides, it's too small for your rain cloud! The beastly thing will just have to stay outside!'

Iggy's face brightened. He said, 'Coo—fanks very much, Mr Ssstubbs, sssir! Dat will do nicely, fanks!'

He scurried to the rear of the car, hopped into the boot and lay down—and Sam pushed the lever back and the lid of the boot swung shut.

Sam punched the big red button and the car rumbled to life.

'Where are we going, Sam?' said Lee. 'We can't go home—that's the first place they'll look for us.'

'I know,' said Sam. 'Wait a minute—let me think.'

Sam furrowed his brow and tapped the front of his teeth with his fingernails. Then, suddenly, he seemed to come to a decision. He reached forward and pushed the button marked A/P.

Yes? came the haughty voice of the car's autopilot.

'A destination,' said Sam.

Where to?

'Lord Octavo's house, please.'

Lord Octavo's house it is, sir.

The car pulled away from the kerb and accelerated down the dark street—and Iggy's muffled voice came drifting out of the back of the car.

'We is goin' to Lord Octopus's house? Coo, dat is good—I like Lord Octopus. He gave me a bissscuit once. And I like it in 'ere, too. It is nice and dry in 'ere. I could live in 'ere, I could. I could live in 'ere, and I could sssleep in 'ere, and I could eat sssweeties in 'ere, and I could—'

Iggy's muffled little voice babbled on and on, as the big green car roared through the night.

And Iggy's tiny black rain cloud—locked out of the boot and thus separated from its master by a sheet of strong steel—tore frantically through the cold night air in pursuit of the speeding car.

THE COURT
OF MAGISTRI

The hearing was going badly.

For the Stubbs family, that is.

The hearing was being held in the same great chamber as the original Inquiry and it was packed. Every wizard and every warlock who could manage to squeeze into the crowded space was there and the court was hushed and expectant. Five elderly judges sat in a line on the platform, their long red robes cascading to the floor in folds. Behind them, on a taller platform, sat Justin Bucket, in a long blue robe with gold stripes on the sleeves. Justin looked pale and frightened—but nobody else did. In fact, Toby Jugg and the five warlocks of the Advisory Committee looked relaxed and thoroughly at ease.

'But can you *prove* all this, Mr Stubbs?'

The judge who had asked the question was sitting next to Lord Octavo and he was leaning forward on his elbows, looking hard at Sam with a disbelieving expression on his elderly face.

Sam and Lee were sitting in a small wooden enclosure, in front—and a little to the right—of the judges' platform. Sam opened his mouth to reply, but Tully Telford interrupted him.

'Of course they can't prove it, my lord,' he squeaked. 'They can't prove it because none of it happened!'

Tully Telford was sitting on a plain bench inside another wooden enclosure. This pen was bigger than Sam and Lee's and was directly in front of the judges' platform. Toby Jugg and the rest of the Advisory Committee were sitting just behind Tully. They all had faint smiles on their faces. Measle thought they looked as if they considered the entire proceedings a dreadful waste of time.

'All these extraordinary accusations!' squeaked Tully. 'Such nonsense! The monstrous suggestion that Mr Jugg somehow drugged the boy's drink in a motorway café and then simply drove him back to the Guild building while he was unconscious! And the rest of it—pictures that come to life! Tiny cows! A murderous grimling! A suit of armour that attacks on sight! I ask you, my lords—how can we take these idiocies seriously? At best, these are mere figments of a lively imagination! Ridiculous, the whole thing!'

'Thank you, Mr Telford,' said Lord Octavo, quietly. 'Thank you for your opinion. Now, Mr Stubbs—please continue.'

Things had gone badly for the Stubbs family from the start—and Lord Octavo had warned them that they might.

Two days earlier, a big green car, with the skull of a baby dragon decorating the bonnet, had rumbled up to Lord Octavo's front door just before dawn. Lord Octavo lived alone in a pretty little thatched cottage deep in the countryside. Sam and Lee had knocked on the front door and soon there were the sounds of bolts being drawn back. The door cracked open, revealing Lord Octavo in his pyjamas and dressing gown. He took one look at the bedraggled collection of people standing on his doorstep—then, without a word, he led them into his living room, sat them down, and listened intently until Sam had finished speaking.

'You must understand,' he had said, his clever old face wrinkled with concern, 'that convening the Court of Magistri is a very serious business. It's hardly ever done—and only in matters of supreme importance. Also, remember, I am not the only judge—there are five of us in total and not all will be friendly to your case. The accusations you're making are extraordinary—and the warlocks you are accusing are all perfectly respectable people, most of them occupying positions of some power and influence. I am the senior judge, which helps you a little—but I can be outvoted, so you must not rely on me. Do you still want me to convene this court?'

'We most certainly do, Lord Octavo,' said Sam, firmly. 'Without the court, I don't see any future for us.'

'And, if we should happen to lose,' said Lord Octavo, slowly, 'I don't see any future for *any* of us.'

The future looked bleak.

The trouble was, there were *six* warlocks on one side, and only *three* Stubbses (and a nasty, sneaky, spiteful, and probably untruthful little wrathmonk) on the other. This made the believability of the two sets of stories decidedly lop-sided. It was getting to be a question of whether the judges believed six very powerful and utterly respectable warlocks—or whether they believed the wild and crazy Stubbs family and a nasty, damp little wrathmonk.

Nanny Flannel, Matilda Stubbs, and Tinker weren't in the court. Nanny Flannel wasn't there because she hadn't been part of the adventure; Matilda wasn't there because Lord Octavo had said that she couldn't possibly be there, because everybody in the Wizards' Guild was terrified of her and they all dreaded the possibility that she might decide to use her powers again; and Tinker wasn't there because Lord Octavo had said that, while a silly little Inquiry might encourage dogs to attend, the Court of Magistri most certainly didn't.

Another problem for Measle and his family was that the story that Sam and Lee had told just sounded so fantastical to everybody there that it was hard to believe. And now Sam was trying to get the truth from Toby Jugg—and he was failing miserably.

'Do you deny, Toby, that you told my son of a plot to change the rules of the Guild? Changes that would result in only warlocks being allowed to stand for the position of Prime Magus?'

'Of course I deny it, old son,' said Toby, smiling gently in Sam's direction. 'We all do, don't we?'

There was a lot of vigorous nodding from the other warlocks, and general murmurs of assent from them too.

'Do you deny that you claim to be the rightful Prime Magus of the Wizards' Guild?'

Toby laughed. 'How can I be the Prime Magus, Sam?' he said, pulling back the two curtains of hair that hung to his shoulders and revealing the Gloomstains on his ears. 'I'm a warlock, old chap. And we all know that warlocks can't be Prime Magus, don't we?'

Again, there was a lot of nodding and murmured agreement from his companions in the pen.

'Do you deny that, for years, Toby, you have *hidden* the fact that you are a warlock?'

'No, I don't deny that, old chap. Why should I? There's nothing illegal about that, you know. Lots of warlocks prefer to be discreet about it—you know that as well as I do, Sam.'

'How about the plot to kill me, Toby? How about the plot to marry my wife, Toby? How about the repeated attempts on my son's life, Toby?' Sam's voice was rising in anger. 'You sent a homicidal grimling, a herd of cattle, and an iron automaton armed with a sword after him! The fact that you failed to harm him is neither here nor there—what you did was the most serious misuse of Prime Magus powers I've ever heard of! And then, finally, you placed him in the hands of a crowd of angry wrathmonks, several of whom were most anxious to take some sort of revenge on him! How do you answer all *that*, Toby?'

Toby put a look of hurt bewilderment onto his face. 'Dear old Sam,' he said, 'there's not a word of truth in any of this! As if I, or *any* of us, would hurt a hair on your son's head! I can't imagine why he would say such things. All I can suggest is that the poor little chap isn't well. Have you had a doctor look him over?'

Measle was beginning to feel the first dark twinges of despair. Everything was going wrong—and that wasn't fair! Nobody had asked him any questions at all! They hadn't asked Iggy any questions either—and Iggy could certainly confirm everything that the Stubbs family was claiming.

Measle glanced sideways at Iggy, who was sitting next to him in the high gallery that overlooked the huge courtroom. Measle and Iggy were in the front row and had been told to stay there until such time as they might be needed to testify. But the investigation had been going on for hours, it seemed, and nobody had come anywhere near them. Nobody had asked them to tell their side of the story either. At least, not yet.

And then something happened that made Measle believe that his side of the story would *never* be heard.

'I would like to propose to this court,' squeaked Tully Telford, 'that all this so-called "testimony" be struck from the record, on the grounds that not a word of it can be proved! I further propose that any evidence from young Measle Stubbs and the wrathmonk Ignatius Niggle be considered worthless—worthless, on the grounds that, as far as the boy is concerned, his mind is obviously seriously disturbed and, as far as Ignatius Niggle is concerned, no wrathmonk has ever been allowed to testify before *any* court assembled by the Wizards' Guild, and now is not the time to change such customs. And, since the testimony of these two witnesses is therefore invalid, I propose that this court—and all the persons charged—be dismissed forthwith! Judges of the Court of Magistri—please raise your hands, those who concur with these proposals!'

To Measle's horror, four hands were lifted slowly in the still air. Only Lord Octavo's remained firmly resting on the desk in front of him.

'A case before the Court of Magistri does not require full agreement of the presiding judges!' shouted Tully triumphantly. 'The Court of Magistri can rule by a clear majority! We *have* a clear majority—of four to one! The case *must* be dismissed!'

There was a general hubbub in the courtroom, as every wizard and warlock there put their heads together and muttered their reactions to each other. Measle looked down at the faces of the six grinning warlocks. Toby's smile was broader than anybody else's.

They're going to get away with it! thought Measle. *And there's nothing we can do about it! If only I could get them to tell what really happened! If only there was some way to reveal the truth, to lay bare their souls, to force them to stop lying—to open them up—*

Open them up.

Open them.

Open . . .

And then the most peculiar idea that Measle had ever come up with dropped into his brain, like a single bead of water falling into a pond. A little drop of water, which plopped silently into his thoughts, sending ripples of further thoughts rolling out across the surface of his mind.

It's crazy! thought Measle. *It's senseless! It doesn't even mean the same thing—but—but it's our only chance!*

Measle came to a momentous decision—and he came to it quickly, because the whole notion didn't bear examining too closely. He turned to Iggy and tapped him on the shoulder and Iggy twisted his head round quickly, spattering Measle's face with rainwater.

'Wot?' he muttered, frowning at Measle to be quiet.

'Iggy!' hissed Measle. 'I want you to do your spell! I want you to do your spell right *now*!'

'Wha' for?' whispered Iggy. 'Dere's nuffing dat needs openin' right now, is dere?'

'Yes! Yes, there is, Iggy!'

'What, Mumps? What needs openin'?'

Measle raised his right hand and pointed straight down towards the wooden enclosure. '*He* does, Iggy! *Toby Jugg! He needs to be opened!*'

Iggy gaped at Measle, his jaw slack and his fishy eyes wide. 'Missster Jugg ain't a *lock*, Mumps!' he muttered. 'He's a *war*lock! Jussst coz it sssounds de sssame, dat don't mean it *is* de sssame! One is made of *perssson*, de uvver is made of *metal*. You can't open a *perssson*, sssee?'

Measle grabbed the front of Iggy's damp,

mildewy coat, pulled Iggy's head next to his and whispered frantically into Iggy's ear.

'Maybe you can't, Iggy! But then again—*maybe you can!* It's worth a try, isn't it?'

Iggy's expression of dumb bewilderment didn't change. Slowly, sorrowfully, he shook his head. 'You is potty, Mumps,' he said.

Down below, the judges were settling back into their chairs. Lord Octavo rapped on the desk in front of him with a small silver hammer.

'Fellow wizards, fellow warlocks,' he said, 'I find myself in a minority of one in this case. Mr Telford has pointed out, correctly, that the judgment of a case before the Court of Magistri does not require full agreement from the presiding judges. A majority vote is sufficient. Therefore—reluctantly I must add—it is my duty to close these proceedings, with the verdict that no fault, blame, or guilt attaches to these persons here before us—'

Measle had one last trick up his sleeve. He pulled Iggy's ear close to his mouth and whispered into it. The whisper was hoarse and urgent and filled with panic—but the words still rang crystal clear in Iggy's head.

'If you do your spell on Mr Jugg, Iggy—I'll give you two hundred red jelly beans—*every day for the rest of your life!*'

This time, Iggy didn't even pause to think. Instead, his pale, thin little face lit up with greedy joy and, in the next instant, he turned away from Measle, leaned over the balcony of the gallery and, staring fixedly down at Toby Jugg, he screamed, '*Unkasssshhhriek gorgogasssshhh plurgholips!*'

Instantly, a pair of lavender-coloured beams shot from Iggy's eyes and sizzled down through the still air of the courtroom, smacking Toby cleanly on the back of his head.

For a moment, there was a stunned silence. Toby himself slowly reached up a hand and stroked his long hair, as if he was smoothing it back into place. Other than this gesture, he seemed not to have noticed that anything at all had happened.

And—and it obviously hasn't! thought Measle, miserably.

There was a buzz of fear from those who had heard the spell and seen the lavender beams. Quite a few of the audience in the great room rose to their feet and several wizards pulled back their sleeves, getting themselves ready to hurl their own spells around—but Lord Octavo held up his hands and shouted over the mounting din.

'Calm yourselves, everybody! That was just the foolish little wrathmonk, Ignatius Niggle, pointlessly performing his only spell! It does nothing other than open stubborn locks! It's quite harmless! There is nothing to fear! Why he did it is anybody's guess—but there's no harm done and now he's mana-less—so, please, all of you sit down again! You too, Niggle—and we shall deal with you later!'

Slowly the hubbub died away and everybody sat down—but there were a lot of suspicious looks directed up at Measle and Iggy and three of the four judges bent their heads together and began an urgent, whispered discussion.

Well, thought Measle, *it's now or never—*

Measle got to his feet and leaned over the balcony. His heart was thumping with nervousness and his tongue felt dry and rough, like a piece of sandpaper.

He gulped.

He licked his lips.

He took a deep breath.

And he knew—as sure as he knew *anything*—that this wasn't going to work.

'WHAT DID YOU PUT IN MY DRINK, TOBY?' he shouted, his voice echoing round the great chamber.

All eyes flicked up to the small boy with the peculiar haircut standing up in the front row of the gallery. Toby Jugg turned slowly, raising his eyes up to where Measle stood. He smiled an affable smile and then he said, quite simply and cheerfully—

'Oh, a marvellous concoction, old son. Dunno what it's called. Got it out of the Alchemy labs. I must say, it worked like a charm—knocked you out cold, didn't it?'

The silence that hung over the great courtroom was thick and heavy. Nothing stirred. Nobody moved. Breathing stopped. Even if a pin had dropped, it almost certainly wouldn't have made a sound.

And Measle was thinking, *I don't believe it! It—it's working! Toby Jugg has been opened up!*

'WHAT DID YOU DO NEXT, TOBY?'

'Popped you back into the car, old son, turned it around and drove straight back to the Wizards' Guild. Put you to bed in the basement labyrinth—when you woke up, I said you were hundreds of miles away, in Caltrop Castle. Then I left you to your own devices. Watched you, of course. Watched you cope with all the dangers I threw at you. Thought you did jolly well, too.'

'ARE YOU THE PRIME MAGUS OF THE WIZARDS' GUILD, TOBY?'

'I certainly am, old son,' said Toby, with a careless little laugh. 'I wiped the floor with poor Bucket. He didn't have a chance against me. I got nearly twice as many votes as he did—'

'Shut up, Toby! *Shut up!*'

The scream came from Dorian Fescue, who was on his feet, his yellow face trembling with fear and fury. The other warlocks were on their feet as well, all staring with furious and frightened eyes at Toby Jugg.

'Be quiet, Mr Fescue,' said Lord Octavo, in a mild voice. 'Be quiet and sit down, please.'

'I will *not* sit down!' yelled Dorian, anger turning his yellow face an unpleasant shade of orange. 'Everything Jugg is saying is a tissue of lies!'

'BE QUIET AND SIT DOWN! ALL OF YOU—BE QUIET AND SIT DOWN IMMEDIATELY!'

All five warlocks sat down as if somebody had suddenly thumped them hard on the tops of their heads—and Measle sat down too. He couldn't help it. There was something in Lord Octavo's new tone of voice that simply forced the listener to obey instantly—

Lord Octavo smiled and then looked up at Measle.

'One of my more useful little vocal tricks, Master Stubbs,' he said, using his normal voice again. 'The last time I used it was on a charging water buffalo. It stopped him dead in his tracks. But that's another story. Now—you're doing extremely well, young man. Perhaps you should think of pursuing a career in the Law—when you're a bit older, that is. Meanwhile, would you object at all if I asked a few questions of my own?'

'N-no, sir.'

'Thank you.' Lord Octavo brought his gaze to bear on the six warlocks, who were now sitting huddled together in their enclosure, with very nervous expressions on their faces. All, that is, except for Toby Jugg, who sat on his section of the bench with a relaxed and cheerful smile on his lips.

'Mr Jugg,' said Lord Octavo, in a cool, quiet voice, 'we would like to know if Justin Bucket is involved in this affair?'

Toby laughed boisterously. 'Justin? That idiot? No, of course he isn't! He's a dope—and a *wizard* dope to boot! Only warlocks need apply here!'

Lord Octavo nodded pleasantly—and, behind him, Justin Bucket's face turned a deep crimson.

'And did you use the Guild building's mana to further your own ends?' continued Lord Octavo. 'And, in so doing, did you place young Measle Stubbs in extreme danger?'

'I can't deny that,' said Toby with a broad smile.

'Did you give Officer Offal money, Mr Jugg?'

'I certainly did,' said Toby. 'Rather more than I wanted to, actually!'

'Why did you give Officer Offal money, Mr Jugg?'

'To get him to open Measle's cell door.'

'And why would you want him to do that, Mr Jugg?'

Toby laughed his careless, booming laugh. 'Well, so that all the wrathmonks could get at him, you see. I knew they would make short work of him if they could get at him.'

'Short work, Mr Jugg? Do you mean—they would *kill* him?'

'I should say so! Well, that was the whole idea, wasn't it? Once we'd discovered the boy had no magic, there was no point keeping him alive, was there? He and his father were of no value to our schemes, you see. No—all we needed by then was the Mallockee and her mother!'

Lord Octavo leaned back in his chair, his eyes twinkling. Then he turned to the two judges sitting on either side of him and said, 'Perhaps my colleagues might like to question Mr Jugg—now that he seems ready to tell the truth?'

For the next hour, all five judges barked question after question at Toby Jugg—and Toby Jugg answered every question with the utter, exact, and absolute truth. Lord Octavo only had to use his special voice twice more—once when Toby was telling the court about the worldwide search for more manafounts (he repeated Ermintrude Bacon's plea for a specially *handsome* manafount husband

and Ermintrude shrieked with embarrassment) and once again when Tully Telford tried desperately to take control of the court by using lots of complicated legal words and phrases which nobody could possibly understand—and then, at the end of it all, when every question had been asked and when Toby had revealed the whole monstrously wicked plan, there was a long, deep silence in the courtroom.

Sam Stubbs broke the silence.

'Well,' he said, getting to his feet and holding out his hand to Lee, 'I seem to remember we've done this before. This time, I hope we shall succeed. So, once again—with the court's permission, I would like to take my family home.'

Lord Octavo smiled and then turned to the other judges. 'I trust nobody has any objections?'

The four other judges shook their heads. They looked a little stunned.

Lord Octavo twisted further round in his seat and peered up at Justin Bucket. Justin's face was very pale and his lips were compressed in a thin line—and his eyes were wide with fear.

'Mr Prime Magus,' said Lord Octavo, his voice ringing out through the whole great courtroom. 'Do *you* have any objection?'

Like the judges, Justin didn't speak. Instead, dumbly, he too simply shook his head.

'You are free to go, Mr Stubbs,' said Lord Octavo, turning back and looking gravely down at Sam and

Lee. 'But before you do so, I would like to say something. This has been a terrible ordeal for you all. On behalf of the Wizards' Guild, I would like to offer our apologies to you and your family. I would also like to express our profound gratitude for bringing this unfortunate matter to our attention. That is all. Go home now, Mr and Mrs Stubbs. Take young Measle with you—and trust us to handle the rest of this dreadful business.'

'Thank you, Lord Octavo,' said Sam. Then Sam and Lee looked up at Measle and they grinned at him. Sam jerked his head towards the door and called, 'Come on, Measle. Let's go home, eh?'

Measle got up—and, instantly, he felt his arm gripped in a small but powerful hand. Measle looked down into Iggy's face, which was doing its twisting, muscle-pulling, grimacing again.

'What, Iggy?'

'Er,' said Iggy, his fishy eyes swivelling madly, 'about dose red jelly beans, Mumps—'

'They'll be at my house, Iggy,' Measle whispered. 'So, if you still want them, you'd better come with us, hadn't you?'

LooSe ENDS

Iggy Niggle came to live at Merlin Manor.

Not *in* Merlin Manor—just *at* Merlin Manor. Nanny Flannel wouldn't let him in the house.

'I don't *care* if it saved you all!' she exclaimed, crossly. 'I'm not having some wet little creature dripping all over my nice clean kitchen! It can live outside!'

Measle spent half a day trying to think of some argument that could change Nanny Flannel's mind— but he stopped trying once Iggy saw the kennel.

The kennel was supposed to belong to Tinker. When Tinker had come to live at Merlin Manor, Sam had gone out and bought the biggest and the best (and certainly the most expensive) doghouse that money could buy.

Tinker had refused to use it. *Wot's the point of that?* he'd thought, firmly turning his back on the kennel and walking away from it with all the dignity that a small, fuzzy, black-and-white dog can muster. *Wot's the point of a little tiny house, when there is a sockin' great big house right next to it—and the sockin' great big house has got all the nice soft furniture in it, eh?*

So the kennel had stood empty, close beside the kitchen door—until Iggy Niggle saw it.

'Wot is dis, Mumps?' said Iggy, his eyes wide with wonder and longing as he stared down at the kennel. It was painted blue and white, with clapboard sides and a real shingled roof. It had a little arched doorway and, inside, a smooth, clean, wooden floor. Sam had put it right beside the kitchen door in the hope that Tinker—who used the kitchen door more than any other door in Merlin Manor—might get used to seeing it there and decide to give it a go. But that hadn't happened, because Tinker insisted on sleeping as close to the smelly kid as he could possibly get, which was certainly *not* just outside the kitchen door.

Measle saw the look of yearning in Iggy's eyes and did a bit of quick thinking.

'It's—it's a little house, Iggy. Do you like it?'

'Do I like it! DO I LIKE IT? It's—it's—*bee-yoo-tee-full*!'

'You think it's beautiful, Iggy?'

Iggy nodded so vigorously that raindrops flew off his head and spattered everywhere.

'Well, that's good,' said Measle, 'because it's *your* house, Iggy.'

Iggy's jaw dropped. 'Mine?' he whispered.

'Yours, Iggy.'

The kennel was the perfect size for Iggy. He still had to lie curled up inside it, but it was a lot less cramped than his old box and, since it had a proper roof, with real shingles on it, the rain slid off it very efficiently and, once inside, Iggy stayed perfectly dry. It even had a little window and a pretend chimney and, when Measle painted 'IGGY'S HOUSE' on the front, just over the arched doorway, Iggy thought it was the finest and the most desirable residence in the whole wide world.

And the Stubbs family found a use for the little wrathmonk too. Idle wrathmonks are worse than busy ones, so there had to be something for Iggy to do—and Lee thought of what it should be. There was a wonderful collection of roses at Merlin Manor—thousands and thousands of them, in many different colours, planted in flower beds all over the vast gardens—and they were always being attacked by aphids. Aphids—those tiny green insects that suck the sap from the stems of roses and spoil the flowers. Iggy's new job was to visit, regularly, all the roses in the Merlin Manor garden and, one by one, gently breathe on them.

Quite soon, the display of roses at Merlin Manor was one of the finest in the whole country.

The business of the two hundred red jelly beans that Measle had promised Iggy might have posed a bit of a problem—but Nanny Flannel solved it by declaring that, if the wet little thing gave her his word that he wouldn't try and come into her nice clean kitchen, then she would *make* him his two hundred red jelly beans fresh every day. And, since Nanny Flannel's red jelly beans tasted much better than the ones from the jar (Nanny Flannel's were made from real strawberry juice and didn't have even a milligram of magic in them) Iggy was about as happy as a wrathmonk can be when he's not allowed to be unpleasant to anybody which, in Iggy's case, was very happy indeed.

Having a Mallockee for a sister turned out to be not quite as disturbing as Measle had thought it might be.

They did several experiments with the little girl—measuring her abilities, testing her magical output, noting her extreme fatigue after performing even the simplest of spells—and the results made everybody in the Merlin Manor household sigh with relief. Matilda's spells were never hurtful, she always fell fast asleep after doing them—and they never lasted longer than ten minutes.

'I bet I know why they're so harmless and don't last long,' said Lee, peering fondly down at Matilda, who was once again fast asleep in her cot. Matilda had exhausted herself by turning Iggy's old black coat a luminous shade of orange and Iggy was very pleased with it—at least, for the ten minutes that the colour lasted.

'Why don't they last, Mum?' said Measle.

'I think it's because we were swimming in dragon's blood that was mixed up with sea water,' Lee said, thoughtfully. 'And there was *far* more water than there was blood—so Arcturion's mana was very heavily diluted, you see. I reckon it might have been something like one part of blood to a thousand parts of water—so Tilly and I were getting only a fraction of the mana that a *real* Mallockee should get.'

'I think we might keep that information to ourselves,' said Sam, who had just strolled into the nursery.

'Why, Sam? What do you mean?' said Lee.

'Well,' said Sam, tapping the front of his teeth with his fingernails, 'I think it might be quite a good idea if we let the Wizards' Guild go on thinking that Tilly's a really *powerful* Mallockee, don't you? It won't hurt them to be—well—a little *frightened* of the Stubbs family. We'll get a lot more respect, I should imagine—and, if those two horrible office boys, Mr Needle and Mr Bland, ever come to visit us again, they might behave themselves a bit better if they know there's a powerful Mallockee in the house—don't you think?'

'I rather think I do,' said Lee.

Several days later, Lord Octavo came to visit.

Lee and Sam and Measle gathered round him, all four of them sitting comfortably at the kitchen table. Iggy was allowed to peer in through the kitchen door—but Nanny, holding a floor mop at the ready, made sure he came no further.

'I thought you might like to know the outcome of the trial,' said Lord Octavo, sipping a cup of tea. 'After all the truth came out, it was decided that Toby Jugg should be sent to the Detention Centre. He'll be down there for quite some considerable time. Officer Offal is currently occupying the next-door cell—and *he'll* be down there for a fairly long time, too. The rest of the gang have been banished from the Wizards' Guild for life. They've been stripped of their magical powers and sent back out into the human world, where, no doubt, they'll continue to make dreadful nuisances of themselves. At least *we* won't be bothered with them.'

'What about those security guards?' said Sam.

'Hah!' barked Lord Octavo, contemptuously. 'Well, they turned out to be employees of Dorian Fescue—they were in charge of protecting his supermarkets up and down the country. They've all been fired, of course. The last thing we need in the Wizards' Guild is a lot of jackbooted thugs running around the place.'

Lord Octavo looked up from his cup of tea and peered at Iggy, who was craning his neck through the open kitchen door.

'Mr Niggle,' he called, 'you'll be pleased to know that you've been given a full pardon and are to be allowed to stay here under the watchful eyes of the Stubbs family—just as long as you don't get yourself into any more trouble. Do you understand?'

'Coo—fanks, Lord Octopus,' said Iggy.

Lord Octavo choked back a small laugh. Then he looked gravely round at every member of the Stubbs family and said, quietly, 'I'm not going to enquire about the Mallockee. As far as I am concerned, she is entirely your responsibility. And I am confident that it's a responsibility that you will all take very, *very* seriously.'

'Oh, we will, Lord Octavo,' said Sam. 'Very, *very* seriously indeed.'

*   *   *

A few days later, it was breakfast time once again at Merlin Manor.

Lee, Sam, Measle, and Matilda were sitting at the big kitchen table. Sam, as usual, was buried behind his newspaper. Tinker was wandering from person to person, hoping for a treat to be dropped down into his open mouth. Nanny Flannel was at the stove, carefully pouring hot, red, sugar syrup into two hundred little oval moulds. Iggy Niggle was standing at the open kitchen door, his fishy eyes staring greedily at the process.

Sam's newspaper started to shake.

'I don't *believe* it!' he muttered. 'The *idiots*! The *cretins*! The stark, staring, barking *lunatics*!'

'What's happened now, Sam?' said Lee, putting down her cup of coffee and leaning forward on her elbows.

Sam lowered the newspaper and they all saw that a heavy frown of irritation was creasing his forehead.

'They've done the stupidest thing you can imagine!' he said, furiously.

'*What* have they done, Sam?' said Lee. 'And, who are "they", may we ask?'

'*They* are the collective morons of the Wizards' Guild,' barked Sam. 'And they have done something so *unbelievably* silly—'

'*What* have they done, Sam?'

'Justin Bucket has resigned. He's no longer the Prime Magus.'

'Well, that's good, isn't it?' said Lee.

Sam sighed heavily. 'Oh, sure—*that* part is good,' he said. 'But it's who they've chosen to take his place—to be the new Prime Magus. Of all the brainless, dim-witted, senseless ideas, this takes the biscuit! How on earth could they have been so irresponsible as to have picked such an *utterly*, *totally*, and *completely* unsuitable candidate!'

Lee snorted with impatience. She rapped her knuckles on the table and said, 'Well, who is it, Sam? Who is this dreadful person they've picked to be Prime Magus?'

'Me,' said Sam, sadly.

And deep beneath the Wizards' Guild building, in a cold, stone cell where not even the faintest glimmer of light could be seen, the Thing with the seven mismatched eyes lay and waited. It waited patiently. It had waited patiently for many, many years. But now it would not have to wait too much longer.

For a moment, a dim light cast a faint, golden radiance around the stone walls of the Thing's cell. The light came from the seven mismatched eyes. They glowed briefly.

Then the Thing lowered its wormy lids over its eyes—and the cell was once again plunged into utter darkness.

Ian Ogilvy is best known as an actor—in particular for his takeover of the role of The Saint from Roger Moore. He has appeared in countless television productions, both here and in the United States, has made a number of films, and starred often on the West End stage. His first children's book was *Measle and the Wrathmonk*, followed by *Measle and the Dragodon*—and he has written a couple of novels for grown-ups too: *Loose Chippings* and *The Polkerton Giant*, both published by Headline. His play, *A Slight Hangover*, is published by Samuel French. He lives in Southern California with his wife Kitty and two stepsons.

Measle Stubbs is best known as a bit of a hero—in particular for his triumphant role as the charge of the evil wrathmonk, Basil Tramplebone, and his defeat of the last of the Dragodons. Measle's latest adventure has been his struggles against the scary monsters at Caltrop Castle with only his baby sister and a very small wrathmonk to help him. Now he has rescued his mum and dad from the warlocks he can relax at home with his family—for a while, at least.